# DARK SON

## A LANCE BRODY NOVEL (BOOK 2)

### MICHAEL ROBERTSON, JR.

ISBN: 9781973178699

"Margie, how 'bout another slice of your pie?"

Hank Peterson was perched on his usual stool at the far end of the diner's counter, an empty pie plate and an opened newspaper set out in front of him. He'd been there for hours. "It's Friday afternoon and I'm celebrating the end of another grueling week."

Margie, rolling her eyes to a customer at the opposite end of the counter as she refilled his coffee, called over her shoulder, "You've been retired for eleven years, Hank. You're not celebrating, you're just a fat old man who can't resist a lady's pastries."

Margie had been working at Annabelle's Apron for a long time, since before Annabelle herself had passed on, and after so long working in a diner in a small town like Westhaven—or any diner, for that matter—you develop a certain rhythm, come to expect a certain pattern of events, causes and effects. You learn types of people and how to play off them, much the same way a bartender might as he pours libations and hopes large tips will pour out of wallets afterward. There's a routine—not just for Margie, but for the customers as well. Everyone knows how to play along; everyone learns the rules of the game eventually.

Which was why it struck a bit of a chord with Margie when her jest at Hank Peterson caused zero reaction from the man for whom she'd poured fresh coffee. The two other waitresses—both currently huddled in a back booth together, counting their day shift tips as they waited for the dinner crowd to start its trickle through the door—had laughed loudly and giggled at Hank's expense, and from through the food window, Margie had heard the cook give a grunt of approval at the joke. The only other customer in the diner, a young teacher from the elementary school whose name Margie was kicking herself for not being able to remember, looked up from the paperback she was reading as she sipped her hot tea and picked at a salad and offered a polite smile in Margie's direction.

Everyone reacted, because that's what you did. Whether you found the joke to be truly amusing or simply adequate, you either laughed or offered a small chuckle or—like the young teacher reading the book—you smiled politely and then went back to your business.

That was the rhythm. That was the routine. Everyone knew it.

The man at the end of the counter had acted as though he'd never even heard Margie's words. Come to think of it, aside from his order of coffee and a cheeseburger, the man had said nothing at all.

Hank Peterson, using one liver-spotted hand to pat his bulging belly, winked at her and said, "Never could resist nothing of yours, Margie."

Margie groaned.

The waitresses laughed again.

Rhythm. Routine.

Nothing from the man at the other end of the counter.

Margie put the coffeepot back on the burner and made a show of turning her back to Hank Peterson to examine a stack of receipts on the counter near the cook's window. But while her head was bent toward the papers, her eyes were shifted upward, taking a nice hard look at the man who hadn't so much as grinned at her and Hank's exchange.

Sizing him up, Margie realized the man looked extremely tired. Not just tired ... beaten down, maybe even demoralized. He could have been fifty, but the deep creases and lines of worry embedded in his forehead and around his eyes made him look even older. His hair was thick, but fully gray, hanging sloppily down around his ears and into his eyes. Margie had noticed him brushing it back out of the way as he'd taken the first bite of his burger. He wore faded blue jeans with a black sweater, along with a threadbare blue sport coat that was either a cheap hand-me-down that had never fit right, or the man had lost a great deal of weight recently. He looked skeletal inside the fabric. As he sat hunched over his half-eaten burger, eyes down, hair splayed across his forehead, Margie suddenly felt an overwhelming sense of sorrow for the man, and she scolded herself for initially considering him rude.

It hadn't even been that good of a joke. She and Hank Peterson went after each other every day and this most recent exchange wouldn't even crack the list of their top fifty all-time hits. She was better than this. The man deserved better than this.

"Margie, my pie?" Hank Peterson said from his stool, his voice sensing something off in his longtime diner pal.

Rhythm. Routine.

"Just a sec, Hank," Margie said, barely finding her voice. She walked over to the man in the too-big sport coat and rested her hands gently on the counter. "Something the matter with the burger, sweetie? Want me to cook you up a fresh one?"

The man lifted his head slowly, an act that seemed to take great effort, and when his eyes met Margie's, she wasn't shocked to see they were glistening with tears. He offered her the sorriest of smiles she'd ever seen.

"No, ma'am. The burger was just fine. Just not much of an appetite is all. I thank you for asking, though. Really, I do." He used both hands to wipe his eyes, no hint of embarrassment. As if the tears were something he'd long since grown used to.

Unable to think of anything else to do, unsure how to respond to the scene before her, Margie asked, "How about a slice of pie? On the house. I bake them myself." She smiled at the man and hoped he found some warmth in it.

"That's very kind of you," he said, "but I think I'll just have the check, please."

Margie wasn't having it, whether because of her own guilt still pushing its way in or because something about the man in front of her with the mop of gray hair and the too-big jacket seemed to be crying out for help regardless of what he said. She had to make one last attempt.

"This is on me, sweetie. You hardly touched your food."

She held up her hand to stop his attempt at a protest. "Now either the food wasn't to your liking, or—and forgive me if I'm getting too personal, but I've been working around people my whole life and I just have to call it like I see it—there's something troubling you. Something troubling you *bad*. And, well, I'd just like to do what I can to maybe brighten your day up a bit."

The man looked at her. He didn't say a word, but Margie thought she could see some form of concession in his eyes, his whole demeanor. Like whatever weight he'd been carrying had suddenly vanished and he could take a deep breath and relax, if only temporarily.

"So, I'm going to ask you one last time," she said with a little bit of playful sass, "is there anything else I can get you?"

The man still did not speak, only turned and looked past the tables and booths and out the row of windows at the front of the diner. Margie looked too, seeing only the darkening sky full of gray clouds and Hank Peterson's ancient pickup truck parked in the same spot it sat in every day. She glanced back at the man and saw he was looking back at her apprehensively, as if he were mulling over what he was about to do. Then he reached a hand into the inside breast pocket of his sport coat.

"I wasn't going to bother any of you fine people with my own agenda," he said. "You all have your own troubles to deal with. No sense in burdening you with mine." He pulled a folded piece of newspaper from the pocket. "I was going to make my way to the sheriff's office, but ... I've just been through this so many times ..." He trailed off and slowly unfolded the piece of newspaper, flattening it out carefully on the counter, next to his half-eaten cheeseburger.

Margie looked down and saw the clipping was a picture from the sports section of a paper she did not recognize. It was worn with age and constant refolding, the crease lines nearly transparent. The photo was an action shot of a boys' basketball game. On the left side of the picture, a defender was in midair and had his hands raised high in an attempt to block his opponent's shot. On the right side of the picture, also in midair, the boy taking the shot was tall and lean and appeared to be unchallenged by the outstretched arms of the defender. He had blond hair and a look of determination on his face that hardened his features.

Margie has seen this boy before. Though he'd been a few years older than he looked in the newspaper photo.

He'd come to Annabelle's Apron twice, a month or so ago. Had sat at this very counter and eaten her food.

And then she'd never seen him again.

Margie looked up from the photo and met the man's eyes, which seemed suddenly on the verge of tears again.

"His name is Lance," the man said. "He's my son." Then,

through a stifled sob and an attempt to hold back fresh tears, he asked, "Have you seen him?"

———

The orange-and-white Volkswagen bus was parked a block away from Annabelle's Apron, on the side of a shopping center parking lot that was mostly hidden from the road and wedged next to a row of dumpsters. The Reverend sat up straight in the passenger seat, his head bowed and his eyes closed. But he wasn't praying, and he certainly wasn't sleeping. He was focusing, reaching out with his mind and otherworldly senses and absorbing what there was to be learned from Westhaven.

Something bad had happened here. But ... it was better now. He tuned himself into the town and tasted the cool sweetness of ... relief? Calmness? He probed deeper, through the layers of newfound happiness and closure and understanding—through the elation that had followed some great victory against ... what?

Beneath those layers, like loose change and sandwich crumbs beneath sofa cushions, there still lurked fragments of some evil, some great sorrow, that had plagued Westhaven. Something that had taken root and sunk its teeth into the town and caused unbearable pain and suffering.

The fact that it was gone now, suddenly vanished with only these small traces of its existence left, only further solidified the Reverend's hunch. They were on the right track.

Movement in the Volkswagen's side mirror caught his eye, and when he looked into the glass, he saw a gray-haired man who appeared to be in his fifties, maybe older, wearing a jacket that was at least two sizes too big and walking across the parking lot toward the bus. His shoulders were slumped and his slow and shuffling gait spoke volumes as to his mood. This was a man with little to live for.

The Reverend smiled.

The gray-haired man passed by the Volkswagen without a word and slid behind one of the dumpsters. Less than ten seconds later, the Surfer emerged from the other side of the dumpster wearing his customary board shorts, flip-flops, and a bright orange tank top that reminded the Reverend of a traffic cone. The Surfer pulled his blond hair back into a loose ponytail, stretched his back, arching his body and looking up toward the sky, and then turned and walked back to the bus, opening the driver's door and sliding inside.

"What happens to your clothes when you do that?" the Reverend asked. "I've always wondered."

The Surfer only leaned his head back against the headrest and stared back at the man with bored apathy. The Reverend could still smell the lingering aroma of grease and strong coffee from the diner on his companion.

The Reverend sighed, rolled his eyes, and then said, "Well?"

The Surfer reached for the key in the ignition and cranked the engine, which choked and whined and then hummed to life.

"You were right." He put the Volkswagen into reverse. "He was here."

The Reverend smiled. They were getting closer.

[ 1 ]

THE BRAKES GAVE OFF A LOW SQUEAL AND THE
transmission chugged and shook the bus hard as it downshifted,
jerking Lance awake. He sat up at once, snapped out of a
surprisingly dreamless sleep. His vision cleared and his heart
settled in his chest, and he looked out the window, which was in
desperate need of some soap, water, and a squeegee.

The water wasn't currently the problem. Through the grimy
glass, Lance watched the downpour of rain curtain the exterior
of the bus station, giving it an out-of-focus, shivering effect. It
pummeled the bus's rooftop with staccato pings that sounded
like a load of gravel being dumped. The bus's wipers worked
furiously to keep up, and only when the bus came first to a slow
crawl, then a complete stop in front of the station's doors did the
visibility become somewhat passable. The driver, a tall, rail-thin
man who unfolded himself from behind the wheel, opened the
bus's doors and stood to face his few passengers. He smiled big
and raised his hand in a wave. "Thanks for traveling with me
today, folks. I hope you enjoyed the ride, and"—he glanced out
the bus's doors, then back to the group—"I hope you all can
make the most of the beautiful weather we're having." He

offered a small chuckle after this, and when he got nothing in return from the group, he nodded once. "Right," he said, and he sat back down in his seat and busied himself with a sheet of paper on a clipboard.

The few passengers began to stir and squirm now, repacking small bags and standing and stretching in the confined aisle. Lance, who had chosen a seat in the second row and was closest to the door, grabbed his backpack from the seat next to him, thanked the driver, and then walked carefully down the bus's steps and out into the rain.

He stood for a moment in the downpour, his hair instantly matted to his head, and closed his eyes, breathing in deep.

He reached out with his mind, feeling the new town. He didn't know quite what it was he was looking for, but so far he'd—

"*Excuse* me." A woman's voice startled him. He turned and saw a line of people waiting to come down the bus's stairs. They looked at him warily and impatiently.

Lance gave a weak smile. "Sorry," he said and then stepped out of the way.

---

A little over a month ago, Lance Brody had lived an ordinary life. As ordinary as a life could be for someone who could see the dead.

It was true. Since Lance's birth, he'd been able to see lingering spirits walking among us mortals. All ages, all walks of life. He'd seen ghosts of those who'd died peacefully in their sleep, and he'd seen the tormented and still-mutilated souls of murder victims, car accident fatalities, and those whose physical bodies had succumbed to terminal illnesses. They almost never appeared to him without cause. Often, they showed themselves in an effort to help, or to be helped. To lead, or to be led. Though the spirits were not always the most straightforward and direct bunch of companions, their assistance, along with Lance's other *psychic tics*—that was what he liked to call them now—had not only helped Lance guide them to whatever closure they might have been looking for but also allowed Lance to aid many people—including his local sheriff's office—in solving a wide assortment of crimes, mysteries, and the all-around generally unexplainable.

It was Lance's ability to help solve crimes that had created his relationship with the only person in his hometown who knew Lance's secret other than his mother, since Lance had never known his own father. Marcus Johnston had been new on the job with the sheriff's office when Lance had been only five years old and had helped find the body of a missing child, who had ended up wandering away from his own backyard and drowning in the small pond at the local park. Johnston had attended high school with Lance's mother, and Pamela Brody had seen something in the man—or perhaps *felt* something about him—that had allowed her to trust him enough to slowly begin to reveal Lance's extraordinary gifts. Looking back and examining his own history, Lance now often wondered just how many of his own gifts his mother might have also possessed, if only subconsciously.

Lance had grown to be a respectable student and had developed the height and quickness to become a superior basketball player for Hillston High School. Though the burden of his unnatural gifts kept Lance from accepting any of the athletic scholarships he'd been offered; instead, he had chosen to remain home, with his mother and with the familiar. Marcus Johnston had grown to become the town's mayor. The bond and trust between the two men had never been broken.

Which was why Marcus Johnston was the first and only

person Lance had called on the night his mother had died. The night Lance had been forced to flee his hometown. The night that had changed his life forever.

The night the Reverend and the Surfer had come for him and his mother had offered up her life in order for Lance to escape.

While most of the spirits that visited Lance were amicable enough, even if their visits were often ill-timed and inconvenient, the lingering dead were not all that Lance's gifts allowed him to see.

He could also see into the darkness. He could see beyond the veil of this world and peer into the shadows of another—and what lurked there, what survived in a place where nothing should be able to survive, was more terrifying than anything you could imagine.

Evil was very real. And evil walked among us. Always present, always waiting.

Lance was still uncertain *what* exactly the Reverend and the Surfer were—while they appeared to be mortal men, the Reverend seemed to possess a similar flavor of telepathic powers to Lance, albeit much more powerful, and the Surfer ... the Surfer seemed to be able to change himself, among whatever other talents he might possess. Shape-shifter was the word Lance wanted to use, but the term carried such a connection to fantasy novels that he found it ill-fitting. The Surfer was terrifying, if not unexplainable.

Whatever the Reverend and the Surfer were, one thing was certain; they knew exactly what Lance could do, and they wanted him. Lance didn't know why, but it was clear their intent wasn't one of friendship and jovial times around a campfire.

Lance had escaped them the night of his mother's death, thanks only to her sacrifice and the quick thinking of Marcus

DARK SON

Johnston, who had gotten him away from the scene of the accident before too many questions could be asked.

Lance had taken the first bus out of town that night and had
ended up in the town of Westhaven, Virginia. There, he'd not
only encountered and barely survived a battle with a demon of
sickening power; he'd also met a new friend who had stolen his
heart. A girl whose beauty lived both outward and deep inside.
Her name was Leah, and leaving her had been one of the
hardest things Lance had done in his twenty-two years of life.
But he knew it was the right thing. He was a hunted man, after
all. He could never jeopardize Leah's life that way. So, on
another bus, he'd left Leah and Westhaven behind.

Lance had been a vagabond ever since. Always moving
forward, always looking over his shoulder and checking for an
orange-and-white Volkswagen bus.

Or something much worse.

Evil was very real.

———

Lance stepped inside the bus station and watched as some of his
fellow travelers greeted friends and family who'd been waiting,
while others slumped off through the rain and stuffed themselves into cars, driving away toward home.

He'd give anything to be able to go home. To be able to walk
down his neighborhood street, take the few steps up to his front
door, and step into his living room where he'd be greeted by his
mother's smiling face and the smells of fresh pie cooling in the
kitchen. They'd enjoy a slice together, her with tea and he with
coffee, and they'd talk and laugh and...

Lance shook away the thought. Which, to his dismay, was
becoming increasingly easier to do after only a bit over a month.
Time heals all wounds—that was the saying, right? Lance

marveled over the weight of its truth. The night of his mother's sacrifice, he had felt an emptiness inside him that could surely never be filled. A sharp pain in his chest whose ache had almost become comforting in its regularity. But both had lessened. Meeting Leah and dealing with the trouble in Westhaven had helped him begin the healing process in ways he still didn't quite understand. It was certainly cathartic, and as he'd helped that town overcome the evil that had been slowly devouring it, one of the last things his mother said to him reverberated in his head.

*My sweet boy. Oh, what great things you'll do.*

He would not let her death become an empty sacrifice. He would go on and he would survive and he would wait until whatever purpose he was to serve presented himself.

He knew—if he stayed alive long enough, and out of the hands of those who hunted him—that he would discover what it was he was meant to do. Or rather, it would discover him. Lance always had a way of stumbling into the right spot at the right time. At times it was so ironically timed that he was certain whatever guiding forces of the Universe controlled his destiny were having a joke at his expense.

Lance watched out the window as the bus pulled away, chugging out a plume of black exhaust, and then glanced to the sky. Storm clouds still blanketed the horizon, and the rain still poured. Lance shifted his backpack off his shoulder and pulled out his cell phone, a no-frills flip phone that offered only the most basic of services. He smiled as he remembered Leah making fun of the phone. For the briefest of moments, he thought about selecting her contact info and sending her a text message. Something harmless, something simple. Ask her how she was doing. Or telling her that he was safe and well.

But then he also thought about deleting her info altogether. The temptation to reach out to her was too great. And what good would it do? It would only remind them both of something that could have been, but likely would never be.

Lance's stomach grumbled, and instead of texting Leah, he sighed and checked the time and saw it was a little after two in the afternoon. He tossed his phone back into his backpack.

After confirming with a very friendly man behind the ticket window that there were places to eat well within walking distance, Lance bought a five-dollar umbrella from a small rack next to the counter and then headed outside, standing on the sidewalk beneath the concrete overhang and looking west toward the town, toward lights that looked friendly and inviting.

He pulled up the hood of his sweatshirt, opened his umbrella and started to walk.

With the steady rhythm of the rain falling, tapping atop his umbrella, and the cool fall air trying to nip at him through his hoodie, Lance felt strangely calm. Oddly relaxed.

It was a feeling he didn't quite trust yet.

[ 2 ]

TWO BLOCKS FROM THE BUS STATION, A SIGN THAT WAS posted along the side of the road as Lance approached the heart of the town welcomed him to Ripton's Grove, and a smaller sign below this encouraged him to "Eat at Mama's."

Even as Lance pondered why so many small-town restaurants in the country seemed to think "Mama's" was a great name for a business establishment (*so much for originality*), he felt his stomach grumble again and assured the sign as he walked past that he would indeed eat at Mama's, despite the generic name. He suddenly found himself so hungry he would happily eat at Toilet Bowl Bistro if presented with an opportunity, and hopefully a well-displayed certificate of passing from the local health inspector.

He stopped as the sidewalk ended at an intersection and tilted his umbrella back a bit to peer out beneath its flap and take in the town. Through the sheet of rain, he saw a small cluster of two-story brick buildings, industrial in design and scope, their fronts painted and repainted over many decades as shops and businesses came and went and came again. Awnings stretched over storefronts, lights glowed from most first-floor

17

display windows. A few cars were parked along the sidewalk, and a single traffic light glowed from an intersection ahead. One car sat, waiting patiently for red to turn to green. It was a familiar scene in rural Virginia, or rural anywhere, really. An ill-preserved snapshot of a place that at one time would have a been bright and vibrant scene straight from a Norman Rockwell painting—soda fountains at the drugstore and all that feel-good mojo from long ago—but had now become grainy and drained of its vividness. It had decayed, yet survived.

Lance was starting to think that if he ever wanted to find himself in a larger city, he might need to start paying more attention to what buses he was taking. But honestly, he preferred the small towns. It reminded him of home … of the time before it had all come crashing down around him.

There was no traffic at the intersection where Lance stood, just two tired and faded stop signs standing guard at the side streets. Lance crossed the road and walked the next block, inserting himself into the cluster of buildings, scanning the storefronts and breathing in the air in search of an aroma that might indicate in which direction he could find Mama's. A car came up from behind him and drove slowly by, not in a creepy way, but in a way that was respectful of the low speed limit. Cautious and courteous. Small-town driving. Its tires kicked up a small rooster tail of water as it navigated the wet road.

The car was a solid black Ford Crown Victoria, not an ancient one, but boring and nondescript except for the dual antennas growing from the trunk. Lance had no doubt it was an unmarked police car. Just as he had no doubt the vehicle's driver had taken inventory of Lance as the car had passed. The sight made Lance slightly uneasy. The last time he'd ended up in the back of a police car, a man had lost his life. A wife had lost a husband. A son had lost a father.

*Because of me.*

*No ... because of* it.

He pushed these thoughts away, a harsh past he could not change, and watched as the Crown Vic rolled through the green light ahead and turned left, disappearing from sight. Lance walked another block, and for a moment it took him a second to realize something was different. Something about him, some feeling had changed since before he'd stopped to watch the Crown Vic make its slow crawl up the street.

*I'm not hungry anymore.* He looked down at his stomach, as if awaiting an explanation, and it did not protest. Lance's hunger pangs had stopped, his stomach's grumbling silenced. He stood for a moment, still and confused, and as he was about to continue on in search of Mama's despite his stomach's change of opinion, a door burst open a little way in front of him, an overhead bell giving off a terribly loud *ring-a-ding!* as a woman spilled out onto the sidewalk carrying a large bouquet of flowers. She called back over her shoulder, "Thanks, Lynn! See you at church!" Then she crossed the street, tucking the bouquet beneath her jacket as she half-jogged to her car and got in.

Lance looked back to the door the woman had come through and saw a large glass display window full of flower arrangements and balloons and teddy bears. Obviously a florist. But it wasn't the florist that was suddenly keeping Lance rooted in place. He turned to his right, toward the door he was standing directly in front of, and read the black block letters painted on the window. R.G. HOMES – REAL ESTATE. And then, stuck in the bottom left corner of the glass, he saw a hand-printed sheet of paper, badly faded by the sun, that read: Rentals Available.

Lance pulled open the door and went inside, his thoughts of food all but forgotten.

The space inside was warm, but not quite inviting. The hardwood floor, presumably the building's original, was scuffed and aged and in desperate need of refinishing, but the only comforting bit of décor. The walls were gray and dull. A few cheap framed prints were hung here and there but did little to lift the mood. To Lance's left was an old metal desk and chair, something that would look more at home in a prison than an office. Atop the desk was a beige desktop computer that had never known speeds greater than dial-up modems, a cup full of pens and pencils, and an opened day planner with a few appointments filled in. There was a fine film of dust covering everything. Two more chairs were in front of the desk, and just as Lance was beginning to think he'd made a mistake, a man emerged from a back office and said, "So sorry! My receptionist is at lunch and I never heard you come in. I really should get a bell like they have next door, but ... between you and me, I hear that thing ringing all day long and I dream about going over there and ripping it off the wall and stomping it flat!"

Lance said nothing.

The man was average height and fairly thin, with the exception of the middle-aged stomach paunch drooping a bit over the belt holding up his khakis. His tie was crooked, but his shirt was clean and pressed. His hair was thinning, but he wore it well, neatly parted on the right side and held in place by—*Oh no, is that hairspray?*

The man gave Lance a quick once-over, just as Lance had done to him, and then, apparently not believing Lance to be any sort of threat, he took three quick strides across the room and shoved his hand into Lance's. "Name's Richard Bellows, but everyone calls me Rich. Pleasure to meet you, sir. What brings you into R.G. Homes today and how can I help?"

The man's enthusiasm toward his potential customer was both amusing and annoying. To Lance, he seemed like a Chihuahua that'd been kept in a cage all day and was now running laps around the living room after being let out.

*Business must be slow.*

Lance said nothing. Instead he looked back over his shoulder, out the windows to the street. The rain was still falling. He looked down at this umbrella, which was dripping water onto the hardwood. Richard Bellows followed Lance's eyes down and immediately jumped to action. "Oh! Right, right! Here, um, here let me take that for you." He swooped in and snatched the wet umbrella from Lance and then carried it over and put it into a metal trash can by the desk. Then with two quick strides, the man was back in front of Lance, a large smile plastered on his face.

"Let me guess, you got a new job in the big city and the folks there told you Ripton's Grove was the place to live? Easy commute, beautiful scenery, friendly people. So, you came on down to check the place out and see what was available before bringing your family along. Am I right?"

Lance said nothing. Rich's mention of family sent a pang of sadness through him. A twinge of pain that Lance quickly shoved aside. He wasn't concerned about the past right now. He was focused on the present. Something had made him come into R.G. Homes today; his vanished hunger was all the evidence he needed to know that for certain. But why? He certainly didn't need—or have the means—to buy a home, and so far he was picking up nothing remarkable from Richard Bellows, aside from his enthusiasm for customer service.

Lance's continued silence finally caused Rich's smile to falter. His face quickly fell, and he looked taken aback, as if he'd made some grave mistake. Without a word, the man turned and dashed back into his office, returning a moment later with a notebook and pen. He opened to a blank page and quickly scribbled something on the paper and then held it up for Lance to see.

Lance read the words and then burst out laughing. Shaking his head he said, "No, I'm not deaf or mute."

Rich's face began to relax at the sound of Lance's laughter and his first spoken words, and Lance apologized. "I'm sorry, I wasn't trying to be rude. I just—"

He was about to say he had no idea why he'd come into Richard Bellows's office, when something familiar jerked his thoughts in a different direction. He looked back down to the notebook Rich was holding in his hand and examined the handwriting. He'd seen that writing before, and he remembered the handwritten sign on the door—Rentals Available.

*Is that it? Am I supposed to rent a place and stay here awhile?*

It wasn't a crazy thought. He'd been hopping around from town to town for a month now, never staying more than a couple days in each, feeling no real sense of purpose or belonging. His gifts of perception and his nudging from the Universe had been all but nonexistent except for a continued urge to move on.

He felt no different today, felt no force telling him this was where he needed to be, felt no threat looming in Ripton's Grove that he needed to attend to, but ... but he wasn't hungry. And he'd been starving.

"I was hoping you might have a place for me to rent," Lance said.

The smile returned in full force on Rich's face. "Of course! Just, um, when you didn't say anything, I ... well..."

Lance said nothing. What could he say?

"Right," Rich said. "Follow me and we'll see what we've got."

Lance followed Rich through the door at the back of the room. It was a small, cramped office with similar furnishings as those in the reception area, except that instead the outdated desktop, there was a modern Apple laptop on the

22

desk connected to a large monitor. Richard Bellows squeezed behind the desk and sat, pointed for Lance to sit as well. Lance sat, resting his backpack on the floor against the desk. He looked around the room and saw that the walls were nearly wallpapered with framed photos of Richard Bellows and his family—nice-looking wife and three small children. Rich caught Lance looking and smiled even larger than before. "My pride and joy," he said. "It's what it's all about, am I right?"

Lance forced a grin. "Sure is."

Rich looked admiringly at the photos for another few seconds and then cleared his throat and turned his attention to his computer. "Okay, first question, Mister, uh..."

"Lance."

"Right. First question, Mr. Lance. How long will you be renting?"

"Just Lance."

"Sorry?"

"My name is Lance. Call me Lance."

"Oh, right, sorry. Apologies. So how long will you be renting, Lance?"

Lance didn't hesitate. "I don't know."

"Three months? Six? One year?"

"I don't know."

Richard Bellows took it in stride, though Lance could sense the apprehension. "Okay, then ... we'll just say *indefinite*." He clicked a few things on the screen. "And what is your price range?"

Lance thought for a moment and then told Rich a dollar amount that caused the man to turn away from the computer and lean back in his chair. He gave Lance an appraising look, as if trying to figure out exactly what he was getting himself into.

Lance could feel the moment slipping away from him and

knew he had to fix things before his opportunity was lost, along with whatever reason he'd come into R.G. Homes today.

"I'm sorry," he said. "I should have been clearer. I can pay that weekly. Do you have anything I can rent by the week instead of a lengthier lease? With the business I'm in, I'm never sure how long a job will last." Then he added, "And frankly, I'm sick of hotels."

This answer seemed to make sense and placate Richard Bellows. He leaned forward again, and though his smile was back, he was clearly disappointed he wouldn't be making much of a profit today. "Lance, I'll be honest with you. We're not a vacation town, nothing touristy for people to come and see or do, so we don't have any weekly rentals..." He trailed off and leaned back in his chair, his brow crinkled as he thought about something.

Lance waited.

"Actually," Rich said, leaning forward again and resting his elbows on the desk, "I might have a place, if you're interested. It's a little way outside of town, and it's been mostly vacant these past few years."

"Mostly?"

"A few folks have come and gone. None have stayed too long."

"So, you've rented it short-term before?" Lance knew all at once that he was on the right track here. Something urged him to push Richard Bellows on.

Rich made a face that said *not exactly*. "The rentals have been short, yes."

This was an omission, but Lance let it slide.

"So, I can rent it weekly?"

Rich actually stifled a laugh before turning his face back to business mode. "Lance, tell you what. I don't know why, but I like you. You seem like a real straight shooter and all-around good guy. If you give me a small deposit. I'll let you rent it by the *day*."

Lance looked at the man and smiled. "Rich, I like you too. So why don't *you* be a straight shooter with me and tell me what's wrong with the place?"

Richard Bellows, his bluff called, could only nod his head and sigh. "The truth?"

"Please."

"People say it's haunted."

And there it was. This time it was Lance's turn to laugh. "I'll take it."

## [ 3 ]

RICHARD BELLOWS HAD PRINTED OFF A LEASE AFTER A FEW clicks on the keyboard and then used a cheap ballpoint pen to fill in details with a rapid, almost robotic pace. He'd moved around to the other side of the desk and handed the pen to Lance, flipping through pages and showing him where to initial and sign. Lance didn't sweat any efforts of entrapment from Rich, didn't ask for any elaboration on what he was signing. He trusted the man ... and his stomach was beginning to grumble again.

On the latest grumble, Richard Bellows had made a comical glance toward Lance's stomach and smiled. "When we finish up here, head on over to Mama's. Best food in town."

Lance nodded. "I intend to. If only because of such an intriguing and creative name."

Rich Bellows didn't pick up on the sarcasm, or simply ignored it. He was too preoccupied with double-checking the freshly signed lease and announcing to Lance the grand total he would have to pay today. "That's the small deposit we spoke of, plus two days' rent."

"I'm really fine paying you for the week." It was clear to

Lance at this point that this was where he was supposed to be, at least for a while. Somebody, or *something*, here needed him.

Rich nodded and said, "I appreciate that, Lance. I do, really. But if you decided to up and take off like the other few folks who've rented the place have, I'd hate for you to be so in a hurry you forget to come by here and settle up, get the rest of your money back."

In that moment, Lance felt a sense of admiration for Richard Bellows. He looked around the small office again at the walls covered in family photos. Here was a man full of pride and joy, swelling with happiness and wanting to show it to anyone who'd happen by. And he was turning out to be an honest businessman as well.

Lance unzipped the front flap of his backpack and pulled out a checkbook—one that was only a few weeks old and had been used sparsely. Lance scribbled on a check and signed it, tearing it free and then handing it over to Rich. As Lance filled out the ledger, Rich examined the check. "PB Consulting?"

Lance nodded as he shoved the checkbook back into his backpack. He offered no more information. Richard Bellows was a smart and polite enough man to take the hint.

During the events in Westhaven, only a blink of an eye after Lance's mother's death and Lance's subsequent abandonment of his hometown, Marcus Johnston had called and left Lance a voicemail he wouldn't be able to listen to until he was finally on a bus, heading out of town once again. Lance had been a little too preoccupied with things in Westhaven trying to kill him to find time to remember to check his phone messages. But as the bus had pulled away from the Westhaven bus station and Lance had played back Marcus Johnston's message twice, he was astonished at what he'd heard.

Lance and his mother had always lived a very frugal life. Pamela Brody had worked at the local library a few days a week and occasionally picked up other part-time work until she grew bored or felt the *need to move on*—that was how she'd always put it. With Lance working at the local sporting goods store from the time he'd been about to enter high school, they'd always had enough money for what they needed, plus the occasional splurge. So when Marcus Johnston called and told Lance that his mother's will had left him not only their house, but a savings account with enough money for Lance to live on for a while, Lance's head had spun with confusion. Where had she gotten all that money? Had she been secretly saving it for all these years? Had she inherited it? Lance had so many questions —questions that would likely never be answered.

In Lance's eyes, Marcus Johnston was practically his guardian angel. He'd been there from the beginning, helping Lance and his mother along the way as they'd all coped and learned to handle Lance's particular skill set. Marcus had been there the night Lance's mother had lain dying on the ground outside the Great Hillston Cemetery, and he'd never doubted Lance's admission that Lance was in some new great danger. That these people chasing him were more dangerous than even Lance himself had understood. Lance's track record spoke for itself.

"What do I do with the house?" Lance had asked once he'd finally gathered the resolve to call Marcus back. Marcus had launched straight into a barrage of questions about Lance's well-being, where he was, where he was going.

"I'm fine," Lance had said, fresh off nearly dying in West-haven. "Probably best if you don't know where I am." Then asked again, "What do I do with the house?"

The house was not completely paid for, so the options were either to sell it or to rent it for enough to cover the mortgage. Lance had chosen to rent it, only because some part of him felt deep down, despite the circumstances, that one day he might return to Hillston. And if he did, he wanted to sleep under his own roof. Sleep in the home his mother and he had made together. But only once he was ready. Once his work was finished. Whatever that might be.

For Lance to start his own business was Marcus's idea. "We'll create an LLC," he'd explained, "and put the money in a checking account for the company that we both have access to. That way, I can help you manage anything you might need help with, and as you're out and spend money on ... whatever it is you're doing out there, nobody will be able to directly trace payments you make back to you. It'll just be billed to the business."

The level of trust Lance held for Marcus Johnston was only surpassed by the trust he'd had for his mother. If Marcus thought this was a good idea—and it did make a lot of sense to Lance—then Lance was fine with it. He didn't need to worry about Marcus running off with any of his money.

"Plus," Marcus had added, "if you have a job—even if it's a fake one—maybe you won't be so damn suspicious all the time."

Another great point.

And so, PB Consulting LLC was born. The PB, of course, stood for Pamela Brody.

"Lance?" Marcus had started as the conversation began to wind down. "Are you sure you can't come home? Let me help you with all this? You know I'll do everything I can."

And Lance *did* know this. But he also knew it was impossible. His journey, wherever he was headed, whatever he was to do, was just beginning.

And the next part had been the hardest. Lance, not one to cry, had nearly choked up as he'd asked, "Just take care of my mother's body, Marcus. Take some of the money and do whatever you think is best to lay her to rest. Nothing extravagant.

You and I both know she wouldn't want anything like that. Just ... simple. Peaceful."

"Of course, Lance. Of course."

Lance found himself surprised by how little he was bothered by not being able to be present for his mother's burial. *I knew her in life*, he thought. *And what is a funeral, a burial, if not a celebration of the life?*

This thought had his mother written all over it, and Lance had smiled at how much he'd become like her.

The sound of a metal filing cabinet sliding on its track snapped Lance out of his thoughts. He looked up and saw Rich riffling through a row of hanging folders, his fingers dancing across their labels. "Ah, here we go," he said, pulling one free and tossing it onto the desk. He flipped it open and retrieved a small key ring with two keys attached. He held it out to Lance, that large smile never leaving his face. Lance let the key ring fall into his palm.

"Now, the place is modestly furnished, so you don't need to worry about furniture or anything like that, but I can't get any cleaners there until tomorrow, I'm afraid. I did have it cleaned after the last tenants left, so..." Rich's face faltered slightly. "Actually, that's been several months. I apologize. Maybe you'd like to stay in a motel tonight?"

"I'm sure I'll be fine," Lance said.

"Of course. Completely up to you."

There was a silence between them then, their business concluded.

"If there's anything wrong with the place, or if you have any issues at all, please," Rich sighed, "let me know." He said this with a tone that suggested he was fully expecting Lance to be back tomorrow morning white-faced, red-eyed, and wanting all his money back.

"I will," Lance said.

"Good. Anything else I can do for you?"

"Yes. You can give me the address."

Rich Bellows's face turned red and he quickly stood from the desk. "Of course! Ha! Silly me. Here, um..." He turned and placed the sheets of Lance's signed rental agreement into the tray of a multifunction printer and made a copy. Lance was amused at how flustered Rich seemed. How distracted. Whatever was wrong with the home Lance was renting clearly had Richard Bellows's mind wandering.

*What am I getting into now?*

Rich handed the copy of the lease to Lance after circling the address with a red pen. The two men shook hands and said their goodbyes, and Lance retrieved his umbrella from the trash can before pushing through the door and heading back into the rain.

## [ 4 ]

With a freshly signed lease in his backpack and the keys to his new haunted home in his pocket, Lance walked down the sidewalk, past the florist with the window full of bouquets and teddy bears, and listened to his stomach grumble loud enough to be mistaken for thunder. He was starving. With his task now complete, the Universe had allowed him to return to his regularly scheduled program.

It was now a quarter after four, and the traffic in town had picked up. The parking spaces along the sidewalk filled up, and now three cars sat at the red light ahead, turn signals flashing through the gray, rain-soaked atmosphere.

But still, things were quiet. Calm. The few people he saw seemed to be in no hurry. The traffic was docile. Maybe it was because of the weather, but Lance figured he was simply witnessing the definition of a sleepy small town. His hometown of Hillston hadn't been a metropolis by any means, and West-haven had been even smaller, but this place ... this was almost comical. Ripton's Grove was the sort of place you drove through accidentally when taking a shortcut to your real destination. The sort of place where, as you looked out the windows when

33

you passed through, you thought to yourself, *Who would want to live here? What do they* do?

This was the sort of place where—in theory—everybody might actually know your name.

Lance started humming the theme song to *Cheers* and listened to the rain continue its patter on his umbrella. He passed by a small law office, a hardware store, a coffee shop—which he was tempted to go into, but refrained, the thought of comfort food from Mama's more appealing to his complaining stomach—and a small karate dojo, lights off and empty of students, before he reached the intersection with the stoplight. He turned left instinctively, allowed a red Ford pickup to pass beneath the green light, the driver raising a friendly hand in a wave, and then crossed the street. There were no pedestrian Walk/Don't Walk signs, and the fear of jaywalking seemed about as insignificant as mismatched socks to Lance after everything he'd been through recently.

His sneakers splashed through puddles in the street, and the sound of water rushing into sidewalk drains echoed between the buildings. Headed perpendicular to the main street now, Lance continued down the sidewalk, passing a CPA's office and a secondhand bookstore before finding the small Ripton's Grove post office at the end of the block, sitting on the corner, back off the road like a child's discarded toy. It was nearly dark now, the heavy rain clouds coupled with the early setting sun making it feel much later than half past four, and through the large front windows, Lance could see a small line of people standing patiently at the counter inside the well-lit post office. Waiting to send messages to the rest of the great big world that existed outside their tiny reality.

Across the street, on the opposite corner from Lance, was Mama's.

The restaurant was an old two-story cottage that had been

converted. Faded gray vinyl siding but a fresh-looking roof. All the lights in the front windows burned bright and seemed warm and welcoming. Instead of a front lawn, there was a crushed-gravel parking lot, half-full. A small marquee sign sat just off the road at the parking lot turn-in, the black plastic letters chipped and cracked but advertising, BEST MEATLOAF IN THE STATE, and beneath this, HOMEMADE PIES!

Lance chose to smile, pushing away the sorrow that could have crept in just then, the fact he'd never taste another of his mother's pies beaten away by the knowledge that she'd want him to enjoy life without her to the fullest. Even if that meant eating another woman's desserts.

Lance checked for traffic and crossed the street in no hurry, heading toward Mama's bright lights as though they were a lighthouse and he a ship lost at sea. Halfway across the parking lot, he saw the solid black Crown Vic, its two antennas standing at attention on the trunk, waving ever so slightly in the wind. Lance slowed his pace, suddenly cautious. The car was parked close to the restaurant, its nose facing those brightly lit windows. Lance changed directions and walked along the side of the car, not stopping, but quickly stealing a peek inside the vehicle. Saw the expected clutter of equipment near the console—sturdy laptop, mounted facing the driver, radio equipment, radar device. All the usual cop fare.

He wasn't afraid of cops, had committed no major crimes that would suggest a statewide manhunt in an attempt to bring him in, but recent events had surely more than made him a person that local law enforcement would like to have a chat with. And if they did, there would be questions that Lance could not answer. Well ... he *could* answer them, but he wouldn't. He wouldn't be believed. Never understood. They'd find him crazy, mentally unstable. Or worse ... they *would* believe him, his secret out and exposed and vulnerable. Ready for the world to pounce on and pick apart and analyze and destroy.

He'd be labeled a freak. Degraded to a test subject, a number. An experiment.

They'd forget he was human.

Lance's stomach grumbled again, almost yelling at him to stop screwing around and send some of that meatloaf down the pipe.

Lance took one last glance at the Crown Vic before pulling open the restaurant's door and stepping inside.

*Something about that car*, he thought. *Or maybe the person driving it.*

---

Unlike the florist, at Mama's there was no bell above the door, but the squeak from the hinges was loud enough for all eyes to instantly look up from their food and away from their conversations and stare at Lance as he entered. He stood there for a moment, the feeling of being put on display nearly toppling him over. After what might have only been two or three seconds—which felt like something closer to a full minute to Lance—Mama's patrons returned their attention to their tables, but Lance figured the hushed whispers were certainly at his expense. *Who is that? Why is he here? What size shoe does he wear? His feet are huge!*

Okay, probably not the last part, but it was a question Lance had heard more times than he cared for in his life.

He closed his umbrella and the door shut behind him, another long screech as the hinges whined some more. There was a coatrack standing in the corner to his right, and Lance rested his dripping umbrella on the floor beside it along with two others that looked exactly the same, probably sold at every shop in Ripton's Grove.

Lance turned and nearly collided with a young woman who'd appeared behind him.

"Whoops, sorry!" she said, taking a quick step back. She was fairly tall for a girl—five-seven or five-eight—and had jet-black hair pulled back in a ponytail. Her skin was pale, and the only trace of makeup was around her eyes—some dark green eyeshadow and a bit of liner. Nothing fancy. She wore black jeans and a white t-shirt tucked in. Lance figured she was still in high school. A year or two out at best.

Lance apologized for the near-collision, and when he said no more, the girl offered, "Can I help you?"

Before Lance could answer, his stomach gave off another low grumble that caused the girl's eyes to look down at it before quickly bouncing back up to meet his eyes. Lance smiled and shrugged. "I was told you have the best meatloaf in the state."

The girl nodded. "It's true," she said, then, after a shrug of her own, "Best I've ever had, at least."

"Good enough for me."

She smiled and pulled a single menu from a stack on a small wooden table by the coatrack that also held a bowl of individually wrapped peppermint hard candies, a cordless telephone with its numbers all but worn off, and small plastic toothpick dispenser. "Table or booth?" the girl asked.

It was then that Lance got his first good look at the place.

The house's interior had been renovated to essentially divide the downstairs into a large dining area and a kitchen at the rear, a metal swinging door allowing employees to pass back and forth between the two. The décor was old, yet comfortable, like a grandma's house. The walls were adorned with faded wallpaper with a flowery print, the carpet a dingy pea-soup-green that Lance supposed did well to hide stains. A cuckoo clock tick-ticked off the seconds from the wall next to the swinging kitchen door. Lance imagined waitresses glancing at that clock incessantly as they passed to and fro from kitchen to dining room, pleading for the minutes to move and their shift to end.

There were twelve tables in total. Small two-tops along three of the walls, and larger four-tops scattered through the center of the open room. Old wooden things with plastic white tablecloths. On the outer wall by the windows were three booths, one in line with each of the front-facing windows. The windows that had appeared to burn so brightly from across the street. The upholstery was lime green and the tabletops were a dark, scuffed and scratched wood.

Lance smiled. This was exactly the type of place his mother would love. A diner meets the touch of home.

Groups of people were seated around four of the tables, plates of food and the hushed murmur of conversation keeping them busy. Somewhere unseen, a radio was playing softly. Country music. Fitting for the scene. There was the occasional clatter of pots and pans, the familiar noise of an oven door opening and closing, coming from beyond the swinging kitchen door. Somebody back there asked what time Henry was delivering tomorrow. Somebody else said they'd guess the same time as always.

Lance saw and heard all these things, but focused on none of it. What drew his attention was the man seated at the corner booth, furthest from the door. His back against the wall. Able to look up and see everything if need be.

It was the driver of the black Crown Vic. There was no question about it.

He was in plain clothes—tan tactical pants, work boots, black sweater, and a black rain jacket—but Lance didn't have to ask if beneath that jacket there was a holster with a pistol. A badge clipped to a belt, maybe. The man was staring down at the table, his head hanging tired on his shoulders. He wore his hair shaggy, but it was thinning on top from where Lance could see. Still damp from the rain. The man was clearly not the owner of one of the other umbrellas by the door.

"Booth," Lance said. "Please."

The girl nodded and led him away from the door, taking just a few steps to the first booth in the row, intentionally leaving the open table between Lance and the man in the corner. Common courtesy, Lance supposed. Or maybe it was more than that. Maybe this was the Universe keeping Lance from getting too close, as if the man in the corner—clearly a police officer—might pick up Lance's scent and know he was trouble. Know he was hiding something.

*Stop it*, Lance scolded himself. *Stop being so paranoid. You're just here to eat. That guy doesn't know you from Adam.*

And he almost believed himself. But as he slid into the booth, keeping his own back to the door, facing toward the man in the corner, he thought back to the sign he'd seen just below the Ripton's Grove welcome sign as he'd walked into town from the bus station—*Eat at Mama's.*

He thought about how his hunger had subsided long enough for him to do his business with Richard Bellows, and how the local real estate agent had also encouraged Lance to come to the restaurant, Lance's hunger pangs returning as they'd finished up in Rich's office.

*No*, Lance thought. *It's just a coincidence. I was supposed to go to the real estate office because of the house. The house is why I'm here. Who better to live in a haunted house than me? Maybe it'll be like having roommates.*

"What would you like to drink?" the girl asked.

Lance realized he'd been staring at the man in the far booth, staring right at the top of his head since he'd sat down. He quickly looked over to the girl who was standing beside him, waiting. "Coffee, please."

"Yes, sir. Be right back."

*Sir? When did I get so old?* He sighed and leaned back in the booth, adjusting his backpack beside him. Truth was, he felt like he'd aged ten years in the past month. His mother's death had taken a toll on him mentally, the stress and the pain and the sadness wearing away at his strength. Things in Westhaven hadn't helped much—nearly dying had done little to improve his mood.

But he had met Leah. That was something. Something special.

He missed her.

He felt another sudden urge to pull out his cell phone and send Leah a text, but the girl returned with his coffee and he pushed the thought away again, tried to bury it deeper down.

The coffee was in a thick plastic mug, and Lance told the waitress she could keep the packets of creamer she was about to set down next to it. She nodded and asked if he was ready to order. Lance hadn't even glanced at the menu. "The meatloaf, of course." He smiled. "It's why I've come all this way, after all."

The girl cocked her head to the side, looking at him with a grin and narrowed eyes. "Really?"

Lance shrugged.

The girl smiled and shook her head and then walked over to the man in the corner. "Refill on the coffee, Sheriff?"

The man lifted his head for the first time that Lance had seen, and his face told a story of somebody who'd seen hard times and come out the other side for the worse. Maybe forty or forty-five, with a heavily creased brow and circles under his eyes so deep and dark he might not have slept in a week. He had a couple days' worth of stubble, spotty and with patches of gray. He offered the waitress a smile that almost seemed to pain him.

"Sure, Susan. A refill would be great." He spoke, and after Susan refilled his coffee and walked away, the sheriff's head went right back down, as if he were staring into the blackness of his coffee.

*Sheriff*, Lance thought. *Wonderful.*

But even from across the space of the empty booth, Lance could feel the cold sense of emptiness the man in the corner carried with him. It was a feeling Lance had recently known all too well. It smelled of the same scent of his own coldness he'd experienced when he'd lost his mother.

The man in the corner—the sheriff of this small and quiet place—had suffered. Had lost something, a part of him that could not be replaced. And at once, Lance no longer feared the man in the corner but felt an odd sense of connection. Two men trying to figure out what life held next. Coping in their own ways. Like eating meatloaf and drinking coffee and watching out the window as the rain continued to fall and the sky turned even darker.

Two of the other tables emptied, and Lance watched absent-mindedly as Susan cleared away the finished meals and wiped down the tablecloth, preparing for the next guests. On the wall by the swinging kitchen door, the cuckoo shot out of its clock and clucked off the five o'clock hour. The sound was muted, not altogether pleasant, but not obnoxiously loud as to intrude into a patron's meal.

Lance continued to steal glances at the sheriff. Watched as the man would lift his coffee mug to his lips and take small, deliberate sips. Then he'd set the mug back down and continue to stare down at the table. He never looked up at the room around him, never looked out the window toward the parking lot and the rain and his town.

Never looked at Lance.

Susan delivered Lance's meatloaf, and while he was no official Virginia authority on the subject, and could make no claim on whether it was the best in the state, he was quick to tell Susan that it was indeed delicious, and honestly the best meatloaf he'd ever eaten. The mashed potatoes on the side were excellent as well. Full of butter and fluffy. No lumps.

When he finished his dinner, Susan offered pie. Which, of course, Lance accepted. He chose cherry.

While Susan was preparing his slice of pie, the other two tables' guests finished up and left, leaving only Lance and the sheriff and an odd, somewhat uncomfortable silence hanging in the air along with the soft-playing country tunes.

Still, the man did not look up, his coffee the most interesting thing in the world.

Susan brought the pie—a huge, heaping slice with a perfectly golden crust—and refilled his coffee. While Lance ate, Susan worked to clean her tables and then reappeared, standing next to Lance as he took his last bite.

"Anything else I can get you?"

Lance contemplated another slice of pie, then toyed with the idea of getting a slice to go instead. In the end, he settled on another idea.

He pushed his empty plate aside and then fumbled inside his backpack until he found the lease he'd signed at R.G Homes. He pointed to the address that Rich had circled in red pen and asked, "Is this close enough for me to walk? And if not, is there a taxi service I can call?"

Susan smiled politely and leaned forward to read the address. As her eyes took in the numbers and words, the smile faltered. She looked up, first to Lance—a puzzled, unsure glance—and then back to the lease, as if to make sure she'd read correctly.

Then, oddly, she glanced toward the booth in the corner, toward the sheriff. His head was still down, staring at nothing.

She leaned in and whispered, "Are you serious? Why do you want to go there?"

Lance whispered too, following her lead only because it seemed right. "I've rented the place for a while." When this didn't seem to be enough, he continued with, "I needed a place to stay, and it was cheap."

Susan scoffed and her face turned sour. "Did Rich do this?"

"Do what?"

"Offer this place to you."

"Yes," Lance said. And then, "He seemed very nice."

Susan sighed. "Oh, he's very nice. One of the nicest guys in town. But nice or not, he should know better than to let you move in there."

"Is there a problem with the place?"

Susan did another quick glance toward the sheriff and then slid into the seat opposite Lance. She leaned forward, her voice more hushed than before. "Rich didn't tell you what happened, did he?"

Lance shook his head. "No. He just said some folks say the place is haunted."

Susan didn't seem fazed by this news. Lance got no sense of disbelief from her. "And that didn't make you think maybe you should find another place to stay."

Lance shrugged. Answered honestly. "It doesn't bother me."

Susan was quiet for a beat. Sat back in the booth and looked at Lance as though he were suddenly a riddle she'd been tasked with solving.

"What happened?" Lance asked. "Can you tell me?"

As soon as the words had left Lance's mouth, the sheriff stood from the booth in the corner, using one hand to quickly down the rest of his coffee and the other to pick up his Kindle e-book reader off the table and tuck it into his jacket pocket.

*So* that's *why he kept staring at the table. He was reading.*

But this fact didn't change the cold feeling that only grew in intensity as the sheriff approached the booth and stopped. Lance's heart suddenly picked up its pace. He looked up at the man and smiled. The man paid him no attention. Instead, he reached into his pocket, pulled out a ten-dollar bill and handed it to Susan. "Thanks, Suze. Have a good evening."

Susan took the money and forced a smile, mumbling a flustered thanks as the sheriff walked out the door and got in the Crown Vic.

Lance watched the car pull out of the lot and head down the street. Then he turned back to Susan but found she'd gotten out of the booth and was heading toward the sheriff's table. She picked up his coffee cup and started toward the kitchen, then turned and said over her shoulder, "You could probably walk, but it's a few miles, and you won't want to do it in the rain. I'm out of here as soon as Joan shows up for the dinner shift. I can give you a ride."

And then she pushed through the swinging kitchen door and left Lance alone in the dining room, wondering what had just happened.

TEN MINUTES LATER, A PAIR OF HEADLIGHTS TURNED INTO Mama's parking lot and a woman made a mad dash from the car to the door, bursting through it in a spray of water and expletives. She cursed the rain and the wet and the fact her shoes were now soaked and how she probably wouldn't make any money tonight because nobody would feel like going out to eat with weather as nasty as it was. She said all these things to nobody, a rapid-fire round of complaining as she hung up her raincoat and tried to straighten her blouse, which had come slightly untucked from her black pants. She was middle-aged, short, plump—*round* might have been the more appropriate word—and had short frizzy red hair in unkempt curls. She somewhat reminded Lance of a more vulgar version of Mrs. Potts from the *Beauty and the Beast* cartoon. She turned around from the coatrack and saw Lance for the first time.

"Oh," she said. "I didn't see you there. Susan taking care of you?"

Lance nodded. "Yes, ma'am."

The woman huffed and nodded once and then quickly waddled across the dining room floor and disappeared into the kitchen. No apology for the foul language or her outburst. No change in personality once she realized Mama's had a customer. Nothing.

Lance smiled. He liked her.

He sat another five minutes, staring out the window at the post office across the street as the rain refused to let up, and just as another pair of headlights began to turn into Mama's lot, Susan came through the kitchen door, laughing. "Joan, you're terrible! See you tomorrow!"

Lance stood, ready to go. Susan looked at him and, as if suddenly remembering her offer of a ride, hesitated just a moment before saying, "Give me just a sec, okay? I gotta make sure Luke's cool with it."

Lance could only nod. No idea who Luke was.

Susan snatched the only other remaining umbrella next to Lance's, pulled up the hood of her jacket, and then headed through the door toward the set of waiting headlights. Lance stood and watched out the window as she opened the passenger door and leaned down, talking to an unseen driver. After a moment, she looked up, back toward the restaurant. Saw Lance watching through the window and waved for him to come out. Lance gave a thumbs-up, regretted it, and then grabbed his own umbrella and hid under it the best he could, heading toward Susan and the car.

The vehicle was a four-door Jeep Wrangler, and Lance pulled open the rear passenger door and jumped inside, sliding his backpack in beside him and closing his umbrella quickly before shutting the door. The inside of the Jeep was warm and smelled faintly of peppermint mixed with sweat. There was a hip-hop song on the radio, turned down low. Lance adjusted himself in his seat and then looked ahead, found the driver—presumably Luke—turned and staring at him with a large smile. "So you're really staying out at the spook farm?" Luke asked.

Luke looked to be about Lance's age and sat tall in the driver's seat. He was thin and long—like Lance—and wore jeans with a frayed and tattered hoodie.

Lance didn't have to ask what Luke was referencing. He just shrugged. "Apparently."

Susan hit Luke in the shoulder. "Luke! I told you not to call it that. It's ... I don't know. Disrespectful."

"Even if it's true?" Luke smiled and then winked at Lance.

Susan smirked and shook her head. "You're a jerk."

Luke leaned forward and kissed her on the mouth. "Yeah, but you love me."

Lance cleared his throat, reminding the people up front they had a third wheel present.

Pushed away the memory of the way he and Leah had kissed that night in the Westhaven bus station. Before he'd left her.

Luke turned his attention back to Lance, then seemed to really look at him for the first time. "Hey," he said. "Don't I know you from somewhere?"

Fear flushed through Lance's veins.

Was his face making the rounds through the local news stations, broadcast on the six o'clock segment as folks were sitting down to eat their dinners? Was there an APB out? Was his photo circulating through county sheriff's offices throughout the state?

Had Leah been forced to give up information about him? Hounded and threatened until she'd been left with no choice but to admit she'd seen him leave on a bus headed out of town? The bus station attendant might remember selling the ticket. Might remember the destination. From there it would only take a bit of amateur sleuthing to potentially follow Lance's trail here to Ripton's Grove and—

Luke snapped his fingers. A strangely loud sound that startled Lance and brought his attention back to the Jeep's driver. "You played ball, right? Not around here, but in-state." Luke closed his eyes and thought for a moment, searching for the right memory. His eye's popped open and he said, "Yeah, you played for Hillston High. We played you guys in the first round of States a few years back. We beat you, but man, you were tough. *You* were tough, I mean. I think you dropped thirty on us."

With the proper context, Lance's memory recalled Luke instantly, remembered the game. "Thirty-four, I think," Lance said. "You guys killed us on the boards." Then he added, "But we never played a team from Ripton's Grove."

Luke nodded. "Yeah, I didn't go to school here. I'm from the next county over. Got a job in the city while going to community college. Rent's cheaper here. I split a place with a buddy of mine a few miles away. Only reason to come here, really. Except for this cutie right here." Luke reached out and squeezed Susan's knee, and she laughed and rolled her eyes.

"All the city girls are out of his league," she said.

Luke shook his head. "Give me a country girl over one of them fake city bitches any day of the year."

Susan looked back to Lance. "See?"

They all laughed, and then Luke asked the question Lance always wanted to avoid. "So, what are you doing here? I figured you'd be ballin' at some D1 school right about now."

Lance shook his head. "I'm here for work." Then, to quickly change the subject and try to get some more answers, "Why do they call it the spook farm?"

Susan looked at the clock on the dash and nudged Luke. "Let's go, we're going to be late for the movie. And I'm telling you right now, there's no way I'm going into the theater wearing this and smelling like meatloaf."

Luke put the Jeep into reverse and started to back out of the parking lot.

Susan sighed and adjusted her seat belt to what Lance considered a very unsafe position that seemed to negate the whole point of wearing the thing in the first place, but also allowed her to turn around nearly backward in her seat and look at Lance while she spoke. The Jeep's windshield wipers flapped back and forth across the glass behind her, almost bringing her in and out of focus as they worked to clear away the water. The large mud tires hummed softly on the wet asphalt.

Susan said, "Did your town have a local haunt?"

"A what?" Lance asked.

"A haunt. A place everybody always said was haunted, or spooky? A place that some stupid kids always broke into during Halloween to show how brave they were, or to drink beer or some dumb shit like that? A place with some history that over time people turned into a local legend?"

Lance knew what she was talking about. Nodded his head. "Sure."

"Okay, well the—God, I hate calling it this—the spook farm is Ripton's Grove's version of that."

Lance had heard these types of stories about places before. Anybody who'd grown up in a small town had. It was what small towns did. They embellished and told stories and tried like hell to keep things interesting.

"So I'm guessing something bad happened there?"

Luke gave off a quiet chuckle. "You could say that."

Susan shot him a glare before returning her eyes back to Lance. "An entire family was found dead."

Lance was smart enough to pick up on Susan's deliberate wording. "And nobody knows what happened? Murder? Suicide? Both?"

Luke turned and looked at Lance, his eyes searching. Susan did something funny with her nose, curious.

Lance tried to recover. "I mean, you said 'found dead,' so I just assumed that the situation wasn't exactly black and white." Then shrugged and added, "I watch a lot of cop shows."

This seemed to put them both back at ease. Luke flipped on his turn signal and turned left onto a rural road. Passed a few small houses, and then the road became lined with mostly trees and field.

Susan's tone was that of somebody eager to tell a tantalizing tale. She seemed suddenly excited, but also, if Lance was correct, a bit unnerved. "Nobody knows exactly what happened in the house that night. I can only tell you what the police found the next morning."

Luke shook his head. "Weird shit, man. Especially the girl."

Susan looked once to her boyfriend, reached across and turned up the Jeep's heater, and then started to tell the story.

## [ 6 ]

"The spook farm has only been the spook farm for maybe ... how long would you say, Luke?" Susan looked to her boyfriend for help. Lance watched in the rearview as Luke crinkled his brow and thought.

"I was a freshman, I think. No, wait ... I was a sophomore. Yeah, I had just gotten my driver's license when it happened. I remember because a bunch of kids were driving up to the house at night after it happened to try and get a look at the crime scene. Just like you said ... dares and dumb shit like that. My parents promised me that if they found out I drove over here to that house, they'd make sure I never drove a mile on my own until I finished high school. So you better believe I stayed away."

Susan nodded. "Okay, yeah. So it's been ... six years." She shook her head. "Damn. I can't believe she's been gone that long."

Luke shrugged. "The way you told it, she'd basically been gone longer than that. Was gone before it all went down."

Susan nodded again. A quiet concession.

"She?" Lance asked.

Susan met his eyes. "Mary Benchley. She was the girl who

lived there with her family. She was my age. Lived on the farm with her mom and dad."

"It's an actual *farm*?" Lance asked.

Susan nodded. "Well, it was. Mary's family inherited it from her great-uncle on her mother's side. Apparently Mary's mom and he were close, and he left it all to her when he passed. It was more of a farm when he owned it—cows, chickens, cornfields, maybe some other stuff. But when Mary and her family moved in, the first thing they did was sell off everything they could. Mary's dad said they weren't farmers and never would be. No sense in pretending."

"Now how could you possibly know that?" Luke asked.

"People talk. It's a small town. I was nosy."

Luke laughed. "Still are."

Susan punched him on the shoulder. "You just remember that." Then she continued. "So they sold everything but the chickens, because Mary's mom argued they could use the free eggs. But otherwise, as a farm, it was just the skeleton of one. Shed, barn, abandoned fields. You know?"

Lance nodded. "So what did Mary's father do? Since he had no interest in farming."

"He was a preacher. Well, that was what he told everybody."

"What do you mean?"

"He didn't actually preach at a church."

Lance was confused, and must have looked it because Susan explained, "Mary's mom got a nursing job at Central Medical, and they apparently got a decent payout when they sold a lot of the farm equipment and the livestock. So Mary's dad didn't have to work. Her mom didn't either, really, but Mary always said her mom loved it too much to quit."

"So what does this have to do with Mary's dad being a preacher?"

"Oh, well, he always walked around town carrying a Bible and would occasionally give impromptu sermons on the street, or in the park. Sometimes he'd invite folks up to the farm to celebrate the Lord and share in the gospel, away from all the distractions of life."

The image of a man walking around town, a tiny black Bible tucked under his arm, brought thoughts of the Reverend into Lance's mind. He shivered at the memory of how the man had spoken to him through his own mind. Effortlessly gotten into Lance's head. And he was still out there. Still coming for Lance. Both of them—the Surfer, too. Lance knew this without knowing how he knew this. He could feel it.

Luke slowed the Jeep for an approaching curve in the road, a steep hill climbing upward where the road dropped off. He made the turn and they began to travel up, rising in elevation as if climbing up the side of a mountain. They drove maybe a hundred yards before switching back around another curve, continuing to climb. "I always forget how high it feels up here," Luke said. He turned his head and looked out the window. Lance followed suit and saw the glowing lights of Ripton's Grove growing smaller below them.

The rain was still falling. Not even a hint of letting up. The Jeep's headlights cut through the falling rain, and the tires stayed firm to the road. Lance figured he'd lucked out with his free ride. And his free history lesson.

His mother did not believe in coincidences.

Lance was finding it harder and harder to find fault in her thinking.

Susan continued. "So yeah, Mary was embarrassed like hell by her dad. I mean, he was nice enough and all, but"—she shrugged—"sorta got the reputation of being a kook, ya know? And once Mary got to middle school, the kids started making fun." She shook her head, then added softly, "I don't think anybody actually thought he was dangerous, though. Crazy? Yes. But crazy for the Lord, ya know? In that way that sometimes makes people seem out of touch with the real world?"

Lance nodded. Said nothing. Tried to figure out where this was going.

Susan was quiet for a moment, then shook her head as if tossing aside a rotten memory. "Anyway, I don't know if it was because the teasing got to be too much for Mary, or maybe just too much for her dad, or if it was something else entirely, but Mary left public school halfway through our freshman year, and her parents shipped her off to some boarding school. Natalie, that was Mary's mom, never told anybody much of the specifics when she'd come into town afterward and people asked about Mary. But something else must have been bothering her, too, because a couple weeks later, she quit her job at Central Medical and was almost never seen after that."

Lance considered this. How bad had things really gotten with the teasing? He knew kids could be cruel. The *world* was cruel. But something about the story didn't seem right to him.

"What do you think really happened?" Lance asked.

Susan replied instantly, her opinion locked and loaded. "Her dad lost his mind, and when Mary came home to visit, he killed her and his wife. Why? I don't know. But he had some sort of plan, and once he was finished, he killed himself, too."

Lance said nothing.

Luke shook his head. "We don't know what happened that night," he said. But from his tone, Lance figured the guy wouldn't be able to offer an alternative story.

Lance hated that he had to ask the next question, but he could tell Susan was waiting, waiting to drop the bomb, the climax of this whole story. "How did he do it?"

"He used a shotgun on Mary's mom and himself," she said. "The police found Mary's mom's body on the front porch steps with a hole the size of a bowling ball in her chest. Like she was trying to run away and got gunned down. Mary's dad killed himself in the recliner in the living room, half his head blown off."

Luke rounded another turn and the land flattened out a bit. Forest on either side, giving way to fields and rugged terrain. He squinted through the windshield and said, "It's up here close, right, Suze? On the left?"

"Yeah, maybe another hundred yards."

Thinking about how far they'd seemed to drive, and the constant switchbacks they'd climbed, Lance asked, "I thought you said I could walk here?"

"Oh," Susan said. "Yeah. I mean, it's possible, but not exactly ideal. There's a hiking trail that comes straight from town up the side of the hill. It's shorter than driving, for sure, but in this rain, it'd be a disaster."

Luke looked to Susan. "You told him he could walk?"

"I didn't lie."

Luke rolled his eyes. He hit his turn signal despite the nonexistent traffic, slowed the Jeep to a crawl, and then turned left onto a dirt road.

Knowing that Susan was purposely dragging out the final bit of information, with a sick feeling in his stomach, Lance asked, "And what happened to Mary?"

Susan sighed, as if telling this part of the story was actually painful. "They found her body burnt beyond all recognition on top of a brush pile in the back field. There was almost nothing left by the time they found her. They had to use her teeth to get a positive ID."

Then, after looking down and giving a long, dramatic pause, Susan lifted her head and added, "They don't know if she was alive or not when she started to burn."

Luke hit the steering wheel with his palm and said, "Jesus,

Suze, you tell this story like you're trying to win a damn Oscar or something. Like you actually enjoy it."

She looked offended. "I do not."

"Yes, you do. You tell it like we're telling ghost stories around a damn campfire."

The two of them continued to bicker, but Lance ignored them. He leaned forward and looked through the rain-splattered windshield. Up ahead, faintly illuminated by the Jeep's headlights, was the house. The *spook farm*.

And Lance was nearly positive he'd seen something move behind one of the front windows.

[ 7 ]

Luke drove the Jeep slowly along the muddy road until the front bumper nearly touched the railing of the farm-house's front porch.

"Jesus, Luke. Why don't you just go on ahead through the front door?" Susan said, sitting up straight in her seat.

Luke shifted the Jeep into park and then leaned over the steering wheel, looking through the windshield and out to the house before them. "I've never seen it up close," he said. "I told you, my parents would have killed me if they ever found out I came out here like the rest of those idiots back then."

Susan didn't look over to him, just continued to stare through the dancing windshield wipers, her eyes locked onto the house. "You never came after? Later on?"

Luke shook his head. "For what reason? I'm not a ghost hunter or anything."

*I'm not either*, Lance thought. *The ghosts tend to be the ones to do the hunting, in my experience.*

Susan shrugged. "I don't know. I guess it's different when you're from here. Me and my friends, we all just felt sorta ... I don't know ... compelled to come see it. Almost like we were paying our respects or something." She shrugged again and asked, "Does that make sense?"

"No," Luke said.

Susan was quiet for a beat. Then: "She was my friend."

Luke had no answer to that.

Lance said nothing.

The rain beat down on the Jeep's top, and the warm glow of the headlights illuminated nearly the entire front of the house. The place wasn't ramshackle exactly, but in the gloomy and wet night, it definitely showed its age, and exposed the neglect it must have endured all these years since the night that ... whatever happened had taken place. Shutters hung skewed and slanted on the dirty gray vinyl siding, the windows cloudy with dirt and dust. A wooden front door looked solid, but the storm door was blown permanently open, plastered against the side of house, the screen ripped completely free of the top of the frame and draped over the bottom half like a man keeled over. A wooden front porch spanned the entire width of the house. Splintery rails and peeling white paint. The overhang sagged a bit on the left side, and rain cascaded off it like a small waterfall.

Lance couldn't see the second story from his position in the rear of the Jeep, but he suspected it would look much the same. There were probably a few shingles missing. Hopefully there weren't any leaks in the roof, because with a storm like this, he'd have a swimming pool inside.

But despite the physical appearance, the house was still standing. And it was the only place Lance had to go. For now, at least. As far as he could tell, this was exactly where he was supposed to be.

The spook farm.

Luke and Susan continued to silently stare through the windshield, and Lance let them get their fill for another full minute before he cleared his throat from the backseat. "Thanks for the ride," he said, grabbing his backpack and umbrella.

They both jumped, as if they'd forgotten Lance was in the car. Lost in their own thoughts as they stared at a place that they likely now only thought of as the site of horrific death.

But to Lance, for now, it was only a house. Though he was certain that would change soon enough.

He reached for the door handle, and Luke and Susan snapped out of their trances. "Wait!" Susan said. "Let me give you my phone number."

"Damn, Suze, I'm sitting right here," Luke quipped.

Susan ignored him. "Seriously," she said to Lance. "You don't have a car right now, and well..." She looked over her shoulder again, back to the house, "If you need something, or ... I don't know. Just take my number, okay?"

Lance smiled. "Sure," he said, pulling his flip phone from his pocket. He ignored the incredulous stares from the two of them as he thumbed his way through his phone's menus and was finally ready to enter Susan's number. He typed it in as she recited it and then returned the phone to his pocket. So far, Susan had been fairly unreadable. Lance's many senses hadn't picked up anything overwhelmingly positive or negative. He paused for a moment, then asked, "Why are you being so nice to me? I'm a complete stranger."

Even in the dim light of the Jeep's interior, he could see Susan blush. She gave another shrug and said, "You seem like a nice guy." She looked at Luke, who was watching her intently, and then back to Lance. "And while I don't really know why you're here, I also don't think you fully know what you're getting into. The town is funny about this place."

Luke shifted at this. "What's that supposed to mean?"

Susan shook her head. "I don't know. But just call me if you think you need to, okay?"

Lance assured her that he would, shook Luke's hand and thanked them both again for the ride, and then opened the door and stepped outside into the rain.

He didn't bother with the umbrella, figuring he only had a few feet to go before he'd be up the three front porch steps and beneath the protection of the overhang. This was a mistake. The wind rushed at him and the rain was relentless, and in the three short seconds it took him to get from Luke's Jeep to the front door of the farmhouse, he was half-soaked. Water dripped into his eyes as he fumbled to pull the set of keys he'd been given from his pocket. Thankfully, Luke was kind enough to keep the Jeep parked in place, the headlights the only source of light to help Lance see what he was doing. There was a small exterior porch light mounted to the right of the front door, just about level with Lance's head, but it was off. Lance looked at the single bulb beneath the cloudy glass enclosure and figured the odds of it working were slim to none.

He moved to insert one of the small brass keys into the dead-bolt, adjusting his body so the Jeep's headlights would shine onto the door, and that's when he heard the voice. It was female, hushed, yet panicked.

*"THANK GOD YOU'RE HERE! YOU'VE GOT TO HELP US!"*

Lance spun around so quickly he dropped the keys, the soft jangling of the brass hitting the wooden boards below drowned out by the constant whoosh of the falling rain. His looked all around, his eyes darting across the porch, before staring like a deer, literally into the headlights of Luke's Jeep. Because of the lights, he was unable to make out Luke and Susan. Could only imagine their perplexed expressions as they watched him become startled on the porch steps and then stare back at them.

But maybe they weren't surprised. This was the spook farm, after all.

Lance stood still for another few seconds, listening. The voice had not come from inside the home. It had sounded as though it were right on the porch with him, circling his head loud and clear.

Now all he heard was the rain and the Jeep's idling engine.

He sighed, bent and picked up the keys. Then he waved farewell to his new friends, signaling all was okay, unlocked the spook house's front door, pushed it open, and stepped inside.

[ 8 ]

ONCE LANCE HAD CLOSED THE DOOR AND RELOCKED IT
behind him, it didn't take long for the dim light coming through
the filthy windows from the Jeep's headlights to fade away and
then vanish completely. Despite Susan and Luke's kindness, it
was as though they'd had all they could handle of the town's
infamous spook farm on this literal dark and stormy night. No
sense in becoming a supporting cast member in an actual ghost
story, if they could help it. They'd done their duty by delivering
Lance here, and now it was time to hightail it back to the real
world.

Lance didn't blame them. They had a movie to catch.

He longed for a life so simple that his biggest worry would
be whether he'd make it to a movie in time for the previews, and
if he wanted popcorn or a box of Junior Mints from the
snack bar.

It was a life he'd never have. Though he allowed himself a
momentary flash of a daydream—him and Leah holding hands,
side-by-side in squeaky theater chairs, laughing at something
funny onscreen; her grabbing his arm and burying her face in
his shoulder as the monster devoured a victim; him looking over

MICHAEL ROBERTSON, JR.

and watching a tear slide down her perfect cheek when the guy finally got the girl.

*"Who's at the door? Is it him? Tell me!"*

A thunderous male voice echoed all around Lance, his heart leaping into this throat as he was snapped out of his moment of fantasy and wishful thinking. His eyes had not yet adjusted to the darkness of the home's interior, and he spun around blindly by the door, eyes searching, body tense and poised to fend off an attacker.

He saw nothing, his eyes slowly focusing and turning the pitch black into a deep gray, his heart like a marching band drummer in his ears. Vague shapes began to take form: a set of stairs to his left, an entryway into what looked like a living room just past them. The amorphous blob of what was probably a sofa pushed against one wall. A smaller object to its right, perhaps an armchair. There was a hallway straight ahead, though the gray faded back into blackness halfway down, the little light from the front windows being swallowed whole.

Lance stayed perfectly still, straining his ears to hear what obviously wasn't there. But even though there were no more voices, he did hear something else. It was as though the outside sounds—the rain and wind—were intensified, louder than they should be. Not coming from behind him, but ahead, from deeper in the house.

As his adrenaline faded and his heartbeat's rhythm returned to normal, a wonderful thought came to him.

*Turn on the lights, Lance.*

It was true. Assuming the weather hadn't caused some sort of damage to knock out a power pole somewhere, the house should, of course, very well have electricity. If it didn't, Lance was going to have a chat with Mr. Richard Bellows about withholding information that could have very well affected Lance's decision (*Ha! Like he had a choice.*) to rent the property. Like

64

the inability to turn on a light, or, you know, charge a cell phone. Even if Lance's phone had long ago been eligible for early retirement.

As Lance was turning around to look for some sort of light switch on the wall near the door, an angry gust of wind screamed through and rattled the walls and windows, and what sounded like a loud clap of thunder exploded from inside the house ... from down the darkened hallway. The noise, like a starter pistol, propelled Lance into motion. He tossed his backpack to the floor and ran down the hallway, toward the source of the noise. He still clutched the umbrella tightly, supposing he could use it as a potential weapon if need be. If Annabelle Winters had been able to fight off a demon with a rolling pin in Westhaven, Lance would be disappointed in himself if he couldn't inflict some damage with an umbrella. It had a pointy end, after all.

He half ran, half fumbled his way down the hall, the wooden floorboards beneath his feet creaking and groaning under his weight. He entered the darkness with a reckless abandon which he only had a moment to second-guess himself on before the tunnel of black faded back into a dimly lit gray as he spilled into the kitchen, where the faint moonlight that was poking through the storm clouds fell through more dirty windows.

Another howl of wind slammed into the house, and this time Lance saw for himself the source of the loud explosion, as the house's back door was caught in the gust and slammed against the wall with enough force to nearly bounce itself back closed.

The back door was open.

This explained the intensified sounds of rain and wind Lance had heard from the front of the house.

But, and more importantly, when combined with the flicker

of movement Lance had sworn he'd seen from behind one of the front windows as Luke's Jeep had approached, it also fed into another theory Lance was forced to entertain.

Somebody had been in the house when Lance had arrived.

Lance stepped cautiously toward the open door. Rainwater had blown just inside the threshold, and Lance's sneakers squeaked on the floor. He gripped his umbrella tightly and cocked it back over his head, ready to swing down should somebody try and rush him.

Nothing happened. Nobody was there.

Lance stood at the open door and stared out into the night, unable to see much further than a few feet out.

"Hello?" he said, almost too quietly to be heard over the rain and wind.

Of course, there was no answer. Just the continued onslaught of water and the purr of the wind.

Lance reached out, grabbed the doorknob and pulled the door shut. There was a deadbolt here as well, and Lance thumbed it locked and stared at it.

*Did whoever was here have a key?*

He made a mental note to make sure to stop by R.G. Homes the next time he was in town and ask Richard Bellows a few questions. "So, *Rich ... Anybody else living in the house you rented to me?"*

Lance turned around in the darkened kitchen and leaned back against the door. He thought of Susan's words earlier.

*"I also don't think you fully know what you're getting into."*

Lance sighed. "Maybe I don't," he said to the house. "Maybe I never do."

## [ 9 ]

LANCE SLOUCHED DOWN IN HIS BUS SEAT AND PRESSED HIS
knees into the seat ahead of him, wedging himself into a comfortable position. There was nobody in the seat ahead of him, so he
wasn't worried about bothering someone. In fact, there was
nobody on this bus at all. For some reason, this didn't strike
Lance as odd. He often felt he was heading places nobody else
wanted to go.

Rain pelted the bus, the sound of the falling droplets
rhythmic and soothing. His eyes were heavy, his hoodie warm,
and he wanted nothing more than to rest his head back and take a
nap until he reached...

Where was he headed? He couldn't remember.

But before he could rest, there was something he had to do.
Something he'd waited too long to do. He slid his cell phone from
the front pocket of his hoodie and flipped it open. A gust of wind
rushed in and shook the bus, water slamming into the side with a
loud splattering of wet noise. Lance thumbed his way to his text
messages and clicked the keys until he had composed a new
message to Leah.

He stared at the screen for a long time. His words were few

*and simple, but they were the absolute truth. They were the feeling he could not shake, could not successfully repress for any extended period of time.*

*He moved his thumb to the button to send the message and—*

*A thunderous pounding rattled the window next to him. Deep, staccato knocks that sounded more like a hammer on wood than glass. Lance dropped his cell phone into his lap, startled, and looked to his right.*

*The bus was moving fast down a highway, the landscape blurring by in a rush of dark sky and rainwater. But despite the noise, the pounding, it wasn't what was outside the bus that caught Lance off guard. It was what he saw inside.*

*Lance's reflection in the bus window was not his own. It was the same shape, mirroring his body exactly, but it was not him. Lance raised his arm halfway from his lap, and the reflection in the window did the same. Only the arm in the reflection was bare, the body in the window wearing a short-sleeved white undershirt instead of Lance's sweatshirt. The arm was blood-speckled, the chest of the once-white shirt now a dark crimson bib, streaks and splatters of blood all over.*

*The head of the body in the window was nearly blown completely off. A gaping hole where the face should have been. Lance could see through it, catching a glimpse of the bus seats behind him.*

*Susan's words floated to Lance:* "Mary's dad killed himself in the recliner in the living room, half his head blown off."

*A strange fear rose in Lance's chest and—*

The pounding noise, rattling wood and glass from somewhere below him, woke Lance from his dream. He sat up quickly, eyes squinting against harsh sunlight coming in through the slats in the opened blinds. Shielded his eyes with one hand and tried to focus his vision. He looked around him, remembered where he was.

After the incident with the open back door the evening before, Lance had gone around the home and made sure all the doors and windows were locked, while also exploring the house's layout. Verdict: it was small by today's standards, old and in need of much work, but plenty big enough for Lance, and it would likely be charming once it had been cleaned and fixed up a bit. You know, assuming you could forget about the horrific murders that had taken place.

The ground floor consisted of the living room, kitchen, small bathroom, and an extra room that had apparently been used as a dining room, due to the large table that took up most of the tiny space. There was a door in the interior wall of the kitchen that Lance had assumed was a pantry or closet, until he had seen the sliding bolt used to keep it locked. When he'd opened it, he'd been presented with a set of wooden stairs leading down into darkness. A basement or cellar. Brave and rational as Lance was, he decided he'd wait until the sun was up to see what might lie beneath the surface of the farmhouse.

Upstairs was even simpler. Two bedrooms—a larger one to the right of the staircase, which Lance had assumed to be the master because of its size and larger bed, and a smaller room with a twin-sized bed pushed against one wall and a small white dresser and makeup mirror pressed against the opposite wall by the door. There was an empty closet next to the dresser, nothing but one empty wooden rod across the top. Not so much as a single clothes hanger left behind. There was a full bathroom in between the two bedrooms, directly above the kitchen below.

Whether the day of travel had truly exhausted him, or the dark evening hour, coupled with the secluded location and the noise of the rainstorm outside, had simply relaxed him in a way he'd not been able to achieve for quite some time, Lance had found himself ready to do nothing but sleep after his brief exploration of the farmhouse, resigned to push aside all sense of duty and desire to understand his new situation until he could rest his body and his mind.

He'd chosen the smaller bedroom—Mary's bedroom, he was certain—and collapsed onto the bed, not moving until now.

Another barrage of pounding rattled the front of the house below, and Lance swung his legs off the side of the bed. He considered grabbing his umbrella, which lay next to his backpack on the floor next to the dresser, but decided the situation likely didn't require melee weaponry and hurried out of the room and down the stairs.

With the thought that a likely criminal or murderer wouldn't be keen on knocking first, Lance quickly unlocked the front deadbolt and opened the door.

The bright sunlight assaulted him, and Lance had to take a step back and shield his eyes again. On the front porch, half-silhouetted by the sun, was the man from Mama's.

The sheriff.

The two men stood silently on opposite sides of the threshold, a sense of appraisal heavy in the air between them. The air blowing in was cool and sweet, the aftermath of the heavy rains the night before, but along with it Lance could also feel the coldness coming from the sheriff. The same sense of loss and sadness he'd sensed in Mama's.

"Good morning," the sheriff said. "I'm sorry if I woke you."

Lance had no idea what the time was. No idea if it was early, or if he'd slept long past any time acceptable for a responsible adult. All he could do was smile and say, "What can I do for you, Sheriff?"

The man did not smile back. "How do you know I'm the sheriff?"

The man was wearing similar attire as the night before. Dark blue tactical pants with black work books, cream-colored sweater beneath that same black rain jacket. The man was maybe three or four inches shorter than Lance, but his body was thick, muscled and strong. But his body language, the way he stood, the way his shoulders slumped and his head hung down, was the opposite. There was a weakness, or maybe an unwilling-ness ... a struggle, carried along with him.

"I was in Mama's yesterday evening," Lance said. "I heard the waitress call you Sheriff."

The man nodded his head. "You're more observant than most."

Lance said nothing.

The sheriff looked as though he was searching for something to say but was coming up short.

Finally, Lance nudged the encounter along by asking, "Can I help you, Sheriff? Do you want to come inside? I'd offer you coffee, but I haven't had a chance to go grocery shopping yet."

The sheriff's eyes looked over Lance's shoulder, darting a quick glance deeper into the house. He shook his head. "No, that's okay. Would you mind stepping out here for me? No sense in leaving the door open."

Lance's heart rate kicked up a bit at this. He couldn't quite pinpoint why the man made him uneasy. Despite Lance's initial fear, he couldn't convince himself the man was here to question or harass him about any of his previous doings—Westhaven, in particular. But Lance was wary as he slowly stepped out onto the wooden porch and gently closed the door behind him.

The grass sparkled with half-melted frost. The dampness of the porch boards seeped through the bottom of Lance's socks, and he wished he'd taken the extra few seconds to step into his sneakers. He pulled his hands into the sleeves of his hoodie and then crossed his arms, trying not to look confrontational. Over the sheriff's shoulder, he saw the Crown Vic parked in the drive-way. The engine was still running.

When he looked back to the sheriff, he found the man

staring at him intently. His eyes focused in determination, as if Lance were a complex equation on a math test. After another long moment of silence, Lance finally asked, "Sir, please don't take this for rudeness, or impatience. It's purely a willingness to help." A short pause, then, "Why are you here?"

As if whatever shroud had been covering the sheriff's visit had suddenly been ripped away, the man raised his head and stood straight. "Actually, that's exactly what I came here to ask you."

"Sir?"

"Why are you here?"

"In town?" Lance asked.

The sheriff shrugged. "Sure. But more specifically, why this house?"

Lance spoke carefully. There was a hidden accusation or suspicion here, though he wasn't sure what it might be. "I'm in town for work," he said.

"Work?"

"I own a consulting firm."

"So what do you do?"

"I consult."

He wanted to take that one back, apply a little less sarcasm. But vagueness was his friend in these types of situations. That was a lesson Lance had learned a long time ago.

The sheriff only nodded and continued with, "And the house?"

"What about it, sir?"

"Why are you staying here?"

"The gentleman at the real estate office in town offered it to me as an inexpensive place to stay short-term." This was only half the truth, but Lance suspected the sheriff cared little for the fact that Lance had felt compelled by other unseen powers to stay here.

"Richard Bellows?"

Lance nodded. "Yes, I believe that was his name. Nice guy."

"Indeed he is. But why not just stay at a hotel, if it's short-term? There's some nice ones in the city."

Lance nodded. "I'm sure," he said. "I guess I'm just partial to small towns. Nothing quite like them, right? Plus, with the nature of my work, I'm never quite sure how long I'll need to stay around."

The sheriff completely disregarded Lance's opinion on small towns and launched right into the meat and potatoes. "Son, do you have any idea what happened in this house?"

Lance looked the man in the eye. "I do, sir."

Nothing more. No need to delve into the details. Especially with local law enforcement.

As if the sheriff had finally cracked the code, finally unearthed some sort of true reasoning behind Lance's visit, he said, "And, let me guess, this consulting firm you own, do you happen to specialize in paranormal investigation? Ghost hunting, if you want to be blunt about it?"

Lance said nothing.

"We get kids come up here all the time, try to break in and have séances or bring fancy equipment to try and catch ghouls on video and then post it on the Internet and make a buck." The man looked down and shook his head, a wave of that coldness Lance had felt before rushing out. "It's disrespectful. What happened here was a tragedy and nothing else, and people shouldn't go poking their noses in it for the sake of their own damn entertainment and profit."

He looked up to Lance with tired eyes that spoke volumes.

"I agree, sir," Lance said.

This seemed to catch the sheriff by surprise. He narrowed his eyes. "You do?"

"Yes, sir."

Lance could understand the man's wariness. Lance was fairly young, and, let's be honest, dressed far below the business casual dress code. He didn't look like somebody in town for work. And he was sure the sheriff really had dealt with all kinds of thrill seekers and paranormal enthusiasts in the years since the murders had taken place here. But, as far as Lance was concerned, the sheriff's frustration, if not downright defensiveness when it came to this house, seemed to carry a personal agenda that Lance was desperate to learn more about. Somehow, the man was connected to this place. Though it occurred to Lance that the connection might only be a tired and downtrodden sheriff not fully accepting the reality of what had happened on the night of what might have been his town's biggest tragedy.

Lance had heard Susan's story about what had happened that night. There were holes in the story, for sure. Maybe the sheriff was desperate to fill them.

"I can assure you, sir, I'm here for neither entertainment nor profit from this house. It was a complete fluke that this is where I ended up when I came into town last night." The part about it all being a fluke wasn't entirely accurate, but Lance tossed this into the "white lie" category for the sheriff's sake. "But, to be honest, I'm happy I found the place. It's very peaceful up here."

The sheriff seemed to be out of ammunition for his line of questioning. He was quiet for a bit, somewhat appeased, it seemed, by Lance's answers. Then he turned and looked around behind him, back toward the Crown Vic in the driveway. Then he turned back to Lance and asked, "How did you get here?"

"Sir?"

The sheriff waved a hand behind him. "No car. How'd you get up here last night?"

"I got a ride with a friend."

"Friend? You know folks around here?"

Lance shrugged. "A new friend, sir."

The sheriff looked as though he was ready to pounce on Lance's vagueness this time, but then his face softened, as if he realized he might be pushing a bit too hard without much in the way of probable cause. This was a good thing, because Lance wasn't ready to give up Susan's name. She was a nice young girl who'd done him a favor. Luke, as well. Lance wasn't going to return the favor by tossing their names out to the sheriff, even if they'd done nothing wrong. To Lance, it was a matter of principle.

Or maybe the sheriff thought he'd get more in the way of truthfulness from Lance if he eased up and started to play a bit nicer. Just about justifying Lance's assumption of this, the sheriff asked, "Everything been okay up here since you arrived? No problems with any trespassers? Haven't seen anything out of the ordinary?"

*Well, sir, now that you mention it, when I got here last night I'm almost positive somebody was here before me and left the back door wide open when they ran away. Oh, and I'm hearing voices. Other than that, everything's peachy.*

"No, sir. Got here after dinner and went to bed shortly after. I was pretty tired after traveling. Didn't wake up until you knocked on the door."

Lance wasn't sure why he didn't want to tell the sheriff about somebody potentially being in the house last night. But sometimes, and usually at the right times, he felt that keeping that sort of information to himself worked out for the best. The sheriff was already on high alert about the house. Lance wasn't ready to dump any additional fuel on that fire.

The sheriff gave Lance another long stare. *He knows,* Lance thought. *Whether it's his police intuition or something else, he knows there's more to me than meets the eye. Knows I'm here for something else. He just can't prove it.*

Finally, the man stuck out his hand. "Sorry to bother you this morning, Mister..."

Lance reached out his own hand. "Call me Lance."

"Sheriff Ray Kruger," the sheriff said as they shook. "Don't hesitate to call the department if you notice anybody strange around, or have anybody bother you. Somebody always shows up this time of year."

The two men released each other's hands, and Lance stood still, his face frozen for just a moment, but long enough for Ray Kruger to notice. "Son?" he asked.

Lance's vision focused back on the sheriff and he quickly asked, "This time of year, sir?"

Sheriff Kruger sighed and started to walk down the porch steps. "It's the anniversary of the murders this week. Always brings the weirdos out the woodwork."

*Of course*, Lance thought. *One weirdo, reporting for duty, sir.*

Sheriff Kruger opened the driver's door of the Crown Vic and then looked back up to Lance. "I'm headed back into town. Do you want a ride? Do that grocery shopping you were talking about?"

Lance wasn't sure how he was going to get back into town, but he wasn't sure he trusted the situation of being locked in a moving vehicle with the sheriff right now. He smiled and waved away the offer. "I appreciate it, sir. But I've only been awake about ten minutes. I'll head in a little later."

Sheriff Kruger nodded once and got into the car, doing a three-point turn in the yard before driving away. Lance stood and watched the Crown Vic grow smaller and smaller before finally disappearing, then he turned and went back into the house.

Wondering what exactly he'd just seen when he'd shaken Sheriff Ray Kruger's hand.

[ 10 ]

INSTANT DOWNLOADS. THAT WAS WHAT LANCE HAD GROWN
to start calling them.

Just another of his unexplainable, uncontrollable gifts.

For as far back as he could remember, Lance had been able
to snatch glimpses of other people's lives with just the briefest of
touches. These glimpses could be montage-like snapshots of a
person's entire life or circumstance, or sometimes a more
specific scene, a random memory or event from a person's past.

Though Lance knew they were never actually random.
What he saw when he received these instant downloads almost
always played a role in something Lance was involved with.
Sometimes as a direct source of information, often an indirect
push or reassurance. They were helpful hints from the
Universe. If life were a video game, these glimpses would be a
cheat code.

Which was why Lance found this particular gift so incredibly frustrating to live with. He had no ability to control which
person's memory he was allowed to peek inside. No sense of
when or where this ability would kick in or what answers it
would provide. How much easier this would all be if he could

simply pick out a target, bump shoulders with them in the supermarket and then get all the answers he needed.

Sometimes he felt the Universe just liked to make him work harder than he needed to. A cosmic joke. Always tested.

Or maybe there was only so much he, as a mortal, could handle. There had to be limits to his abilities, sure. He understood that, if nothing else about who he was and what he could do.

But the Reverend and the Surfer...

They were more. They were stronger.

And that was why they terrified him.

Lance stood on the front porch of the farmhouse and leaned against one of the splintering banisters. His eyes looked toward the end of the driveway and the mountain forest beyond, where the sheriff's car had just driven out of sight, but his vision was unfocused. He was recalling what he'd just seen. When he'd shaken Sheriff Ray Kruger's hand, he'd been expecting nothing, too focused on the strange conversation he'd been engaged in, but instead of nothing, he was hit with a flash of memory of

*A young girl, maybe six or seven years old, and a boy maybe a year or two older. Outside. A backyard. A small vinyl-sided house in the background. Simple porch with two patio chairs and a child's plastic picnic table. The boy and girl were both wearing bathing suits. The boy's a solid blue pair of trunks. The girl's a matching blue one-piece that tied around the back of her neck. They both had globs of white sunscreen on their noses, running through the grass in a chorus of giggles and squeals as they headed toward a small round inflatable pool. A dull green garden hose snaking from the house, through the yard, and then climbing up the side of the pool and resting inside, filling the plastic with ice-cold city water. It was summer. The sun was hot. The water would feel good. They jumped in and splashed and giggled some more. There was a plastic submarine from the bathtub and a rubber frog that would squirt water from its mouth. They played for what seemed like hours, until the water was warm and the sun was getting too hot on their bare backs and the boredom set in and they grew annoyed with each other, as kids tend to do. The girl splashed the boy and water got in his eyes. He didn't like it and splashed her back. She yelled at him not to splash her and she splashed him again, this time with more effort, more water finding his face. The boy, a kid with a temper, lunged forward and grabbed the little girl's head and pushed it under the water. Not long, just enough to scare her. Two seconds. But it was enough. When the girl's face resurfaced, there were tears and cries of anguish. She slapped at the boy's arms and chest and scrambled over the edge of the pool running on wobbly legs back toward the house crying out, "Mamma! Mamma! Ray tried to drowneded me!" The cries and the looming fear of his mother's anger sparked his temper again, and he lashed out, not thinking of further consequences. He grabbed the nozzle of the garden hose from the pool and lifted it, grabbing the hose with both hands. He watched the girl's feet run through the grass, closer and closer to the patio, and then, timing it perfectly, the boy yanked on the hose, drawing it taut, creating a tripwire in the yard. The hose snapped up at the girl's ankles and her feet tangled, and that's when the boy realized he'd been too late. Saw what was going to happen and suddenly wished more than anything he could go back in time, just a few seconds, and do things differently. Because the little girl had gotten too close to the porch, and when she fell, she fell forward, going down down down, her knees hitting first, thankfully, before her chin cracked on the concrete edge of the patio. The boy was running then. Running before the piercing cry of pain, a wail of agony only a child can produce, hit his eardrums like a siren. He reached the little girl at the same time as his mother, who'd just come running through the back sliding glass door. His mother had swooped the girl up in her*

79

*arms and the boy had seen it at once. The split in the girl's chin, just to the left of center. The blood that had begun to pour. So much blood.*

That's what Lance had pulled from Sheriff Ray Kruger with a quick handshake. A memory from what had to be the man's childhood (*"Mamma! Mamma! Ray tried to drowneded me!"*). But the relevance was lost on Lance.

He knew it meant something. The downloads always did. But Lance was smart enough to know he wasn't going to piece it all together standing on the front porch any longer. He filed the memory away, and when his stomach grumbled he remembered he had no food in the house.

It was time to go back into town.

Lance stood in front of the upstairs bathroom mirror and brushed his teeth. Traveling light had proven not to be much of an issue for him over the past few months, which he attributed to the simplistic lifestyle he'd been raised in. Pamela Brody had never been much for possessions. Books and family and pie and tea. Walks to the park. Farmers markets and friends and the feel of a fall breeze rolling in. These were the things that mattered most to her.

They'd never needed much to be happy. And Lance didn't need much now. Aside from the few thing's he'd kept in his backpack in general—the things that had come with him when he'd been forced to flee his hometown the night his mother had died—he'd been traveling from town to town for the past couple months with nothing but a few changes of clothes, his small toiletry bag (a purchase he'd made at a small drugstore on his first stop after Westhaven), a first aid kit that was really nothing more than a couple Band-Aids, a small roll of gauze and a tiny tube of antibacterial ointment, and his cell phone and charger. He picked up items now and then that might serve some purpose to him—a small butane lighter, a pair of cheap sunglasses, some hand sanitizer. Normal things people might carry around with them. He also always tried to keep a few snacks and at least one bottle of water in the backpack as well. For emergencies.

If he was being honest with himself, despite the tragedy that had unfolded that awful night in Hillston—the night that officially ended the longest chapter of his life and started another—Lance was proud of how he'd been doing since leaving home. He wouldn't go so far as to consider himself sheltered—he'd attended public school and lived a fairly normal adolescent life (aside from, you know ... the ghosts and the visions and everything else completely *not* normal about him)—but his world had been confined to a fairly small geographical location. Any trips outside of this area had been brief and infrequent. The night he'd stepped onto that bus in Hillston, he'd essentially stepped into the rest of the world.

He finished brushing his teeth and put his toothbrush back in the toiletry pouch. The bathroom was spacious enough, with the sink and vanity, toilet, and a standalone bathtub with showerhead against the back wall, just beneath a window that overlooked the backyard. The fixtures were grimy with soap scum and mildew, and cobwebs hung from the corners and along the tops of the windows, but again, if the place were cleaned and fixed up a bit, it would be perfectly suitable. Lance didn't need much. He leaned over and rinsed his mouth with cold water from the tap. It was cool and clean-tasting, likely water from a well this far outside of town. He dumped out the travel-sized bottle of shaving cream and his disposable razor and lathered his face. But when he looked up from the sink to the mirror hanging on the wall, he froze.

Something was different.

He'd stared at himself in the mirror as he'd been brushing his teeth and decided that he'd needed to shave, and while the image of himself now looked the same—except for the white beard of foam on his face—he couldn't shake a sudden tingling at the base of his skull that told him there was more to the mirror now than there had been before.

He kept staring. Looked into his own eyes for a full ten or fifteen seconds, waiting for something to happen. He couldn't say what, but a sudden expectation filled him. He looked at the reflection of the room behind him in the glass. It likewise seemed unchanged.

And then it occurred to him that perhaps the expectation was actually on *him*. As if the mirror itself were waiting, urging him to take the next step.

If that was the case, the mirror was out of luck. Because Lance had no idea what he was supposed to do here. He took a step back and looked at the mirror in full, studying its shape and its position. Nothing looked out of the ordinary at first, except that it seemed to be hung a little high up on the wall. Lance himself was six-six, and most household bathroom mirrors only just managed to capture the bottom half of his face. Here, however, he almost appeared a normal height. Maybe close to a foot of mirror still visible above where his head's reflection stopped.

But aside from this small anomaly, everything looked just as it should.

He stepped back toward the sink and leaned to the side, seeing the mirror had some depth to it, a good four of five inches off the wall. *A medicine cabinet*, he thought, feeling as though he'd finally gotten the clue. He reached out and grabbed the bottom of the mirror and tugged gently. It popped open with no trouble, swinging out wide on its hinges.

The inside was empty, two dead flies legs-up on one of the shallow shelves.

Frustrated, Lance closed the mirror again and stared once more, still feeling an unseen hand at his back, pushing him toward the mirror. And then another idea hit him, one that seemed ridiculous at first, but not all impossible when you'd seen some of the things that Lance had.

He reached his hand out, slowly, tentatively, fingers hesitant as though they might suddenly get burned, or chopped off. Or somebody might reach out from the other side and grab his hand and pull him into...

Into what?

He sucked in a deep breath and pushed his hand forward the last few inches, and when his hand hit the glass, nothing happened.

Nothing at all.

And all at once, the invisible hand nudging him along disappeared and he felt completely silly.

Another quick succession of knocks on the front door rattled from down the stairs. Lance whipped his head toward the sound.

*Another visitor, and I still haven't had breakfast.*

So far, the entire situation had been strange and, as usual, completely unpredictable. Lance had stepped off a bus less than twenty-four hours ago, and since then he'd somehow rented a farmhouse for himself, made two new friends after dining on the best meatloaf he'd ever tasted, heard voices from unseen sources, probably had a home intruder, slept in a dead girl's bed, and been woken from some sort of nightmare by the local sheriff, who suspected Lance was up to no good.

So naturally, with his curiosity piqued and his senses on the highest alert, desperately searching for anything that might be valuable information, when the knock came from the front door, he didn't hesitate. He rushed from the bathroom, bounded down the creaking stairs two at a time, and pulled open the door so fast he nearly ripped off the handle.

"Oh! God bless America!"

A tall woman with blond hair pulled back into a ponytail, wearing slim-fitting blue jeans, sneakers, and a red-and-white long-sleeved flannel shirt with the cuffs rolled up to her forearms, jumped, shouted, and took two steps back. A plastic bucket full of various cleaning supplies swung wildly from one hand, a pair of yellow rubber gloves draped over the side.

She laughed, a nervous giggle, and then tucked a stray strand of hair behind her ear. Then she stood, smiling. A relaxed posture. Friendly. "Sorry," she said. "You startled me."

Lance studied the woman on the porch, raising one hand to shield his eyes from the sun that was still rising further above the trees and hilltop in the distance. He glanced behind her and saw a Mercedes SUV in the driveway, parked in nearly the same spot where Sheriff Ray Kruger had parked less than fifteen minutes ago. Heck, the two of them might have passed each other on the road.

Lance looked from the Mercedes to the cleaning bucket, then back to the woman's face. She was likely late thirties, early forties, slim build. Fit. Like somebody who probably did yoga and drank smoothies for breakfast. Attractive.

(*I can't get any cleaners there until tomorrow, I'm afraid.*)

Lance remembered Richard Bellows's words from yesterday afternoon. And then ... it clicked. Lance took himself back to that backroom office. The cramped workspace. All the pictures of the man's family on the wall. Remembered the faces.

"You're Mr. Bellows's wife," Lance said.

The woman laughed, made a face of mock disgust. "Oh, please. That's way too official." She stuck out a hand. "Victoria. And, yes, Rich is my husband. You're Lance, right?"

Lance shook her hand, bracing himself for another rush of memory, another download. He got nothing. Of course. Never did when he was ready for it. Her hand was cool and soft, but her grip was strong. She smelled faintly of strawberries. "Nice to meet you," Lance said. "So you're the 'cleaners' I was promised?" He pointed to the bucket full of supplies.

Victoria Bellows held the plastic bucket up to her face and grinned. "I'm afraid so. Hard to find good help around this town. So you're stuck with me." She laughed, and it sounded genuine and pleasant. She struck Lance as a woman who lived a very happy and comfortable life. And there was good in her. Somebody to whom the word *self-importance* did not apply; someone who didn't hold herself above anyone, despite circumstance. She'd just driven a vehicle that Lance guessed could easily cost fifty grand to come clean an old farmhouse for a stranger. And she was doing it with a smile and a laugh.

"Uh ... Lance?"

"Yes, ma'am?"

"Did I catch you in the middle of something?" She made a quick gesture at brushing her face with her index finger, and Lance felt the heat rise to his cheeks, suddenly very aware of the layer of shaving cream lathered onto his face. Right on time, a glob of the stuff fell from his chin and plopped onto the boards of the porch, splattering like a drop of bird shit.

The two of them stood and stared at the mess for what felt to Lance like half an hour. Then, to his horror, another glob fell and splattered next to the first one, the porch beginning to look like a crude Rorschach test.

Victoria Bellows let out a quick, explosive laugh when the second drop hit, falling into a fit of giggles and shooing Lance back inside the house. "Go," she said. "Finish up. I'll wipe this up and then start downstairs."

"Sorry," Lance said. "But thank you." He turned on his heel and bounded up the stairs, marveling over just how much of a doofus he could make himself out to be with women. He wasn't one to embarrass easily, but even he knew that the anorexic-Santa-Claus-in-comfy-clothes look wasn't his best first impression.

He shaved quickly, but carefully. He'd like to avoid bloodshed today, especially his own, if he could at all help it. As he ran the razor over his face, he couldn't keep his eyes from occasionally refocusing on the mirror itself instead of his reflection in it. Continued trying to look deeper at the object itself, reaching out again, cautiously, for that sense of expectancy that'd seemed to be calling out to him earlier. He looked past his reflection and into the background, at the wall and linen closet door behind him.

He got nothing. Saw nothing but what was supposed to be there.

A sound of running water from somewhere below him shoved the possibility of the mirror having more meaning to the back of his mind. He finished shaving, rinsed his face, and then stripped down and pulled fresh boxers, socks, and a t-shirt from his backpack, changing into them. He gave his hoodie a sniff, found it more than acceptable, and then tugged it back on. After the day on the bus yesterday, and then the walking in the rain, he wanted a shower badly, but that would have to wait until later. He shoved his dirty clothes into a plastic shopping bag at the bottom of his backpack, tossed in his toiletry bag, and then zipped the whole thing up and swung it over his shoulder. He didn't like to leave anything behind when he left places he was staying. Mostly because he couldn't quite trust the idea that he'd ever return to retrieve them. Better to be prepared. At least, as prepared as he could be.

He found Victoria Bellows in the half bathroom downstairs, yellow rubber gloves nearly up to her elbows, bent over the sink, scrubbing hard on a green ring around the drain. Lance watched the muscles in her back and shoulders work beneath the fabric of her shirt and thought maybe yoga was only the tip of the iceberg.

Victoria caught sight of him behind her in the mirror above the sink, and instead of asking him why he was being creepy and just standing there staring, she used a yellow finger to point up toward the light fixture. Two of the four bulbs were burnt out.

"I've got a pack of bulbs in the car, too," she said, halting the scrubbing for a moment and turning on the hot water tap. Pipes gurgled and groaned somewhere in the wall before water spat from the faucet. It was murky at first but cleared quickly. "Rich said you might need a few. Been a while since anyone's been here."

She rinsed the sink out, scrubbed away another bit of grime, then rinsed again. Satisfied, she stood and turned to look at Lance, eyed the straps of his backpack. "Headed out?"

Lance nodded. "I am. Though if you want some help, I'm more than happy to stay."

This wasn't exactly true. Lance, though he tended to be well-organized and neat, hated the act of actually cleaning as much as the next guy. But, as a gentleman, he felt obligated to at least offer his assistance. Especially since Victoria Bellows seemed to be doing this work as a favor.

She waved him off, pulling off one of her gloves and wiping a small droplet of sweat from her brow. "Hot in here," she said. "I might open the windows, if you don't mind."

"Be my guest."

She nodded and slid past him in the hallway, pulling the cord to raise the blinds on one of the front windows and then unlatching the lock and throwing the window open. Immediately, the cool fall air found its way inside. She repeated the process for the remaining windows in the front of the house and then turned, saying, "Okay, that's better."

Lance stared at her, trying to work something out in his mind. Something that had at first seemed normal but now seemed out of place. She saw him looking her over and cocked her head, smiling. Not suspicious. Curious. "What?"

"I've got to ask," Lance said. "Why are you here?"

She didn't miss a beat. Held up her rubber gloves. "To clean."

Lance nodded. "Right. But why you? Why not an actual cleaning company? Somebody who does this for a living, or a part-time job, or whatever. Surely you don't clean all of Mr. Bellows's rental properties. He's got to have a company or business he uses, right?"

Victoria's face fell, slightly. Not in a disappointed look, but more in a "So I guess we have to have to this conversation" look. She sighed. "He does usually have somebody else do it, yes. A local crew. They do great work. But..." She paused, as if contemplating whether she wanted to actually say it all out loud.

Lance finished for her. "They won't come here because of what happened. Because of the murders."

Victoria's posture relaxed again and she winked at him. "Bingo."

"They think it's haunted?"

Victoria opened her mouth to speak, but paused again. Only shrugged and said, "Something like that."

"Something like that?"

Victoria sighed again. "Look, I don't want to fill your head with a bunch of nonsense. Scare you out of here over something so silly."

"You won't scare me. I promise." Lance said it so matter-of-factly that Victoria gave him a hard, silent look. Lance didn't elaborate.

Then she smiled big and bright and shrugged again, as if about to reveal the punchline of a joke. "Fine," she said. "The cleaners won't come because they think the place is haunted, but it's a bit more than that. They believe the girl that lived here —Mary was her name—they think she was a witch."

Lance said nothing.

"And they think her spirit is still here and is actually evil. Ready to dole out harm and misfortune to anyone who trespasses on her property."

The way Victoria Bellows said it, all with an undertone of complete mockery and disbelief, as one might when discussing the latest Elvis sighting, or ridiculous tales of alien encounters whose only witnesses were backwoods hillbillies with barely enough teeth to chew gum, told Lance all he needed to know about her opinion on the subject.

He smiled at her, posing the question lightly. "And you don't believe any of it?"

Victoria shook her head. "Not a word." Then asked, "You?"

"I'll believe it when I see it." *And if anybody is going to see it, it's me.* "So the cleaners are afraid of a witch, and you decided you'd come clean instead?"

"What can I say?" Victoria said, making her way toward him, back to the bathroom. "I love my husband, and he needed some help. He said you seemed like a really great guy and he felt terrible renting the place to you, knowing it was likely filthy inside. He said he should have been more adamant about not letting you stay here until we could get it in order."

"He said I was a great guy?"

Again, the shrug. "You must have made an impression." Then: "Was he wrong?"

Lance smiled. "I like to think he wasn't."

"Good. Now it's my turn to ask the question. Why are *you* here?"

Lance leaned against the wall, watching Victoria remove a spray bottle from the bucket and start spraying disinfectant on the bathroom counter. "You know you're the second person today to ask me that question?"

"Oh, really? Who was first?"

"Sheriff Kruger."

The spray bottle stopped spraying and she turned to look at him, seriousness in her eyes. "Ray was here?"

Lance nodded. "Maybe fifteen minutes before you."

"Interesting." She gave Lance a look, chewed on her bottom lip for a moment, thinking. "I didn't think he actually came up here anymore. Rumor is he always sends somebody else. A deputy, or some lackey. Though I think most folks have sorta forgotten about this place."

"Why doesn't he come up here?" Lance asked, feeling close to something, some explanation as to why the sheriff was so suspicious of him, why he carried with him such a coldness.

Victoria looked down and shook her head. Spoke softly. "He just took it all so hard, and he's never really completely gotten over it. But who would, really?"

Lance said nothing.

"The worst part—or maybe the saddest part—is that after it happened, he went on for days, mumbling how he knew nothing good would happen here. That too much evil had already happened in this house and it only made sense it would happen again. He said he should have never let her move here. But he thought he was doing the right thing. Thought he was helping her out."

The comment about too much evil in the house completely derailed Lance's train of thought. "Wait, are you saying that the *sheriff* thinks this place is haunted?" He thought back to the conversation he'd had with Ray Kruger less than an hour ago. Nothing the man had said really made it seem like he was pro-ghost, so to speak. Quite the opposite.

Victoria only turned and started spraying the countertop again. "Nobody really knows what Ray thinks anymore. He's never been the same since it happened." She pulled a cleaning rag from the bucket and started scrubbing the counter. "Don't get me wrong," she said, "he does a fine job as sheriff. But ... well, I guess you'd just have to have known him before to see what I mean. It's like the Ray we have now is only pretending to be Ray. Like outwardly he's the same, but inside ... it's like he's empty. Cold. Does that make sense?"

Lance saw the image of the man alone in Mama's, tucked into a booth away from everyone, silently reading his Kindle. Remembered that coldness.

"It does."

Lance's stomach growled loudly, and he was quickly hit with just how hungry he'd grown. With nothing to eat or drink since his meal at Mama's, he was running on empty. Victoria heard the growl and shooed him away again.

"Go," she said. "You've got things to do."

Lance thanked her again for cleaning and turned to leave, deciding to head out the back door and attempt to find the trail that supposedly led down the side of the hill and into town. He'd made it as far as two steps into the kitchen when there was another rattle of knocking at the front door.

Lance stopped and turned back. *What is this, a bed and breakfast all of a sudden?*

Victoria Bellows stuck her head out of the bathroom. Looked at him and asked, "Expecting somebody?"

"No," Lance said, walking toward the door. "But I hope they brought coffee."

## [ 12 ]

FOR A PLACE THAT EVERYBODY HE'D MET SO FAR HAD indicated was avoided and feared, there sure were a lot of visitors at the spook farm this morning. But Lance couldn't honestly say he was that surprised. He had a tendency to accelerate otherwise dormant situations.

With Victoria Bellows still half out of the bathroom, looking toward the front door, Lance turned the knob and opened the door.

"Did you rent a Mercedes? What exactly is it you do again?"

Luke stood on the front porch, wearing basketball shorts and a baggy hoodie, a huge Nike swoosh emblazoned on the front. He had bedhead, and his face was peppered with stubble. He looked like he hadn't been awake long. He looked at Lance, waiting for an answer.

Lance shook his head. "Not mine." He looked over his shoulder, saw Victoria Bellows poking her head out from the bathroom. Apparently satisfied the person at the door did not require her attention, she disappeared back into the room and returned to her work, the squeaking of the cleaning rag on the counter faintly heard.

"Oh, right," Luke said, "So you've got company, then? Sorry. I didn't know. But I mean, how would I, right? This was Susan's idea. I mean, not that I mind, but ... you know." He paused. Took a breath. "Shit, man, I need some coffee. Brain ain't working right yet. I came to see if you wanted a lift into town. But if you're busy..."

"That'd be great," Lance said, stepping out and closing the door behind him. "I was about to start walking."

Luke took a step back and looked from Lance back to the Mercedes and then at the house. Raised an eyebrow.

"Somebody here to clean," Lance said, offering no more unless pressed. Just like with Sheriff Kruger earlier, Lance tried to make a habit of not throwing people's names into the mix unless necessary.

Luke grinned. "Is that a euphemism?"

Lance shook his head and started walking down the steps. "I'm not that lucky."

"Yeah," Luke said, following toward his Jeep. "I hear ya."

Lance got into the front passenger seat and Luke backed all the way down the driveway, staring intently into his rearview mirror. He pulled out of the driveway and started the winding road down the hillside, an awkward silence all at once heavy in the air.

Lance broke it. "How was the movie?"

"Shit," Luke said. Then he sighed. "I mean, it was okay I guess. Some rom-com Suze wanted to see. I made her see the new *Transformers* last time we went, so I figured I owed her one."

Lance smiled. "How chivalrous."

"Right? I'm still stuck at third base, though."

Lance didn't know what it was that made Luke feel comfortable enough with him to divulge this sort of information. Maybe it was their similar age, or their odd connection from their basketball days. Maybe Lance just had an honest face.

"She's worth it, though, man. Totally worth it. You know what I mean?"

Lance thought of Leah, then quickly pushed the thought away. *Not now.*

"Yes," Lance said. "I do." Then, to change the subject, "I appreciate you stopping by. I'm starving."

"No sweat, man. Seems like you sorta had your evening rushed last night, what with getting in later in the day, and then all the damn rain. I was headed to grab a coffee and hit the gym, and Suze thought maybe you'd need a lift. Are you going to rent a car today? I think we've got a couple Uber drivers around, but I can't guarantee that. Most of them are closer to the city. And there's a taxi service, I think."

"I'll figure something out," Lance said, then asked, "Hey, what day is it?" He tried to think back, count the days in his head. "Saturday?"

Luke kept his eyes on the road, but Lance could feel the shift of his gaze toward him. A quick, questioning look. "Yeah," Luke said. "It's Saturday. Man, you must stay busy if you don't even know what day it is."

Lance nodded. "Something like that."

The roads were still damp in places, but the sun was doing a good job of drying everything off. The sky was bright blue, few clouds. No traces of the heavy rains from the night before. Luke drove the Jeep expertly around the sharp bends in the road, and soon they were spat out onto flat ground, headed in the direction of town. Lance was hungry and craving coffee, but something tugged at his gut, an odd sensation that he should not have left the house. He tried to swallow it down, blaming his hunger and caffeine deprivation.

But then the thought about the bathroom mirror again. How it had seemed to be reaching out to him.

But that had been a bust. He'd seen nothing in the mirror. Found nothing inside.

"So where to?" Luke asked.

Lance was about to tell his new friend to turn around, take him back. But then his stomach grumbled loud enough to be heard over the rumble of the off-road tires, and he asked, "Does Mama's serve breakfast?"

"Best in town."

Lance grinned. "Of course it is."

A few minutes later Luke had pulled the Jeep into the small parking lot in front of Mama's, and Lance opened the passenger door. "Thanks again," he said.

Luke reached across the center console and balled his fist. "Sure thing, man."

Lance bumped Luke's fist with his own, an action that brought to light a sense of normalcy and regularity that seemed so unfamiliar it was almost overwhelming. Just two guys hanging out. Two friends saying goodbye. It was moments like these that startled Lance into realizing just how abnormal his existence was. Sometimes he felt so inhuman, so detached from the real world it was like drowning in a blackness so deep and dark nobody could hear you scream. On the surface, he appeared to be a functioning member of society. But inside, at times he felt like nothing more than a tool the Universe was using for its own bidding.

Lance closed the Jeep's door and watched Luke back out of the parking lot and drive away. Then he went inside.

The aroma of bacon and biscuits and coffee sent all negative thoughts fleeing from his mind. He could practically taste the food on the air, and he had to refrain from doing his best snake impression and darting his tongue out of his mouth to try.

"Sit anywhere you like!" a voice called from the kitchen. A familiar voice. One full of energy and slight irritation.

Joan.

Lance looked around the restaurant and saw most of the tables where full, but the booth in the rear corner, the booth Sheriff Kruger had sat in the night before, was empty, and Lance walked over and slumped into it, facing the door. A moment later, Joan emerged through the swinging kitchen door, scanned the room, saw the new face, and waddled over to him, sliding a plastic menu onto the table.

"You were here last night," she said. Her face was red from the heat of the kitchen, or maybe she always looked like that. Forever flushed.

Lance nodded. "I was. So were you."

Joan was unimpressed with his observation. "Coffee?"

"Please," Lance said.

She walked away, saying something to the group at another table, causing them all to laugh. Lance smiled and looked over the menu. It was full of all the makings of a hearty country breakfast: pancakes, country ham, eggs, bacon, biscuits, grits, sausage—the only remotely healthy item Lance could see was a blueberry muffin. But that was fine. His metabolism was in perfect working order. Plus, he walked a lot.

Joan returned and set a coffee mug on the table and then filled it right to the brim with black coffee. "You seem like a black guy to me," she said.

"Sorry?" Lance asked.

"Coffee. You take it black, don't you?"

"Oh. Yes, I do." He smiled up at her. "How'd you know?"

Joan shrugged, the skin around her neck rolling up and down like rippling waves. "Been doing this a long time." She winked and then got back to business. "What'll you have?"

Lance ordered pancakes with eggs and bacon and asked

Joan if she could double however many pancakes they normally served. She nodded, turned to leave, and then turned back. "You really staying up at that place?"

Lance took a slow sip of his coffee. It was hot and wonderful. He didn't need to ask for clarification. "I am."

Joan crinkled her brow, Lance's neutral tone causing her to pause. "And you know what happened?"

"I know a family was killed there."

Another sip of coffee. Nobody actually knew what had happened that night, and Lance wasn't going to support any theories quite yet.

Joan looked at him hard, then nodded again and walked to the kitchen, disappearing through the swinging door. Lance held his mug to his lips and blew on it, cooling the coffee before taking another sip. He looked out the window and watched a few cars drive by lazily, the Saturday morning traffic slow and sleepy. The asphalt was dotted with wet spots and puddles, the sun heliographing off the wet surfaces. It was a tranquil scene. Relaxing. Lance felt momentarily at ease, ready to enjoy his meal.

And then there was a rocking of the table and booth and Lance turned and saw Joan sliding into the seat across from him.

"So what are you?" she asked. "A reporter? Are you writing a book? Doing research?"

"What?"

"I know you're staying at that house, and I know you're telling everyone you're a consultant. To me that just means you're hiding the truth."

Small towns. No secrets.

Lance said nothing.

Joan kept going. "I don't think you're up to anything bad, mostly because little Susan seems to have taken a liking to you, and that girl's got about some of the best intuition I've seen for somebody her age." She held up her hands when she saw Lance's face. "Oh, no, not 'like you' like that. She's dating that Luke fella. I just mean she seems to think you're one of the good ones. And I believe her. Like I told you, I've been doing this a long time. You work in food service long enough, you start to get good at reading people. Do you understand?"

Lance nodded.

"Good. So listen. I don't know what you're really doing up there, but I know you're involved somehow. I don't believe for a second that you randomly ended up there. You came here with the intention of staying at that house. So, if you *are* writing a book or an article or researching whatever project it is you're working on, I want to tell you something. You can quote me, but I want it to be anonymous."

Lance was about to hold up his hands, try and slow Joan down so he could end her conspiracy about him. But then he thought better of it. If she was willing to divulge information to him that might help him figure out what this mess was all about, he might as well let her.

Lance looked around at the other tables. Nobody seemed to be paying him and Joan any mind, so he set his mug down and leaned in close over the table, playing the role of interested listener. "Okay. What is it you want to say?"

Joan leaned in, her ample bosom spilling onto the tabletop. "And you'll keep my name out of anything you write?"

Lance nodded. "I promise." It was an easy promise to make. He'd never write anything about this, period.

Joan's eyes flicked to her right, out toward the dining room. "Shit," she said. "One sec." Then she heaved herself out of the booth, rushed across the room to refill a glass of water, and then was back, the booth shifting again with her weight as she slid back in across from Lance.

"Look," she started. "I know what they say about me around

here. 'Ol' Joan's nothing but a gossip. Nosy. She'll say anything to anyone for a bigger tip.' Sure, folks seem to like me okay, but I don't know that a one of them actually trusts me. Not sure anybody has since my husband passed."

"I'm sorry for your loss," Lance said.

She waved him off. "S'okay. Henry was a pain in the ass." She said it jokingly, but Lance felt the twinge of pain flash through her at the memory.

"Anyway, my opinion might not mean much to the folks round here, but I'll just go ahead and set the record straight for you, okay?"

"Okay."

Joan looked over toward the rest of the dining room again, only this time it was apparent she wasn't checking for empty glasses or dirty dishes that needed to be bussed. She was seeing if anybody was eavesdropping. Satisfied, she leaned in close again and said, "I don't know what happened that night, but Mark Benchley didn't kill his family."

## [ 13 ]

Lance sat back and lifted his coffee cup to his mouth, taking another sip. It was cooling now, and he would soon need a refill. He looked at Joan, who had sat back as well after her revelation, and saw the conviction in her eyes. She was as serious as a heart attack.

"I've only heard one version of the story," Lance said, downing the rest of his coffee. "And in that version, Mr. Benchley killed his wife and daughter and then shot himself in the living room."

Joan rolled her eyes and nodded. "Yeah, yeah ... that's what everybody thinks. Easiest explanation, right? Blame the God-fearing lunatic?"

"But you don't think that's what happened."

"I know it's not what happened."

Lance made a sympathetic face, tried not to sound harsh with his next words. "Were you there that night? Did you see what happened?"

Joan's face softened. "No, of course not. That's ... that's not what I mean."

"So you can't say for sure."

She eyed him, as if suddenly suspicious. "Yeah … you've got reporter written all over you."

Lance had never considered a career in journalism. He suspected too many of his sources would be of the spirit variety for him to be taken seriously. He backed off a bit, tried to lighten his tone. "Help me understand."

Joan leaned forward again, eying his coffee mug and asked, "You need a refill?"

Lance waved her off. "No, thank you. I can wait till you're finished." This answer seemed not to sit well with Joan, as if her inner waitress was jumpy, twitching at the thought of a customer in need of a refill.

"You sure?"

"Positive."

She took one last glance at the mug, then shrugged, as if to indicate there was nothing else she could do. Then she leaned back, crossed her arms, and started talking.

"Mark came in here at least twice a week for breakfast. Wheat toast, two eggs over easy. Coffee with a splash of cream. He'd sit right here in this booth," she said. "Right where you're sitting now."

Lance felt a strange chill at this. Joan continued.

"He was always friendly, always polite. Never bothered anyone. Sat here and would read the paper, both the local and national. And then," she sighed, "yes, he spent a lot of time going through his Bible. He was always making notes in the margins, underlining passages. To say he was well read in regard to scripture would be an understatement. He took his faith very seriously." Then: "It made some people uncomfortable. But otherwise, there was nothing out of the ordinary about him, except he was a tall drink of water. Had a good couple inches on just about most men."

"I heard he liked to walk the streets and give impromptu

sermons," Lance said. "And folks didn't necessarily think he was in his right mind. Is that right?"

Joan gave another eye roll. "*Folks* like to gossip. *Folks* like to blow things out of proportion for the sake of a good story. Now, I'm not saying Mark didn't try to witness to his fair share of people in town, and, yes, I do believe he did speak to a small gathering of people having a picnic one day in the park—unwarranted, possibly. But it didn't take long for people to label him as a crazy person. Honestly, the fact he had no job and not much to do to occupy his time during the day is probably what made folks so uneasy about him. He seemed like a bum, a lazy freeloader with nothing better to do than to shove his ideology down people's throats." She paused, looked around the dining room. Still, nobody looked their direction.

"But it wasn't like that. I won't say Mark wasn't a tad fanatical—old-school, even. But he was gentle. And he was *smart*. Boy, you could ask him about any topic you could think of and he'd be able to carry on a conversation with you. He'd either read a book or read an article about it, and just seemed to know. He was a joy to talk with. Not dull and boring like most of these people."

After she'd said it, she quickly turned her head to look and see if anybody had heard, not meaning to offend. She looked back at Lance, her cheeks redder than before.

"And here's the other thing, the part that makes me certain he didn't kill them. Mark was absolutely in love with his family."

Lance said nothing. Waited.

"He talked about them all the time. Loved to boast about how Natalie was helping to save lives over at Central Medical, and you could just tell he thought she was the most beautiful thing on earth. And with Mary..." Joan smiled, her eyes unfocused, clearly lost deep in memory. "Mary was his absolute pride and joy. He was so proud of her. So excited to see the woman she was growing up to be." She shook her head as if to clear it, then looked Lance dead in the eyes. "Mark would have died if anything had happened to Mary. He'd have killed himself to save her. And that's why I'd bet my life there's no way he could do something so horrific to his girl."

Lance waited to see if there was more, but Joan had apparently told all she needed to. He asked one last question. "So what happened at the end? With Mrs. Benchley quitting her job and Mary going off to the new school?"

Joan's face grew heavy. "Mark stopped coming for breakfast, too." She sighed and pushed her way out of the booth, grabbing Lance's coffee mug as she stood. "You're the reporter," she said. "Maybe you can figure out the rest. Because nobody around here knows a thing more than I just told you."

Lance watched as Joan carried his mug to a server station against the wall next to the kitchen door and began pouring coffee from a nearly full pot. He couldn't help but think she was wrong. Maybe not about Mark Benchley, not all of it. But she was wrong if she thought she had all the answers. *Somebody* in town had to know more about the Benchley family's situation. *Somebody* was hiding something. Even if Mark Benchley actually did kill his own family, there was more too it. Of this, Lance was all at once certain.

Joan returned and set his full cup of coffee on the table with the deft hand of a practiced server. It was completely full and she hadn't spilled a drop. "If you want to call somebody a kook— a crazy person—look at Natalie's uncle." She stood at the side of the table, hands on her hips, as if she'd just challenged Lance to prove her wrong.

"Thank you," Lance said. "And also, *what*?"

"Natalie's uncle, Joseph. He was the weird one. Ask anyone who knew him around here. The last ten years or so of his life, he was basically a hermit. Only came to town once a week for groceries and whatnot. Was some sort of engineer in the Army. Could build anything, s'what I always heard. Once he retired, he lived up on that hill all by himself the rest of his life, it seems. Never married, never dated. Kept to himself. But every time somebody tried to talk to him when he came to town, ask him how things were going, he'd go on these long-winded rants about government conspiracies, how the commies were taking over our government. He said the US would be part of Russia or China in no time."

Lance took a sip of his coffee, letting Joan finish her venting about something Lance felt had absolutely no bearing on the Benchley family's murder. Maybe she was a gossip, after all. Though that didn't necessarily mean she was spreading false information.

"Rumor has it," Joan said, "he'd even gone so far as to build himself some sort of fallout shelter up at the farm. A bunker, or something. And knowing what I know about Joseph, I wouldn't put it past his crazy ass. It's like he only felt safe up at that farm."

Lance couldn't ignore the irony. Nobody seemed to feel safe at the farm now.

"Anyway, your food's ready," Joan said. Then she turned and vanished through the kitchen door, returning a moment later and delivering Lance his plates of food. "Enjoy," she said.

Lance ate in silence, devouring the food—which was very good—and thinking about everything Joan had told him. Tried to see how any of it fit together, explored what he knew, looking for possible holes. But the truth was, if this situation had been a logic problem, the answer Lance would circle would be *Not enough information*.

When he'd finished eating, he paid his bill, leaving what he hoped Joan considered to be a generous tip, and then slung his backpack onto his shoulders and left the restaurant. He walked across the parking lot and then crossed the street, cutting across the post office's parking lot and turning right on the sidewalk. He wanted to see if Rich Bellows was in his office. Lance thought the odds were pretty slim, considering it was a Saturday, and with Rich's wife currently cleaning the farmhouse, somebody had to be watching the children Lance had seen in the office photographs. But still, he'd try. He wanted to ask whether anybody else had keys to the farmhouse, or if by chance the back door could have somehow been left unlocked the last time anybody had been there.

Lance made it two blocks from the post office when a quick *whoop-whoop* from a siren made him jump and spin around. A sheriff's office cruiser was idling in the street, the passenger window rolled down. The officer behind the wheel motioned for Lance to walk over. Lance did, leaning down to look through the opened window. "Yes, Officer?"

"Are you Lance Brody?"

*This can't be good.*

"Yes, sir."

The officer nodded with his head to the back door. "Need you to get in, son."

*Nope. Not good at all.*

LANCE DIDN'T HESITATE, BECAUSE REALLY, WHAT WOULD his options have been? Try to outrun a vehicle? Unlikely. Talk his way out of it? He didn't even know what *it* was. So in the end, he simply asked, "Where are we going?"

The sheriff's deputy said, "The station." And Lance nodded and opened the back door and got in.

All at once, the memory of the near-life-ending ride in the back of a police car in Westhaven hit him hard. It was an almost nauseating sense of fear and déjà vu. But Lance was nothing if not strong-minded, a realist, and he took a couple deep breaths and calmed his nerves. Westhaven was different. There was unspeakable evil there. And he'd defeated it. Well, with the help of a few friends. Right now, in Ripton's Grove, he was simply sitting in the back of a police car, being driven to the local sheriff's office. Which in its own right caused an unshakable sense of dread, but on a more earthly level.

When the deputy was certain Lance was inside and situated, he picked up the radio from the dash and told whoever was on the other line what had happened and that he was en route to the station. The deputy had used the word *suspect* when referring to Lance, and Lance didn't like that at all. He thought about asking more questions, but in the end decided to be quiet and see how things would play out. Unless people in Westhaven had somehow tracked him down to Ripton's Grove and had questions, he suspected he was either currently being brought in because Sheriff Kruger still had a hair up his ass about Lance's being in town, at the farm, or because of a misunderstanding. Misunderstanding had a habit of following Lance.

The deputy pulled the car away from the sidewalk and started to drive, slowly and carefully, occasionally glancing at Lance in the rearview. They drove in the direction of the bus station, a few curious pedestrians standing on the sidewalk and staring at Lance in the back of the car as he rode by, concerned expressions plastered on their faces. Lance had to wonder if Joan was already telling all the new customers at Mama's that the new guy in town had just been picked up by the sheriff's department and being brought in for questioning. The rumor mill would be churning hard and fast. The deputy made a right turn just past the bus station parking lot. Lance glanced toward the building and wondered what he'd be doing right now if he'd stayed on the bus, gone somewhere else. But he knew it was a silly thought. He was meant to be here. That much was becoming quite certain.

"You're awfully quiet," the deputy said, giving Lance an accusatory glare he didn't appreciate.

Lance met the man's eyes in the rearview and said, "Sorry, I didn't know this was *Taxi Cab Confessions*."

The deputy's mouth opened, closed, and then the man shook his head and mumbled, "S*mart-ass*."

Lance had been called worse. He felt only a little guilty for his outburst. He knew he was innocent of whatever situation they suspected he'd been a part of, and this entire side trip to the sheriff's office was doing nothing but wasting Lance's time. Not that he was pressed for time, exactly, but still, it was the principle.

The Ripton's Grove sheriff's office was a dated-looking one-story brick building that looked as though it might have once been a bank. The parking lot was large and mostly empty. A cluster of county vehicles and police cruisers much like the one Lance was riding in sat behind wire fencing to the right side of the building. The gate to this parking area was open, and Lance had no difficulty spying the black Crown Vic that had visited him earlier this morning. Lance looked back to the building. Kruger was in there somewhere. Waiting for him.

Lance's deputy chauffeur pulled the vehicle up to the front of the building and parked, getting out and making a big show of stretching his back and checking his cell phone. If he thought this would irritate Lance—being forced to wait longer in the back of the vehicle with no explanation—he was sadly mistaken. Lance was incredibly patient. And, again, had nowhere he needed to be.

After the deputy was apparently satisfied he'd stalled long enough to get Lance's blood boiling, he slowly walked around to Lance's door and opened it. Lance hadn't moved an inch before the man said, "Nice and easy, now. Take it slow." He placed a hand on Lance's upper arm and pulled. Lance grabbed his back-pack from the seat next to him and allowed himself to be "helped" from the rear of the car. Standing at his full height, Lance was easily a foot taller than the deputy, and as if underestimating Lance's height, the man took a small step back and said, "You aren't going to be any trouble, right?"

Lance said nothing. Waited.

The deputy nodded, as if he'd somehow made his point. He

stepped forward and grabbed Lance's upper arm again, although this time he was noticeably gentler, and led Lance into the building.

They made their way through the lobby/waiting room, and the deputy waved to a middle-aged woman behind a pane of glass. She didn't even look up from the romance novel she was reading to reach down and push a button that caused the door at the end of the wall to buzz and a lock to disengage. The deputy opened the door and nudged Lance through it. From there, Lance was forced to surrender his backpack to be searched—for evidence, they told him—and he agreed, only adding, "There's dirty underwear in there," which drew an uncomfortable stare from the other deputy, who'd been tasked with the job. Then the deputy who'd driven him here marched him to what felt like the back corner of the building and stuck him in a small interview room, telling Lance to sit down and not move and that somebody would be by shortly.

Lance sat. The door closed. Lance sighed and looked around the room.

At once, it looked like something you'd see on one of those TV crime dramas. Small, cramped space. Single metal table in the middle of the room, with two chairs. There was dull fluorescent lighting overhead and a large mirror on the left wall (two-way, Lance presumed). No windows. The walls were a faded gray. Dingy was one word that came to mind, but depressing might be more apropos. Lance understood; this room was meant to make a person uncomfortable, meant to make them give answers and admit to crimes and do what they needed to do to get out and see a shred of sunlight again.

While Lance was mostly unfazed by the room—his life had prepared him well for less-than-pleasant situations—he felt the slow swell of impatience rise in his chest with each passing minute. Something was afoul here, and his curiosity was growing. Time was being wasted.

He leaned back in the uncomfortable chair and closed his eyes. Began to take a couple of deep breaths when he heard a man laugh and say, "Boy, we don't even have time for all the stories I could tell you of the idiots I've had come through this room—on *both* sides of the table, mind you."

Lance's eyes shot open and found a man seated directly across from him in the other chair.

The man smiled, showing coffee-stained teeth, and winked. He wore dark khaki pants and a matching shirt. The sleeves of the shirt were rolled up around thick forearms; the buttons looked strained against a substantial stomach and broad chest. His face was weathered, the skin drooping around his neck and cheeks. His eyes shone bright, but the bags under them told a different story altogether. His hair was gray and lay in short, sloppy curls around his ears and forehead. To Lance, he looked well into his fifties, maybe early sixties, but he likely felt much older.

What struck Lance as more interesting than the man's sudden appearance was what was pinned on the man's shirt, chest-high and opposite a folding pocket with what looked like a pack of cigarettes tucked neatly away.

A gold star. The word *Sheriff* emblazoned on it.

Lance looked up and met the man's eyes.

"Heart attack," the man said. Then he looked around the room and smiled, as if recalling pleasant memories. "Right here in this very room." He laughed. "Brought a kid in for shoplifting, couldn't have been more than twelve or thirteen, and I was just having some fun with him, trying to put the fear of God in him, if you know what I mean. Wasn't nothing serious. I knew his pops, and was just waiting on the old fool to get down here and pick his kid up. Well, about halfway through my fake interrogation I felt the ol' ticker seize up and *bam!* Lights out." He shook his head. "The whole town always said if I didn't slow down some and take better care of myself, something like that would happen. But nobody would have thought it would go down while I was just trying to have a little fun."

Lance said nothing. Waited.

"Not real chatty, are ya, kid?"

At this point in his life, Lance wasn't certain of a great many things, but he had come to understand that spirits—ghosts, if you like—weren't always visible to him. Lance had a theory that they had to expend some sort of energy to make themselves seen, and after a while they'd have to slip back beyond the veil to recharge their batteries, so to speak. Sure, Lance had had social visits from the lingering dead. That wasn't unusual. But more often than not, they came with a purpose. Lance felt this was likely one of those times.

Instead of answering, Lance asked a question of his own. "How long ago were you sheriff?"

The man's head looked down to the star pinned to his chest, his eyes suddenly looking sad. Then he grunted. "I was taking care of this town when Kruger here was still shittin' his diapers." He sighed. "Been a long time."

"Why are you still here?" Lance asked.

The man smiled again, then shrugged, as if he knew his answer was going to disappoint. "This is what I was born to do. I got nothing else."

Lance didn't claim to have any understanding of what followed our mortal lives, no evidence specific to a Heaven or hell. But the simple fact that there were such things as spirits—like the man sitting across the table and countless others before him—did suggest that our souls have the ability to move on from this world and into another.

Beyond the veil, and then further still.

"Besides," the man said, "I got nobody waitin' for me anywhere. Been a loner my whole life. And don't go getting sad for me, I preferred it that way."

Lance said nothing. He was beginning to understand what it meant to be a loner himself.

"Anyway," the man continued, "I didn't pop in to talk about me—though you'd love some of the stories, trust me on that! I wanted to help you with the case you're working on."

"Case, sir?"

The man sat back and looked at Lance like he was trying to pull a fast one on him. "Yes, son! The case. The Benchley house. You're here to figure out what really happened, right?"

Now it was Lance's turn to sigh. "Apparently."

The deceased sheriff nodded and leaned forward, resting his thick arms on the table. "And what have you learned so far? Got any leads?"

Lance began to feel even more like he was in a TV crime drama. He had to suppress a sudden urge to get up, slam his hand on the table and yell, "You can't handle the truth!"

Wait ... that was in a courtroom. Close enough.

Lance didn't bother with asking such trivial questions such as how this man knew who he was and why he was in town. He went straight into the details. "I've got two sides of things. The most popular opinion seems to be that Mark Benchley was crazy and killed his wife and daughter before shooting himself. The second and most recent opinion I've heard is that Mark Benchley would never have hurt a hair on his wife and daughter's head, so there was another sort of foul play involved." Lance stopped and considered what he'd said. Shrugged. "So really, either Mark Benchley killed them all, or somebody else did. Not exactly a groundbreaking investigation I'm conducting here."

The Ghost of Sheriff Past looked disappointed. "That's all?"

Lance thought some more. "I've heard voices at the farm. A man and a woman. There's nobody there but me."

"So the voices are like me?" the man asked.

"I'm not sure. I know they're otherworldly, so to speak, but I don't see or feel any other presence along with the voices. It's just sound."

The man considered this for a moment, then sat up straight, excited. "Maybe it's a message? A ... recording of some sort? A clue that's been waiting for somebody to find it?"

Lance crinkled his brow. "Waiting for *me*?"

"Waiting for you or someone like you."

Lance didn't allow himself to dwell on thoughts of other people in the world who shared his gifts. He'd never met anyone else who could do the things he could except for the Reverend. Though he liked to hope that they did exist out there somewhere.

"It's not much of a clue," Lance said.

"Maybe there's more, and you just haven't found it yet."

"I don't exactly know how to look."

"You will," the man said. "I can tell. You'd have made a hell of a deputy."

"You've only known me a couple minutes," Lance said.

The man smiled again, and Lance knew it was only a trick of the mind that he could smell the nicotine on the man's breath. "You don't know what it's like on this side of the table, son." He winked.

Lance got the meaning. Didn't know what to say.

The man said, "Listen, I've got to go. They'll be here soon—don't worry, by the way, they've got nothing on you. But let me tell you this. I've been here for every interview they've ever performed regarding the Benchley case over the years. I've read every case file, every note. Heard every discussion, opinion, argument, and theory."

Lance waited. Let the man enjoy his buildup.

"Something happened in Mark Benchley's life after he moved here that changed him," the lingering sheriff said. "And not in a good way. But my gut tells me there's a lot more to that night than anybody around here has even tried to understand. And I need you to help these idiots around here figure out what it was."

Lance was about to ask for more, anything else to go on, but then, out of the corner of his eye, he caught the presumed two-way mirror to his left and he felt a cold chill of fear down his spine. *What if they've been watching the whole time? What if they've been watching me talk to myself?*

As if suddenly sensing Lance's panic, the man turned to look at the mirror, laughed, and then raised his middle finger to the glass. "They can't see, son."

Lance didn't take his eyes from the mirror, "I know they can't see *you*, but I've been sitting here probably looking like—"

He stopped talking. Focused his eyes on himself in the mirror and then slowly and deliberately said, "I'm talking, but my mouth isn't moving."

And it was true. Lance felt all the muscle and movement in his jaw and mouth, heard the words leaving his throat, but the image of Lance in the mirror simply sat and stared.

"You didn't know that's how it worked with us?" the man asked, sounding genuinely curious.

Lance said, "No." Lance in the mirror said nothing.

"Hmm," the man grunted. "Interesting. People would think you were crazy if you just went around talking to people who weren't there."

Lance tried hard to remember if he'd ever been able to see

himself while talking to a lingering spirit. A mirror, or reflective surface ... anything. He couldn't recall a single moment.

Amazed he was just now finding out this little secret of his, he turned back to the man who had once been the sheriff of Ripton's Grove but found only an empty chair.

Then the door to the interview room opened, and Sheriff Ray Kruger walked in.

[ 15 ]

THE SHERIFF—THE CURRENT AND VERY MUCH ALIVE sheriff—closed the door softly and turned to face Lance. Looked at him with weary eyes and sighed, as if he'd known this moment was inevitable.

Lance smiled. "Well, Sheriff, I hate that you had to waste the gas to come visit me this morning. Apparently we could have just waited a couple hours for our proper introductions."

Ray Kruger didn't even so much as smirk.

*So much for that approach*, Lance thought. Kruger appeared to be all business. Lance couldn't say he was surprised.

The sheriff walked to the table and sat down opposite Lance, his knees popping as he fell into the chair. Then he ran a hand through his hair and leaned back, still not saying a word.

The silence sat heavy. Lance's stomach gurgled, his digesting breakfast deciding to break the ice. Lance smiled again. "Mama's," he said. "So much good food."

"Can you tell me everything you did and everywhere you went after I left the farmhouse this morning, please?"

*Yep*, Lance thought, *all business.*

He straightened in his chair and took a deep breath. "Absolutely. After you left, I went upstairs to change my clothes and shave and brush my teeth. In the middle of shaving, the doorbell rang and I answered it. It was Victoria Bellows. Her husband mentioned to her that the farmhouse needed to be cleaned, and the cleaners apparently won't come to the property out of fear of ... well, you know. Victoria and I chatted briefly and then she started to clean. About that time, the doorbell rang again and it was Luke—one of the new friends I mentioned to you." Lance hated dropping Luke's name but understood the situation well enough to know it was going to be required one way or the other.

Sheriff Kruger held up a hand to slow him down. "Luke who?"

Lance shook his head. "I don't know his last name, sir. He drives a Jeep." Then, after a slight hesitation, "He's dating Susan. The waitress from Mama's."

Kruger nodded and motioned for Lance to continue.

"Luke asked if I wanted a ride into town, and I accepted. He drove me straight to Mama's and I had breakfast. After that, I left the restaurant and started walking. I hadn't gotten far when your very pleasant and overly charming deputy picked me up and delivered me here, to this very room."

Again, not so much as a hint of a grin at the crack on his deputy. The sheriff was stone-faced. He was quiet for a moment, perhaps thinking through all that Lance had said. Then he nodded once, stood and said, "Be right back."

He walked out of the room, leaving Lance alone again.

Except he wasn't, really. As soon as Sheriff Kruger had left the room and closed the door, Lance swiveled his head back to the chair across from him and found the ghost of the deceased sheriff had returned.

"Don't worry about Deputy Payton," the man said. "There's

always ones like him in every station in the country. Big badge, big attitude, small pecker. Literally, in Payton's case. I've seen him in the locker room."

Lance wasn't sure what to do with this information, so he asked a question of his own. "What's your name, sir?"

The man's face did something funny, as if he wasn't sure what Lance was asking him. Almost as if he had to dig deep, search for the answer. "Willard," he finally said. "Sheriff Bill Willard." Then he shook his head, as if to clear it. "Sorry," he said. "It's been a long time since my name's mattered."

"Nice to meet you, Sheriff Willard. I'm Lance."

Willard nodded. "I know, son. I know. Listen to me, okay? I may not be alive, but I've got a few tricks up my sleeve. I have a way of making things happen around here from time to time, if you catch my drift."

Lance didn't catch anything, but he nodded all the same.

"You need answers," Willard continued. "And the only way you're going to get them is to dig, to talk to folks. Learn things that these morons here didn't."

Lance said nothing.

"I know you're special, son. I know you've got gifts beyond this world's understanding. And maybe that's all you need— your talents and whatever clues the other world you can see and hear lends you. But I think you might be surprised just how much you can still learn from the living. When you know how to listen, that is.

"So when you get your bag back, maybe in the smaller front compartment, you'll find a list of names. Maybe those names were all people of interest in the Benchley case. Not because they were suspects, necessarily, but because they were thought to maybe have information that could help in discovering the truth. Maybe," Willard said, "you can call on a few of them and see what they remember. Maybe you'll get more out of them than just their words." At this, Sheriff Bill Willard winked, and the interview room door opened and Sheriff Ray Kruger appeared.

Lance looked back to the chair and found it, expectedly, empty.

Kruger walked over and resumed his position opposite Lance. "Where were you headed when my pleasant and overly charming deputy picked you up?"

Something about the question made Lance feel uneasy, but he pressed on with his honesty. He knew he'd done nothing illegal. Today. "I was walking to Rich Bellows's real estate office."

Kruger's face was expressionless. "Why?" he asked.

Lance decided not to lie, specifically, but not to offer up more information than was required either. "I had some questions about the house. Thought maybe he might be in for a few hours on a Saturday. He seems like that sort of guy."

Kruger nodded. Sighed again before saying, "Well, it's a good thing you didn't run across him this morning."

Lance took the bait. "Why's that, sir?"

"Because his wife was assaulted in the house you're currently renting from him, and he's convinced you were her attacker."

Lance felt a cold stone drop in his stomach. Not because he was fearing prosecution, but because he felt sorry for Victoria Bellows. She'd been so nice to him, friendly and energetic. He'd liked her. And once again, Lance had managed to get somebody hurt because of a situation he was involved in.

How many times would this happen in his life? How many people would suffer because of him?

"Anything to say, Lance?" Sheriff Ray Kruger asked. He didn't look all that concerned.

Lance looked the man in the eye. "I didn't do it," he said. He felt a new vibe coming off Kruger, and then slowly added, "But you already know that, don't you?"

Kruger leaned back and nodded. "I do. I just called over to the YMCA and got them to track down Luke—that's the thing about small towns, right? Easy to learn people's routines. He verified your story and also said that when the two of you left, he did see a woman matching the description of Mrs. Bellows in the house. Unharmed."

Lance was relieved, but only a little. "Is she okay? Mrs. Bellows?"

Kruger nodded. "A nasty bump on the head, but she'll be fine. The assailant struck her just above the temple and she blacked out temporarily. When she came to, she had the good sense to call an ambulance, and they took her over to Central Medical."

"Has she said anything about her attacker? Any idea who it might be?"

"Like I said, her husband thinks it was you." Kruger had a small smirk on his face as he said this.

"But you know it wasn't," Lance said. Then, after a beat, "Are you planning on sharing that information with Mr. Bellows anytime soon."

"Of course. As soon as we're done here."

"I'd appreciate that," Lance said, unsure what sort of game he was stuck playing with Sheriff Kruger. There seemed to be more the man wanted to say.

"So am I free to go?" Lance asked, making a small move to stand up from the chair.

Kruger held up a hand. "Not quite yet. If you'll humor me for just another minute."

Lance had expected this. He sat. Tried to look uninterested.

Sheriff Kruger cleared his throat and asked, "Do you have any idea who might have attacked Mrs. Bellows this morning?"

Lance almost answered too quickly. Of course he didn't know who'd attacked her. But then he thought back to the previous evening, the open back door, the movement behind the blinds when he'd arrived. Kruger picked up on his hesitation. "Well?"

"To answer your question, no, I don't have any idea who specifically might have attacked her."

"I feel like you've got a 'but' coming."

Lance nodded. He didn't necessarily feel his back was against the wall, but now that folks were getting hurt, it was time to share the one bit of information he'd been keeping to himself. "When I got to the house last night, I thought I saw movement behind the blinds in one of the front windows, and then when I got inside, the back door was wide open. I didn't see anybody, but I assumed somebody was in the house."

Kruger sat up straighter at this. "Why didn't you tell me this earlier?"

Lance fibbed, but only a little. "With everything folks have been telling me—including yourself, sir—about the reputation the farmhouse has, I sort of, I don't know, figured it was just one of those weirdos who wanted to come by and see the place or have a séance or whatever they do. I figured maybe the back door was left unlocked and they sneaked in and then fled the place when I got there." Lance shrugged. "I locked the door and didn't hear or see anything else the rest of the night. I didn't think it was that big a deal."

Kruger sat silently, appraising Lance enough to make him feel a bit uncomfortable. Finally, he said, "So you're either very brave or very stupid."

Lance grinned. "Are they mutually exclusive?"

At this, Sheriff Ray Kruger finally offered a small, yet very apparent smile. But he followed it with a question Lance was starting to get tired of. "Lance, be honest with me. Why are you here?"

Lance was quiet for a long time, trying his best to get a better read on Kruger. There was kindness buried beneath the toughness and the sorrow. At last, Lance shrugged and said, "Right now, Sheriff, this is just where I'm supposed to be."

And that wasn't a lie.

[ 16 ]

IF SHERIFF RAY KRUGER THOUGHT LANCE WAS BEING A
smart-ass or simply evasive with his answer, he didn't show it.
Instead, he sighed, nodded, and then stood, telling Lance he was
free to go, but that he'd better call the police the moment he
suspected anybody trespassing on the farmhouse's land.

"I'm serious, son," he said as he handed Lance his backpack
on their way back through the office area. "You have no idea
how tired I am of dealing with that place. No idea at all. Don't
give me a reason to bring you back down here again, okay?"

Lance wanted to say he could make no promises in that
regard, given his past experiences, but he decided to play it safe.
He smiled, nodded, and said, "Yes, sir. Of course. I'm terribly
sorry for all the trouble. Please let me know if there's anything I
can do to help further."

Lance thought the conversation was going to end at this
point, but the sheriff surprised him with saying, "You can leave,
if you really want to help."

"Sir?"

The sheriff shook his head. "Nothing good happens up
there, son. It's easier when the place just sits empty."

127

Lance gave Kruger the only answer he could. "I promise I won't stay a minute longer than I need to."

With that, Kruger opened the door leading to the lobby, let Lance walk through it, and then closed it behind him, leaving Lance alone with just the outdated furniture and the same woman behind the glass partition, chewing gum and twirling her hair as she read her novel. "Have a nice day," Lance said as he left.

She didn't respond.

Outside, the sun was blinding and Lance raised a hand to his eyes and squinted as he looked across the parking lot. The cruiser he'd arrived in was gone, and the lot was empty except for a black pickup truck parked alone in the corner. A passenger bus drove slowly down the street, air brakes hissing as it slowed to make a turn, headed for the bus station. Lance stepped off the sidewalk and followed it back toward town, a strong breeze blowing at his back. The air felt alive and fresh compared to the stuffy interview room. Chilly, but not uncomfortable.

He kicked pebbles down the sidewalk as he walked, not too concerned with where he was headed. Stopped briefly across the street from the bus station and contemplated going inside and buying a ticket. Moving on to somewhere else. Somewhere that made more sense. He couldn't understand why he was in Ripton's Grove. The tragedy at the farmhouse was a terrible thing, no question. But aside from the alternative theory that Mark Benchley hadn't been the one to kill his family and himself that night, what was Lance's purpose here? Was that his only task, to bring to justice a killer who'd flown under the radar for too long? Not that that was anything to shake your head at, but still ... he felt there was more.

The loud ringing of a bell startled Lance out of his thoughts, and he looked up, finding a bell tower off in the distance, ringing in the noon hour. He thought about lunch but then dismissed it. *Not yet*, he thought. *You've obviously got work to do.*

He had so many questions, but the one he was interested in at the moment was, who had attacked Victoria Bellows? His gut told him that the attacker was the same person who'd been in the farmhouse the night before. He found the timing of two different home invasions at the same property within twelve hours of each other to be too coincidental, regardless of the home's infamy.

He kept walking, and as a short, balding man came out of a small hardware store to Lance's left, Lance said, "Excuse me, sir —could you tell me how to get to Central Medical?"

The man stopped and eyed Lance suspiciously. Lance wasn't bothered by this, was in fact used to it. He remained still and smiled, trying to look pleasant.

"Are you hurt?" the man asked.

"No, sir. Need to visit a friend."

The man nodded slowly, as if Lance was trying to pull a fast one on him, then huffed and puffed and gave Lance the directions. Followed it up with, "It's going to be a long walk."

Lance thanked the man and added, "It's okay. I like to walk." Then he walked across the street to Rich Bellows's real estate office. The door was, unsurprisingly, locked and the lights off. Lance moved on and ducked inside the florist next door. Ten minutes later, he emerged carrying a small bouquet of flowers and headed off to find Central Medical.

---

The man from outside the hardware store was correct. It had been a long walk to Central Medical. It took Lance half an hour to end up nearly two miles on the opposite end of town, well past the downtown section he'd become somewhat familiar with. He'd made a right turn at Mama's, passing by the building with the bell tower, which turned out to be a courthouse, then followed the sidewalk along a rural route for nearly the entire way before the sidewalk eventually ended and Lance was forced to walk along the shoulder the remainder of the trip. Traffic was light, thankfully, and the weather was cool enough that the walk wasn't that tiring. He'd glanced down every so often at the bouquet he was carrying, hoping the flowers remained presentable long enough to be delivered.

ʹAnd now he stood in a large, freshly paved, mostly empty parking lot, looking at a medium-sized two-story beige building sitting unassumingly in the corner of the lot. It was dull and plain and boring, darkened windows dotting the faded exterior. The words CENTRAL MEDICAL CENTER were positioned above a set of automatic doors in the center of the building's front. On the left of the building, accessible by another, smaller entrance road, was a gray parking overhang with the word EMERGENCY advertised in red letters on all sides. An ambulance was parked beneath the overhang, its lights off and doors closed. It looked tired, almost as if it were napping in the quiet afternoon.

Lance stood and stared at the building for a long time. Despite Central Medical's lack of size and flash and energy, there was still no misunderstanding what the place was.

A hospital.

Lance did not like hospitals.

This wasn't an odd fear or phobia or general dislike to have as a human being. A lot of people didn't like hospitals. Hospitals often brought to mind illness or injury—and for some, an acute awareness of their own mortality. Death walked the halls of hospitals. It stood in the corners of rooms and waited its turn to slip in and do its job, lurking in the shadows but hidden from no one. Hospitals were a relatively unhappy place if you were a guest, despite the cheerfulness exuded by friendly staff. Nobody went there to have fun.

But for Lance, the dislike of hospitals extended beyond the common tropes of mortals. Because he could see into the shadows, beyond the veil. Lance could see newly appointed spirits lingering at the bedsides of their deceased bodies, watching as loved ones mourned and said final goodbyes. Lance walked hallways crowded not just by passing nurses and hustling doctors and concerned visitors, but also by the ghosts of those who'd not yet passed on to whatever lay on the other side. Sometimes they were peaceful, almost contemplative as they moved along and grasped their new situation with a sort of wonder, testing the waters of their new being. But others ... others were completely distraught, frantic. And it was them—those for whom the idea of their death had stricken such fear into their souls—who disturbed Lance. They always seemed to sense what Lance was, and that he could see and hear them. They flung themselves at him and begged and pleaded for help, for answers he did not have. They wanted another chance, they wanted more time with their wives and husbands and sons and daughters. Some asked if they were going to hell ... or to Heaven. They asked what they'd done wrong—both in life and in their own dying.

Aside from his birth, Lance had only been inside the walls of a hospital twice. Once when he was only ten years old and had fractured his wrist after falling out of a tire swing at the park, and again when he was sixteen and had gone to visit a friend of his from high school who'd had to have an emergency appendectomy. Her name was Mariah and she played softball and volleyball, and Lance would never forget the look of hurt in her eyes when he'd been unable to stand in her room any longer and had nearly run down the hallway and down the stairs and out into the fresh air.

The episode with his wrist when he was ten had been traumatic—a memory forever burned into Lance's mind. But when he'd been older, he thought he would have been better equipped to handle the hospital. He understood more about who he was at that point, and thought himself accustomed to dealing with the spirit world.

He'd been wrong.

So much sadness and so much anger and so much pleading had driven him away.

He'd apologized profusely to Mariah when she'd returned to school, but he'd never forgiven himself for making such a stupid mistake, for being so over confident in himself.

Yet here he stood, again. Outside a building that undoubtedly held—at least on some small scale—the things that Lance did not want to face, did not want to have to deal with right now. But there was also the chance that Victoria and Richard Bellows were still inside, and he needed to talk to them both. Needed some answers.

Lance sighed heavily and looked up to the sky. Heavy clouds rolled across, shading the parking lot. But they weren't dark and foreboding and promising of storms. Instead, they were white and cheerful, creating a cool, comfortable fall afternoon. A breeze blew across the parking lot, and Lance enjoyed the momentary chill, inhaling deeply and beginning a mental pep talk to convince himself that no matter how badly he didn't want to step through the doors of Central Medical, he was old enough now—if not wise enough—to understand that much of his life had very little to do with what *he* wanted. There were much bigger things at play, and no matter how much he hated to admit that on some larger scale, he might be nothing but a tool, a vessel the Universe used to do its bidding, he carried the burden with respect.

Especially now. After what his mother had done, and what she'd said to him as she'd passed on.

Lance started across the parking lot, his feet feeling heavy, as if he were slogging through a marsh. His heart beat faster in his chest the closer he got to those automatic doors, which began to look more and more like a robotic mouth, ready to open and swallow him whole, swallow him into a prison of despair.

He felt a trickle of sweat slide down his temple.

He was still ten yards from the doors when they slid open with a *whoosh* so sudden and unexpected that Lance actually jumped back a step. He stopped and stood and stared, a momentary flit of an absurd thought that the building had become self-aware and was taunting him. But then the thought vanished, the fear abated, and he was quickly overcome with a cool, refreshing stream of relief.

Richard and Victoria Bellows walked out of Central Medical. They both stopped just outside the doors and stared at Lance as if he were an exotic animal—the last thing they'd expected to see at that moment.

Lance stood perfectly still and waited, not particularly feeling like making the first move. Victoria Bellows's eyes looked more tired than before, but they were still kind. Rich stared at Lance with what looked like gritted teeth and a crinkled brow, as if he were working out a complex word problem and struggling to find the answer.

*He's still not sure*, Lance thought. *He still thinks it might be me.*

After what felt like minutes but was likely only a matter of seconds, Victoria gave Lance a small smile and said, "I'm hoping your morning went a lot better than mine."

Lance returned a smile of his own and slowly walked forward to meet them on the sidewalk. "Had a great breakfast," he said. "But it sort of went downhill from there, what with the whole police interrogation and all."

"Police what? Wait ... did they...?" She shot a glare at her husband. "*Rich.* I may be concussed, but I very clearly remember telling you it wasn't him."

Rich was staring directly at Lance. He spoke slowly and said, "You don't know who it was. You said you never saw who hit you."

Victoria sighed, and Rich and Lance continued to stare at each other. Rich looked ready for blood, but Lance stood and tried to look indifferent to the whole thing. After an uncomfortable moment of silence, Lance held the bouquet of flowers out to Victoria. "For you," he said. "A get-well present, I guess. Or a 'thanks-for-cleaning-my-house-and-I'm-sorry-you-got-attacked-while-scrubbing-toilets' present, if you'd prefer."

This elicited a snort of laugher from Victoria, which caused Lance to chuckle, and he watched as a bit of the tension Rich Bellows had been holding in his shoulders and neck began to loosen. Victoria took the flowers from Lance and smelled them, closing her eyes and inhaling deeply. "Wonderful," she said. "Thank you so much."

Rich allowed himself a small grin and put a protective arm around his wife. He looked at Lance and said, "I admit you'd have to have some pretty big gonads to attack my wife and then show up with flowers at the hospital."

Lance shrugged. "I suppose I could just be playing an angle. Trying to appear innocent by hiding in plain sight. But I think that only works in mystery novels."

Rich narrowed his eyes. "Did Kruger really bring you in?"

Lance nodded. "Yes, sir. I got a behind-the-scenes look at Ripton's Grove's finest at work."

Rich Bellows was silent.

Lance gave him what he wanted. "My alibi checked out," he said. "Sheriff Kruger was supposed to let you know."

Rich used his free hand to pat the pockets of his jeans. After not finding what he was looking for, he snapped his fingers and said, "I left my phone in the car. Sorry, I was in a bit of a panic when I got here."

Lance held up his hand. "I understand. But I want to promise you, I had nothing to do with what happened to your wife. I feel terrible for the whole thing, truly. If I hadn't been renting the place, she would have never been there and this would have never happened."

Victoria said, "Don't be ridiculous. This is in no way your fault."

*You have no idea*, Lance thought.

Rich removed his arm from around his wife and stuck out his hand. "I'm sorry I jumped to conclusions," he said. "It's just ... well, that place ... and you showed up and ..." He stopped. "I'm sorry. You didn't deserve that."

Lance shook Rich's hand. "I don't blame you," he said.

Then, as if they were approaching the inevitable, Rich asked, "I suppose you'll be wanting to find somewhere else to stay now?" He shook his head, disbelievingly. "I swear ... it's always something with that farmhouse. First it's haunted, and now we have violent home invaders." He sighed. "Come by the office after church tomorrow and I'll get you your deposit back. I tend to pop in for an hour or so after services to catch up on some paperwork."

"Actually, sir," Lance said, "I think I'd like to stay there a bit longer, if that's okay with you."

Both Rich and Victoria looked shocked at this. "Seriously?" Rich asked.

Lance nodded. "Yes, sir."

The Bellowses waited for more, but they weren't getting anything else from Lance right then.

Finally, Rich nodded. "All right, then. Just let me know if you change your mind." Then, "Well, as you know, we've all had a bit of an adventurous day." He moved to step off the sidewalk, off to their vehicle. "I think Victoria would like to get home."

Rich and Victoria, hand in hand, had made it a few feet past Lance when he called after them. "I hear there's a trail, leads from town up to the farmhouse?"

The couple stopped and turned together. Rich looked done with the entire conversation but nodded his head. "Yeah, there is. Straight up the damn hill. Maybe a little less than mile."

Lance started walking back across the parking lot, toward Rich and Victoria. "Any chance I could have a ride to where it starts? If you're going that direction."

Lance knew they were going that direction. Somehow, he knew. Just like he knew Victoria would never let Rich deny Lance's request. They both had kind hearts.

Sure enough, Rich looked to his wife, saw something unmistakable in her eyes, and then said, "Sure. Come on."

Lance smiled and said thank you and followed them to their car.

If they were locked in a car together, it would be harder for Rich Bellows to avoid answering Lance's questions.

[ 17 ]

Rich Bellows drove a late-model Ford Explorer, that new car smell still faintly clinging on. Lance waited while Rich opened the front passenger door for Victoria and helped her in. "Easy does it," Rich said as he held his wife's hand and she stepped up into the vehicle. "No need to rush."

"I got hit in the head, Rich. I don't have a spinal injury, for goodness sake. I'm fine."

Rich said something Lance couldn't hear and Victoria laughed. Then he closed the door so gently it was as if he were trying to keep from waking a napping infant. Victoria made an I'm-not-amused face through the window, and this time it was Rich who chuckled. But when he turned and saw Lance standing by, waiting for the couple to finish their moment before he'd allow himself into the backseat, Rich's face fell just the tiniest bit. Enough that Lance noticed. Rich recovered quickly enough. "Hop on in, Lance. Apologies if you sit on something sticky. Kids..." Rich shrugged and walked around the front of the car and slid into the driver's seat.

Lance folded his feet and legs enough that he was able to slide into the backseat of the Explorer with little trouble. The rear seats were a bench that stretched all the way across, so Lance chose to sit in the middle, giving him a better view out the front, and also allowing him to stretch his legs out to either side for more room. When you're tall, you learn these sort of things—a unique set of survival tactics for the long-limbed. He buckled his seat belt and adjusted his backpack on the floor between his feet.

Rich started the engine and drove the vehicle through the parking lot and out onto the road, headed back toward town. He cranked up the Explorer's heater like a blizzard was fast approaching and looked to Victoria. "Warm enough, sweetie?"

Victoria quickly shot her hand out and snapped off the fan. "Burning up. Seriously, Rich. Again, I have a head injury, not hypothermia. It's got to be in the high fifties today!"

Even from the backseat, Lance could see Rich's cheeks redden ever so slightly. After a moment of silence, given as ample time for Rich to regain his dignity after his wife's scolding, Lance started with his questions. He knew his time was going to be limited, he'd need to make the most of it.

"Mr. Bellows, I figure I should tell you, I'm fairly certain there was somebody in the farmhouse last night when I got there."

Rich's head spun around so fast Lance thought they might end up back at Central Medical to treat the man for whiplash. "*What?*" Then, almost under his breath, "Damn teenagers. Can't they find someplace else to smoke their pot and drink their warm beers?"

"Don't forget about the sex," Victoria chimed in.

Rich looked at her as if she'd spoken Latin. She gave him a playful wink that made Lance a little uncomfortable. Lance cleared his throat, pushed on. "I don't know if it was teenagers, sir. I mean, I can't say for sure, but I think it might have just been one person."

Rich sighed. "Certainly isn't the first time folks have broken in. But I figured by now everybody was too afraid to have to deal with the wrath of Ray Kruger to bother having a go at it. Like I said, that place used to be sort of the go-to hangout spot for the ones that weren't too creeped out by what happened there and —" He stopped, as if merely alluding to the murders was more than he wanted to get into.

"That's the other thing, sir," Lance said. "I don't think they had to break in, exactly."

Rich shot Lance a look in the rearview. "What do you mean?"

"The back door was wide open when I got there. There was no sign of forced entry that I could see."

The car went quiet. Lance continued, in case Rich wasn't coming to the conclusion himself. "So, in my opinion, that means either the door wasn't locked to start with, or somebody has a key."

Rich shook his head. "The door was definitely locked. I was the last person there. I make it a point to visit all the vacant rental properties once a month, just to do a quick walk-through. Though I'll admit I usually only get up to the farmhouse once a quarter—I know Kruger sends a guy up that way a couple times a month, so I figure it sits quietly enough."

"Does the sheriff have a key?" Lance asked.

Rich opened his mouth to answer, then stopped. Closed it and thought a moment. Finally, he shook his head. "No. I'm fairly certain he doesn't have a key. Not anymore..."

Lance sat up a bit straighter. "*Anymore*, sir?"

"Ray Kruger did *not* attack me," Victoria said, almost too quickly. Lance and Rich both turned their heads toward her. Ahead, a yellow traffic light turned to red, and Rich eased on the brakes. When the car was stopped, he said, "I thought you told us you didn't see who attacked you."

139

If Rich Bellows was trying to gain some redemption from his wife about entertaining the possibility of Lance being her attacker, he wasn't going to get that satisfaction. Victoria eyed him with what appeared to be a well-practiced look that only married couples can become familiar with. Rich flinched, almost as if he'd taken a small blow, and offered with some forced cheerfulness, "Right?"

Victoria looked straight ahead and sighed. "Nobody in this town is dumb enough to believe Ray Kruger would do something like this to me. Unless you'd like to try and prove me wrong."

Rich sighed as well, heavier and deeper than his wife, then nodded. "I agree."

Lance let a little more silence pass between the couple, then asked, "Mrs. Bellows, I know you didn't see the person who hit you, but do you have any idea where they might have come from? How they got in the house?"

Victoria closed her eyes for a moment and bowed her head down, as if she were about to pray. Then she said, "I had just come down the stairs. I turned left to head toward the kitchen and had made it about halfway down the hall when I got the feeling that something was behind me. Turns out, I was right. I didn't even get to turn around before my lights went out. They could have come in anywhere. The front door was unlocked. I know that for sure, because I'd gone out to the car a couple times."

Rich smacked the steering wheel with his palm. "The car! I forgot all about your car. It's still up there."

"We can get it later, Rich. It'll be fine," Then, to Lance, "But I didn't touch the back door. Was it locked, as far as you know?"

Lance nodded. "Definitely."

Victoria shrugged. "Well, we may never know. Heck, I had

the windows open, remember. They could have climbed right in if they wanted to."

This conversation was giving Lance nothing. Rich Bellows drove the Explorer past Mama's and then made a turn just past the post office, turning into what looked like a small park. A few picnic tables were scattered about under the shade of some large trees. A baseball diamond, basketball court, jungle gym and swing set completed the picture. Lance felt his time slipping away.

"Mr. Bellows, why did you say Sheriff Kruger doesn't have a key 'anymore'?"

Rich pulled the Explorer into a parking space along the fence line bordering the park. "See that walking path there?" He pointed to a paved path leading away from the parking lot. "Follow it around the baseball field and turn right. You'll see the entrance to the trail that leads up the hill and to the farmhouse. It's a nice little hike, but you look like you're in good shape."

Lance waited. Said nothing.

Rich reached up and switched on the fan again, this time letting it blow cool air instead of heat.

Lance picked up his backpack, moved to leave. Then stopped. "Sir, with all due respect, there's something you're not telling me."

Rich looked to Victoria, his eyebrows questioning. Victoria nodded and turned around to face Lance. "He's not doing it out of spite, or to be a hindrance. It's just ... Ray's a part of this town. A big part. And, well, he's been through a lot, and..." She shrugged. "We tend to respect his privacy." And then for good measure, "We don't tell Ray's business, and he respects ours."

Lance sat back in his seat, possibly even more confused than he had been when he'd gotten into the car. He wanted to push forward, demand more. But he couldn't think of a tactful way to go about it.

Finally, when Rich Bellows must have decided Lance had sat there long enough, he looked at Lance with a stoic face and said. "Son, my wife's right. It's not really your business. *But*"— he said this cautiously, looking to Victoria with a face that said *just bear with me a second*—"since you're staying in the house, and because of the events of last night and today, I suppose I can tell you this much to appease you a bit."

Lance still wasn't a fan of the vagueness, but he waited patiently for Rich to finish.

Rich sighed again and looked out the windshield, staring at the picnic tables. "After the murders, Ray Kruger was the owner of the farmhouse. That's why he had keys."

LANCE SAT BACK IN THE SEAT, THE WHIR OF THE Explorer's air-conditioning fans quietly filling the cabin. Rich Bellows's assertion of Ray Kruger's previous ownership of the farmhouse seemed to have stunned them all. Lance because it was information he hadn't expected—and now his gears were spinning so fast in his head he was surprised they weren't audible; Rich and Victoria because they seemed to be almost ashamed that the information had come to light, and now they were weighed down with guilt, unsure how to proceed.

The farmhouse had once belonged to Ray Kruger. The sheriff, who seemed to carry such a distaste for the place, who seemed to get agitated at the very mention of the home, not to mention having to drive out to it and give Lance a stern talking-to, had been the farm's *owner*. This raised so many more questions in Lance's mind, he didn't know where to start. But ... on the other hand, it did somewhat explain why the sheriff— although the place clearly raised his blood pressure— also seemed to carry along with him a sense of protectiveness about the place. It was as though he both despised the farm and wanted to make sure nothing happened to it. Or at least, maybe, to the people in it.

Lance didn't know what to do, what to ask. With his head still spinning, and the look on Rich Bellows's face clearly unhappy, Lance thanked the couple for the ride, apologized for all the trouble, told Victoria he hoped her head felt better soon, and then grabbed his backpack and got out of the Explorer.

He offered a wave as he passed by the side of the car, and Victoria gave him a smile and waved back. Rich put the Explorer into gear and was driving the car out of the parking lot before Lance had even made it to the start of the path.

Once the sound of Bellows's engine was gone, it was replaced with nature—a few birds chirping, wind rustling the leaves, water trickling from somewhere. A stream, perhaps—and the sounds of life. The chains from the swing set creaked softly, and a few children laughed as their mothers pushed them gently back and forth. Four boys were playing two-on-two on the basketball court. The echo of the ball bouncing on the asphalt would always be one of the sweetest sounds to Lance. He was more than half-tempted to walk over to them and ask if he could join. Only for a game or two. But the numbers would be uneven. Plus, he wasn't here to play basketball. At least he didn't think so. At this point, he was more confused than he'd been in a long time.

But now he did have one piece of information that might at least help point him in the right direction. Ray Kruger played a bigger part in all of this than Lance had originally thought. Lance had first thought the sheriff to be an unlucky casualty of the aftermath of the murders, unhappy about the crime and angry that the truth might never surface—no matter what sort of opinion he presented to the town. Now, it turned out the sheriff was more deeply connected to the farmhouse.

But how?

Surely he wasn't the one who'd pulled the trigger. Impossible. Right?

Lance knew better than to completely discredit possible scenarios, but this seemed too much. He thought again about the flash of memory he'd received from Kruger when he'd shaken the man's hand—the little boy and girl playing in the backyard kiddie pool. Would the Universe really make Lance work so hard that it wouldn't show him a vision of the sheriff committing the crime instead of some childhood play day?

Lance sighed. Boy, did he want to play basketball right about now. Just let his mind wander away from the real world for a moment and disappear into the game.

He walked by the courts and watched as one of the boys swished a three-pointer, the chain net jingling as the ball fell through. Then Lance kept going, following Rich's directions until he'd wrapped around the empty baseball field and turned right and found a clearing in the tree line that had to be the start of the trail. He headed for it and heard the jingle of the basketball net again, fading into the distance.

The terrain was mostly flat for the first fifty yards or so, but then it quickly increased in its incline, starting a winding path up and around the hillside, much as the road did from the other side. The trail was mostly dirt and rock, the occasional gnarled tree roots surfacing and crisscrossing the walking path like booby traps, waiting for an unsuspecting ankle. The sky was blotted out by the tree growth, an umbrella of limbs and leaves. Lance heard small animals scurrying through the bed of fallen leaves and pine needles that blanketed the ground on either side of him, among the trees and bushes and overgrowth. He wondered if some of them stopped to watch him, wondering if he were friend or foe. He wondered if animals could see the dead like he could. Dogs, particularly, always seemed to get this sixth sense associated with them when you watched horror movies. Lance would like a dog like that. A companion that shared his gifts, a loyal and understanding friend.

He kept walking.

The sounds of nature were soft and gentle: the leaves rustling, the breeze whistling through limbs and gaps in the trees, the creatures going about their business without a care in the world. It was soothing, peaceful. Lance let his mind slow down a bit, tried to relax and focus on one thing at a time. Tried to recap his day so far and make any sense whatsoever of everything he'd learned.

He sighed and gave up after only a few minutes. Let himself disappear into the forest and the trail, enjoy the quiet, appreciate the simplicity of it all, if only for just a brief moment. He adjusted the straps of his backpack and continued to walk, climbing the small inclines and carefully stepping through the rock and roots. It was cooler under the tree cover, and Lance breathed in the fresh air, smelling pine and soil and, faintly, his own sweat.

He imagined himself back in Westhaven, him and Leah sitting at the Sonic Drive-In, eating hot dogs and slurping slushies and laughing so freely it felt illegal. He could see her, sitting there with the windows down, the breeze teasing her blond hair, making it curl around her face, framing it in such a way it made his heart skip. He watched as she shivered at both the coolness of the air and the icy bite of her slushie and pulled her hands into the sleeves of her blue Westhaven High School sweatshirt and wrapped her arms around herself. And that was when he couldn't take it anymore and leaned across the center console so fast he nearly spilled his slushie and went in to kiss her and—

"That's close enough, Ethan. You wanna keep all your fingers, don't ya?"

A male voice grabbed Lance and pulled him out of his

daydream. The words were followed by a sharp crack and a dull thud. "See, Ethan? See how sharp the blade is?"

Lance resurfaced back in reality and looked up, not even having realized he'd been staring only at the ground for who knew how long, absentmindedly following the trail up and around the hillside. But now, the ground around him had flattened out, and when he looked to his left, he could see where twenty or thirty yards out, the trees began to thin out and give way to land that had been cleared. A small one-story house that looked more hunting cabin than home sat on a few acres of land. To the left of the house, Lance could make out a man and a small child standing by a stacked pile of wood. The man wore blue jeans and no shirt, his chest and arms smeared with sweat and dirt. He was lean and roped with muscle, his skin bronzed by the sun. On the ground at the man's feet were split pieces of wood, waiting to be added to the pile. He held an axe in one hand, its sharpened blade gleaming in the sunlight that made it through the cracks in the clouds as he moved about, and with the other, he was motioning for the child to move back, further away.

"A little more ... little more ... there, that's good. You can watch from there. You can help me stack it and bring some in the house when we're finished, okay?"

Either the boy didn't answer, or he spoke too softly for Lance to hear. But all the same, he stood where he was told and watched dutifully as the man set another piece of wood on the block and gave the axe a mighty swing, sending two perfectly halved pieces to the ground.

Lance watched the man split two more pieces of wood, took another glance at the small house in the distance, and then turned and continued to follow the hill. He was almost back to the farmhouse, he felt, and as the ground began to rise up again, a gentle swell that he was positive led to the precipice that his temporary home was perched, Lance turned and looked over his shoulder, back toward where he'd seen the man and the boy.

He wasn't positive, but it looked like the man was staring straight at Lance. Through all the cover of the trees, and with the small elevation change, Lance wasn't sure it was even possible for the man to see him from his vantage point, but nonetheless, Lance wasn't particularly in the mood to make new friends at the moment. He turned and hurried along, nearly jogging the rest of the way.

The tree line began to thin more and the ground flattened out again and soon he spilled out into the side yard of the spook farm, approaching the house from its south side. He passed by what was left of an old barn that he was too tired and too frustrated to bother taking a look inside and continued toward the rear of the house. To his left, the sun was beginning its descent, dipping below the clouds, and as Lance got closer to the farmhouse, he found himself pulled in that direction like iron to a magnet. He stopped and stood maybe fifty yards from the farmhouse's backdoor, looking straight ahead, out and over the edge of the hilltop.

The sun was perched beautifully in the sky, the early fall evening setting in quickly. Below the highlight of orange and pinkish light, the rooftops of downtown Ripton's Grove looked like a child's plaything. Decorative accessories to a model train set. The fall foliage was only just getting started here, but already the bit of color the leaves provided added to the landscape's beauty. Lance felt as if he could reach out with two fingers and pinch one of the buildings and lift it up to eye level. It was a stunning scene. Beautiful and serene and the epitome of bliss.

He wished Leah could be there to see it. She'd love it, he just knew she would.

And at the thought of his friend, Lance felt his emotions

shift away from the happiness he'd attempted to allow himself to enjoy and turned quickly to look at the farmhouse. Stared for a long time, his shadow growing shorter on the ground before him as the sun continued to sink.

"What do you want from me?" Lance asked the house, his voice carried off on a breeze.

The house did not answer.

Lance didn't bother to take another look at the scene behind him. Instead, he walked around to the front of the house, glanced at Victoria Bellows's Mercedes SUV in the driveway, and then took the porch steps two at a time. He gripped the doorknob and turned it and—

"*THANK GOD YOU'RE HERE! YOU'VE GOT TO HELP US!*"

The woman's voice, same as the night before, echoed all around Lance on the porch.

"Well," Lance said as he pushed through the door, "I see we're playing this game again."

[ 19 ]

L<small>ANCE STEPPED INTO THE FARMHOUSE AND CLOSED THE</small> door behind him. The house had a chill to it and smelled faintly of pine and disinfectant. The air felt fresher than before, and Lance turned and saw that the windows were still thrown open from earlier, the cool fall air pouring in. It helped to abate the stuffiness, but the sight of the open windows only recalled the memory that Victoria Bellows had been attacked in this very house earlier today.

Lance positioned himself so his back was against the front door, letting his eyes fall across the stairs, and then focus on the back door in the kitchen down the hallway. All was still and quiet.

"Honey, I'm *hooooome!*" he called out, like a devoted husband after a long day at the office. If his intuition was correct, he should be getting his response any second now.

Sure enough, just as he was about to make his way forward, down the hall and to the kitchen, the man's voice bellowed from nowhere, like an overhead loudspeaker that only Lance could hear.

"*Who's at the door? Is it him? Tell me!*"

151

Lance paused, waited to see if there would be more, then announced, "It is I, Sir Lancelot, protector of this land, drinker of coffee, and eater of pies. I demand you tell me at once with whom I'm speaking!" A pause, then, "Please."

A breeze from outside picked up some speed and gusted through the window to Lance's right, and the wooden frame of the house creaked and groaned along with it, but otherwise there was silence. Lance's request had fallen on deaf ears. Or, more correctly, dead ears. He'd expected this much but figured it was worth a try. He waited another full minute by the door, listening for anything else, then gave up and started toward the kitchen to check the lock on the back door.

He got halfway down the hall when the man's voice hissed with anger.

*"She doesn't want to see you."* A pause. *"No. Never. You'll never see it. We're leaving, for good."* A longer pause this time. And just when Lance thought the man had said all he was meant to hear for now, the final, chilling words came. *"You've got three seconds to get off this property or I swear to God I will fucking kill you. You see this? You think I don't know how to use this? You think I'm* afraid *to use this? Go ahead. You've ruined us, and you're lucky you're not already dead."*

Lance stood motionless in the hallway, holding his breath as the words around him crescendoed in intensity. He waited, ears strained, hanging on for the conclusion of the argument.

Nothing happened.

No more words. No more yelling.

Lance threw up his hands in disgust. "Really? You're just going to leave me hanging like that? What a tease." He thought about giving the house the finger, but he'd never flipped off the spirit world before. Wasn't sure it would have the same impact or satisfaction. Plus, he doubted his mother would approve of such juvenile behavior.

He walked into the kitchen and set his backpack down on the table, pulling out a chair to sit and retrieving a bottle of water from his bag. He twisted off the cap and downed half the bottle in three big gulps.

Then the gunshot boomed and rattled the walls and shook the glass, and Lance dropped the bottle onto the floor. He jumped up from his seat at the table and turned to look back down the hall...

...just as the door to his right, the one leading down to the basement, began to rattle in its frame, the sounds of pounding fists beating against the other side almost in perfectly synced rhythm with Lance's heart as it danced in his chest.

*"Let me out!"*

A female voice, younger than the voice from before and sounding very weak. Exhausted, and also terrified.

Lance lurched forward and ripped the door open.

There was nothing there but blackness and the sight of the first couple wooden stairs that led down into the dark mouth of the house's belly.

Lance stood and waited, listened for a long time.

He heard no more. The house was finished for now.

---

The house creaked occasionally, and the breeze still trickled in from the front windows, stirring up the air. A few floorboards groaned as Lance walked around the kitchen, pacing back and forth and thinking.

"Three voices," he said to the kitchen. "If you count the girl from behind the basement door." He glanced at the door, which he'd decided to close, promising himself that he would inspect whatever lay down there very soon. But first he needed to think, go over things while they were still fresh in his mind.

Playing on the theory that the voices he was hearing were in fact a message, some sort of cosmic reenactment meant as a clue to assist Lance in figuring out what had happened at the farmhouse, Lance felt it was safe to assume that the woman's voice he'd now heard twice on the porch belonged to Natalie Benchley. Which meant that the man's voice, that angry, inquisitive voice, likely belonged to her husband, Mark Benchley.

"And the girl's voice was Mary," Lance said aloud, stopping and again looking to the basement door. He didn't know how he knew, but he was certain. It'd been Mary Benchley pounding away on the basement door, sounding weak and tired and crying to be let out.

Lance eyed the sliding bolt meant to keep the door locked. "Why was she down there?"

He sat down at the table and finished what was left of his bottle of water. Stared at that bolt. His first thought was that Mark Benchley, while being a suspected murderer, had also been some sort of psychotic child abuser and had locked his daughter away. After all, if you could stomach murdering your whole family, what was throwing one of them down into your home's very own dungeon?*

But then Lance thought about his conversation with Joan earlier that day, as she'd sat across from him in the booth at Mama's and poured her heart out to him.

*Mary was his absolute pride and joy. He was so proud of her.*

Joan was adamant that Mark Benchley hadn't killed his family.

The ghost of Sheriff Bill Willard had a similar opinion.

One was the town gossip, the other was an ever-present fly on the wall at the local sheriff's office. Both were privy to all sorts of information. Lance trusted both of them, though he knew he'd need a lot more than just his trust in a waitress and a spirit to prove anything.

He eyed the bolt again.

"Protection," he said. "He put her down there to protect her." Then, "But from who?"

The answer seemed obvious.

Lance replayed the voices in his head again. The initial shock from Natalie Benchley ("*THANK GOD YOU'RE HERE!...*"), and the argument Mark Benchley had followed with ("*You've got three seconds to get off this property or I swear to God I will kill you*").

Lance had heard three voices ... but there had been four people in the house that night. The fourth was somebody that wasn't supposed to be there. Somebody who was not welcome.

(*You think I'm* afraid *to use this?*)

Lance envisioned Mark Benchley holding a shotgun up into the face of whoever else had been in the farmhouse that night, angry, his words full of intent. Threatening.

Yet it was the Benchley family who'd ended up dead that night.

And if Lance was only hearing the voices of the dead, that meant the fourth person who'd been in the house that night was still alive. And they might be the only person who knew the truth.

Lance sighed and looked up to the ceiling. "What the heck happened here?"

Then his stomach grumbled, and he realized he'd never made it to the grocery store.

THE SUN HAD GONE DOWN COMPLETELY, ENCASING THE farmhouse in darkness. Lance had closed the windows and locked them, then turned on all the lights on the house's first floor, bathing everything in yellowish tinge that unfortunately brought to mind seventies slasher films. But he preferred this look to the darkness. Not that he was afraid, but the light helped the place feel more alive. Less like the crime scene everybody seemed determined to cement it as. He sat on the steps and waited for his guests.

Susan and Luke were on their way. Lance had gambled that their curiosity about the farmhouse, Susan's past friendship with Mary Benchley, and the fact that there might not be a whole lot to do in a town as small as Ripton's Grove on a Saturday night might be enough to entice the two of them to come over and spend some time with him. The only stipulation was that they were required to bring dinner. And maybe answer a few questions.

Headlights dotted the distance and grew closer. Lance stood and opened the front door, stepping out onto the porch and waving blindly into the lights. Luke's Jeep took form and parked, two silhouettes jumping from the doors and approaching the porch steps as the headlights cut off.

"Hi," Susan said. "I hope pizza's okay." She offered a large pizza box, stained with grease.

"Perfect," Lance said, taking it from her and stepping aside so the two of them could enter the house.

Luke, carrying a six-pack of soda, offered his fist and Lance bumped it. "Not exactly how I expected to spend my evening," he said. "But that's not necessarily a bad thing."

Lance followed them inside and closed the door.

Luke and Susan stood motionless in the foyer, ramrod straight, heads tilted up and swiveling slowly back and forth along the walls, rooms, stairs, hallway. They took it all in silently, like two patrons at a museum admiring a piece of art that both captivated and stunned them.

Lance waited. Said nothing.

Finally, Luke turned and said, "I feel weird being here. Do you feel weird?"

Lance shrugged. "It wears off. I guess I've gotten used to it."

Susan was still silent, staring down at the floor. Lance noticed a single tear spill down her cheek. Luke took notice as well. "Suze? Everything okay?" He put his arm around her, and she nodded and laughed and shook her head.

"It's surreal, I guess. I mean, I *played* here a few times when I was little. Once or twice was all. But..." She stifled a sob, then shook her head again and smiled. "Sorry. It's been a long time, but I guess it just seems more real now that I'm actually standing in the house."

Lance mentally kicked himself. "I'm sorry," he said. "I shouldn't have asked you to come. It was completely insensitive and—"

"It's fine," Susan cut him off. "Really. I'm glad you invited us. Honestly, and this might sound strange, but by being here I sort of feel like I'm keeping Mary's memory alive a little longer in my head." She waited a beat, and when neither Lance or Luke said anything, she shrugged and wiped away the tear. "Anyway, I'm starving. Let's eat."

They walked into the kitchen and sat around the table— Susan giving it an appraising glance, probably recalling another memory. A meal she'd shared with the Benchley family at this very table, or maybe an after-school arts and crafts project with Mary. Lance swallowed down his guilt. Susan was old enough to make her own decisions. If she wanted to leave, she was more than welcome to. But he didn't think she would.

Luke flipped open the pizza box and grabbed a slice, his eyes darting around the kitchen as he chewed, taking it all in. Then he asked, "So I've been dying to ask you, why exactly did I get a call from the sheriff while I was finishing up my workout at the Y?"

"*What?*" Susan said, head swiveling toward her boyfriend. "What do you mean?"

Luke didn't answer. Instead he looked to Lance, eyes full of curiosity more than any hint of anger or irritation.

Lance grabbed his own slice and started to eat. He saw no sense in being coy. Besides, he was hoping his two friends could answer some of his questions. Figured it better to divulge some of his own information first, level the playing field as best he could. "Victoria Bellows came by the house this morning to clean the place. She was doing it as a favor for her husband because the cleaning people he usually uses for rentals are terrified to come here because..." He paused and gave Susan a quick glance before continuing, "They believe Mary Benchley was a witch."

Susan scoffed at this and rolled her eyes. Luke took another bite of pizza.

"But that's not the problem," Lance continued. "Shortly

after Luke picked me up to take me into town, somebody entered the house and attacked Victoria Bellows. Hit her over the head hard enough she blacked out. She didn't see who it was, and the sheriff's department thought it prudent to eliminate any potential suspects as quickly as possible, which included me. Luke verified my alibi."

"*Shit*," Luke said in between chews of pizza. "Weird day this's been, huh? First I get used as an alibi, and now I'm eating pizza at the spook farm. I wish I had a vlog. This would get bigtime views."

Susan looked at him and shook her head. Lance laughed, though he wasn't positive he knew what a vlog was. "It's been interesting. I'll give you that. But there's more. Somebody was here when you all dropped me off last night. I didn't see anybody—other than some movement at one of the windows when we pulled in—but the back door was wide open when I got inside. I'm positive somebody took off when they saw us arrive. My suspicion, and this is nothing more than a hunch, is that whoever was here last night attacked Victoria Bellows earlier today. Aside from the main question of who, I'm almost more curious as to what it is they want. I mean, there's nothing here." Lance held out his arms, gesturing to the empty kitchen around them. "It's an empty old house."

"Squatter, maybe?" Luke suggested. "Some homeless drifter who's pissed somebody showed up to boot him out? I mean, nobody's been here for a while, right?"

"Maybe," Lance said. "But there's no sign of forced entry anywhere I've seen. So whoever got in, they either found a door or window unlocked, picked a lock, or—and this is the one that I'm a bit concerned about—they had a key."

Silence around the table. Lance had laid it all out, and it appeared his two companions were just as out of answers as he was. He wasn't surprised. He sighed and grabbed a slice of pizza and wolfed it down in three huge bites. Started on a second slice.

Susan popped open one of the soda cans and took a long swig. "Mmmm," she said. "Nothing beats warm soda."

The three of them chuckled, the tension slowly evaporating. "I've got a couple bottles of water," Lance offered. "Also warm, but maybe better than the soda?"

Susan politely declined, but Luke took Lance up on the offer. "Sure, I'll take one. I don't need all that sugar in those things," he said, pointing to the remaining five cans. Lance couldn't help but think he and Luke would be good friends under different circumstances. In another life that Lance tried to keep himself from fantasizing about too frequently.

"I completely agree," Lance said and reached down under the table, where he'd stowed his backpack. He unzipped the front pouch and then sighed to himself. *Wrong pouch.* But as he was about to close it, something caught his eye. There, sitting on top of all his other small items he kept for ready access in the front pouch of the backpack, was a sheet of paper, folded in half. Yellow legal pad, from the looks of it. Lance reached in slowly, as if the paper might scurry away if frightened, and plucked it out with his thumb and index finger. He kept his hands below the table, his torso still bent over toward the bag, and unfolded the paper.

It was a list of names, handwritten. Scribbled in a hurry, from the looks of it.

And Lance was back in the interview room at the sheriff's office, the ghost of Sheriff Bill Willard echoing softly in his head.

("So when you get your bag back, maybe in the smaller front compartment, you find a list of names. Maybe those names were all people of interest in the Benchley case. Not because they were suspects, necessarily, but because they were thought to maybe have information that could help in discovering the truth. Maybe...")

Lance read over the names, surprised that he recognized a few.

The first name that jumped off the page was the most confusing. It sat atop the list, the most neatly printed of them all.

Ray Kruger.

Lance crinkled his brow and had to calm his brain from racing to figure out why the current active sheriff would be on this list. Did his previous ownership of the house somehow implicate him?

He shoved the thoughts aside and looked at the second name that stood out to him. He had no solid knowledge to verify that the name belonged to who he thought it did, but, as with many things he couldn't explain, he knew all the same.

He opened the main compartment of his backpack and tossed Luke a bottle of water. "Sorry if it smells like a gym bag," he said. "I sort of live out of this thing most of the time."

Luke waved him off and cracked open the bottle, taking a large swig.

Lance, hopefully not sounding as somber as he suddenly felt, looked at Susan. "I know this is random, but what's your last name?"

Susan swallowed a bite of pizza and without hesitation answered, "Marsh." Then, after a quick pull from the soda can, "Why?"

*Because you're on the short list of people who might know what happened here the night the Benchley family was killed,* Lance thought.

[ 21 ]

THE PROBLEM WITH TALKING TO THE LIVING WAS THAT they tended to ask more questions than the dead.

Lance needed to ask his own questions to Luke and Susan, see if they could help him piece together some of the puzzle, but in doing so, they'd undoubtedly question the information he already possessed and, more importantly, how he'd come by it.

These were questions Lance could not answer honestly. Not with the two new friends sitting around the table with him, eating pizza and drinking lukewarm beverages. They were good people. Mostly honest, Lance felt, but he would not trust them with his secrets, his abilities. There were so few whom he had.

His mother.

Marcus Johnston.

And most recently ... Leah.

He'd felt the connection with her the moment they'd met. Explored it, treaded its waters that first day, and in the end he had told her everything. And she'd accepted him completely. Believed him wholeheartedly. Had developed more faith in him than he'd ever had in himself. She was special. He knew that beyond any doubt. And she'd felt it in him as well, able to see there was much more to Lance Brody than was on the surface.

And when he'd held her hand, when their lips had met for the first kiss, it'd felt more right than anything he had ever felt before. For those moments, Lance was normal. Just a guy kissing a girl and wondering if this was what love felt like. Wondering if it was possible to be hit with it so fast, and under such unexpected circumstances.

But since when had life ever followed any sort of script? Since when did life care about the circumstances? Things happened when they happened, and you could drive yourself mad trying to make heads or tails of it.

"Well?" Susan said.

Lance's eyes refocused on the room, the table, his friends. They were both looking at him expectantly. Lance shook his head, resurfacing from the deep waters of his daydream. "I'm sorry, what?"

"What are you looking at?" Luke said, starting on yet another slice of pizza. "What's that in your hand? It looks like it spooked you."

Lance sat up and laid the sheet of paper on the table, running his hand over it to press it smooth, his mind scrambling for some sort of plausible explanation. Something he could work with to drive this conversation where he needed it to go.

And then it came to him. Something so convenient he almost laughed. His mother's words echoed in his head, an adage of hers that Lance consistently found validated.

(*Do you, a person with your gifts, honestly believe things could be so random?*)

He picked up another slice of pizza and took a bite. Chewed and swallowed, wiping his mouth with the back of his hand. "Susan, what's everybody in town saying I'm here for?"

Susan's eyes widened, like she'd been caught in some sort of lie. "What? Why are you asking me?"

Lance smiled, held up his hands to show he meant no harm. "It's okay, it's okay. I know people are gossiping. Joan made that pretty apparent this morning at breakfast. I just figured you'd probably heard something through the grapevine." He waited a second, then asked again, "Why do people think I'm here?"

Susan sighed in a sort of admission. "They think you're a reporter, or journalist or something like that. They think you're going to write one of those true crime books about the night of the murder, or some big exposé piece for a big magazine. Try and win a Pulitzer. Whatever reason they believe, they think you're here for money. Blood money, to be specific."

Lance wasn't surprised by any of this. He supposed it could be worse. "So I don't have a lot of fans, huh?"

Luke and Susan both shook their heads.

"And what do you both think?"

Luke shrugged his shoulders and finished off the bottle of water. "You seem like a cool dude, and you don't seem to be hurting anybody by being here, so I don't really think it matters what you're up to. You say you're here for work, that's good enough for me. Innocent till proven guilty. That's America, right?"

Lance looked at Susan. She seemed a bit more apprehensive than her boyfriend, but her eyes were still soft, kind. "I agree with Luke," she said, "but I also don't think you're telling us everything."

And Lance wouldn't. It was better for everybody if they never knew the truth.

"I can promise you this," Lance said. "I'm not here to hurt anybody or disrespect anybody's memory, and I'm certainly not here to cause any trouble."

Luke and Susan waited. Knew there was more coming.

"So, I'm asking you to trust me here, okay?"

The two of them looked at each other, then back to Lance. Nodded.

"For the sake of everything going forward, let's assume that I am a journalist. And as a journalist, I have to protect my sources. So please, don't ask me how I've gotten certain information, because I can't tell you. I'm sorry if that sounds harsh, but believe me, all I'm trying to do is get to the bottom of this. I want to know who really killed the Benchley family."

Susan sat forward at this, alert and eyes glinting with ... was it excitement? "So you don't think Mark Benchley did it, do you?"

Lance heard the voices in his head—the argument between who he presumed to be Mark Benchley and the mystery fourth person who'd been in the house that night. "I think there's more to it," Lance said. Then, without any other preamble, he slid the sheet of paper across the table to Susan. Luke slid over close to examine it with her. "What do you make of that list of names?" Lance asked.

Before Susan could answer, there was a knock at the front door.

"Expecting somebody else?" Luke asked.

Lance stood from the table. "No," he said. "I usually never am."

[ 22 ]

LANCE WALKED TO THE DOOR SLOWLY, HEARING LUKE AND Susan's steady footfalls behind him. Keeping their distance, but curious all the same. The yellow light from inside the house reflected off the windows next to the door, making it impossible to see out, try to catch a glimpse of who'd knocked.

Then another knock at the door. Not urgent, not angry, just a simple one-two rap of knuckles, loud enough to hopefully be heard. Lance reached the door and then turned, whispered to his friends. "It's probably fine, but just in case, get ready to go out the back door." He nodded back toward the kitchen, but neither Luke nor Susan turned to check. They nodded and kept staring at the door, waiting with breath held to see who was on the other side.

Lance turned the knob and opened the door, slowly, only a third of the way. Peered out.

Saw the man and the boy who'd been chopping wood earlier as Lance had walked up the trail. The boy held the man's hand, standing shyly, almost hiding behind the man's leg. He was wearing jeans and dirty sneakers and a red flannel shirt. The man, also clad in jeans and wearing a tight-fitting black t-shirt

167

despite the cool night air, held a battery powered lantern in the other hand, its light bright and fierce. Lance felt his body loosen, his muscles relax and his lungs suck in a full breath of air that almost sounded like a sigh as he exhaled it. Then he opened the door completely and said, "Hi."

"Miss Susan! Miss Susan!" The little boy shot from the porch and ran on still-unsteady legs across the threshold and into the foyer, rushing to Susan's side and wrapping her leg with a hug.

"Hey, Ethan! How are you, sweetie pie?" Susan squatted down and kissed the little boy on the top of the head and returned the hug. Ethan started to talk rapidly, and to Lance, mostly incoherently, using his hands to animate what appeared to be all sorts of adventures and fascinating tales. Susan smiled and nodded and played along and encouraged.

Luke stood and watched, disinterested, rubbing the side of his face and then looking to Lance, as if to ask, *What's happening?*

Lance had the same question. He turned and found the man still standing politely on the porch, eyes locked onto the boy as he continued his rapid-fire storytelling. Then the man's gaze shifted back to Lance, and his smile broadened and gleamed in the darkness.

"Hi," he said. "Sorry about that. Ethan loves Susan. More than me, I'm afraid." He laughed, and Lance offered a small grin. It was all he could force. His confusion was still overpowering the rest of him. The man, seeming to sense this, said, "Oh, sorry." He stuck out his hand. "Jacob Morgan. I'm sorry it's getting so late, but I'd heard there was somebody new staying here, and then I saw you walking up the trail earlier, so I figured Ethan and I would come and introduce ourselves. You know"— he shrugged—"since we're basically neighbors and all."

Lance shook Jacob's hand. It was rough and calloused and

the grip was strong. "Lance Brody," he said. "It's nice to meet you. I saw you chopping wood when I walked up. I didn't figure you could see me, though, because of all the trees."

Jacob nodded, as if this was a story he'd heard a hundred times. "I mean, I probably couldn't have picked you out of a lineup, but I got the general idea. Human. Male. Tall. Not Sasquatch." He smiled.

Lance looked back to Susan and Ethan. They were sitting on the floor together. Luke had joined them and was playing a game of hot hands with the boy, which he was pretending to lose at terribly, each slap of his hand causing Ethan to squeal in laughter.

"She watches him in Kids' Group at church on Sundays," Jacob said. "And she gets the cook at Mama's to make him Mickey Mouse pancakes when we get breakfast there sometimes. He thinks it's the funniest damn thing."

Lance nodded. Said nothing. He wasn't great with kids, and not great at talking about them either. Grasping for a talking point, he asked, "So how old is he, your son?"

"Just turned six," he said. "And he's not my son. I mean, at least not by blood." Then, briefly, Jacob Morgan's face dropped, his eyes went unfocused. Sadness seemed to creep in and then out. "He's my nephew. My half-sister's kid. She passed away right after he was born."

Lance kicked himself for accidentally bringing up the topic. "I'm so sorry," he said.

Jacob's eyes reignited with life and he smiled. "It's okay. Little guy is the best thing ever to happen to me." Then he laughed. "Don't get me wrong, he can be a complete pain in the butt, but it's in the best way. You know?"

Lance nodded. What else could he say to that?

"Anyway," Jacob said, "I didn't mean to interrupt your evening. Just wanted to say hi and let you know that if you need

169

any help with anything—want to borrow a cup of sugar and all that neighborly stuff—just come on down. It can get a little lonely up here sometimes."

"Thank you," Lance said. "I appreciate it."

Both he and Jacob looked back to Ethan and Susan and Luke, playing on the rough wooden floor. Ethan was demonstrating to Luke how to chop wood properly, setting imaginary pieces of wood and then swinging an invisible axe, making a *whooshing* sound with his mouth as he did so. Luke pantomimed the action, purposely screwing up and making Ethan laugh and shake his head and say, "No, like *this!*"

Lance watched the boy make another imaginary swing and then looked back to Jacob. "You know, I think there might be a slice or two of pizza left, if you want to come in and let Ethan play a little longer."

Jacob looked to his nephew for a moment, then back to Lance. Then Lance watched as the man's eyes fell over the rest of the house's interior, the same way Luke and Susan's had earlier that evening when they'd arrived, as if he were remembering things the way they used to be, like he'd been here before.

"If you're sure it's no trouble," he finally said. "We won't stay long. Ethan needs to get to bed."

Then he stepped inside and Lance closed the door, happy he'd convinced the man to stay.

Something inside Lance was sending up signals, picking up something unusual in the air. His senses coming to life and recognizing something that might be important to everything he was here for.

Not about Jacob.

Ethan.

There was something special about the boy.

Susan helped Ethan pick out a slice of pizza, and after some pseudo-protests from Jacob about the sugar and caffeine, the boy sat on his knees in one of the chairs, eating over the opened pizza box and sipping one of the warm sodas like he was at the best party in the world.

Lance sat where he'd been before, as did Susan. But Luke was now leaning against the counter by the sink, arms crossed and watching Jacob and Susan sitting next to each other, chatting like old friends. Which apparently they were, to a certain extent.

Susan wasted no time launching into explaining the relationship to Lance. "Jacob's parents used to own the hardware store down on South Street," she said. "I used to go down there with Daddy on the weekends just to see if Jacob was working!" She blushed then, as if she'd forgotten Jacob was capable of hearing. She laughed. "I had the biggest crush on you! And what are you, five, six years older?"

Jacob looked up to the ceiling, apparently doing mental math. Nodded his head. "Yeah, I think that's about right."

Susan made a noise that sounded like a squeal and groan. "I was so stupid. I couldn't have been more than twelve ... maybe thirteen at the time."

Jacob laughed. "I remember you coming in. You always stood over by the paint section, pretending to look at the color sample cards."

"So you *knew* I was pretending?"

Jacob shrugged. "You were comically obvious. Like you said, you were young."

Lance looked to Luke, whose face remained passive, but he was uncrossing and recrossing his arms a lot, clearly not thrilled with what he was hearing.

"I was surprised to see you here." Susan laughed. "We had

no idea who was at the door. We thought you might have been one of those ghost hunters!"

Jacob grinned and shook his head. "I must say, I could say the same thing about you." Then, "What are you guys up to up here, anyway?"

Lance felt a twinge of panic. Susan was obviously still crushing on Jacob Morgan, and Lance feared this was going to make her open to discussing a lot more with the man than Lance really wanted her to.

Thankfully, Luke was on the same page.

"I used to play ball with Lance here," he said, uncrossing his arms again and this time shoving his hands into the pockets of jeans. "We ran into each other last night and thought we'd try and catch up some. I haven't seen him in years."

Jacob nodded, eyeing Lance. Lance smiled and said, "Yeah, one of those small world moments, I guess."

Susan caught on, smiled and nodded.

Jacob asked, "And what brings you to Ripton's Grove, Lance? Why are you here?"

*Boy, am I getting tired of that question.*

He shrugged. "I heard you had the best meatloaf in the state."

Susan laughed. Luke smirked. Jacob Morgan gave one of his grins.

That was that. Lance wouldn't offer more unless provoked. He was getting tired of everyone prying into his business. He was getting tired of all the lies, despite their inevitability.

Jacob's eyes shifted over to his nephew, the boy had finished his pizza—half the slice sitting upside down in the box—and was gripping his soda can with two hands as he said something to Susan. She laughed and nodded and asked Jacob, "Okay if I take him to the bathroom? He's just informed me—very politely,

I might add—that he has to pee and he doesn't know where to go."

This got a chuckle from the group, and Jacob said, "Are you sure you don't mind?"

"Not at all."

The two of them walked hand in hand the short way down the hall, and Lance heard the bathroom door open and close and then Susan calling out, "Don't forget to wash your hands!"

The three men sat alone in the kitchen together, and even though Susan was right down the hall, they might as well have been on a desert island together. Susan had taken all the conversation with her, and the three of them sat there, trying not to look at each other and be forced to make mind-numbing small talk.

Luke didn't like Jacob Morgan. That much was obvious to Lance. Whether it was insecurity or jealousy or both, Luke was doing his best to try and look unfazed, but Lance read it in his body language easily enough.

Jacob Morgan didn't seem to care one way or the other about Luke's presence in the kitchen, as he hadn't even gone so far as to nod in his direction, or shake his hand, or even offer a hello.

Lance didn't care about either of the other two men right then, because he was still fascinated with the boy.

He'd felt it as soon as Ethan had rushed across the threshold into Susan's arms, a sudden, gentle pull, magnetic-like. No, maybe that wasn't quite right. It was more like an energy, a cold feeling that was also warm at the same time, like a pulsing wave. A crackle of electricity that made the hair on Lance's arms and the back of his neck tickle with static.

And the longer Ethan had been in the house, the stronger the sensation had become. As Lance had sat across from the boy, trying to keep his attention focused on the adults and the conversation, he'd been sneaking glance after glance toward Ethan, studying him, and also trying to reach out to him.

Because there was something familiar about the sensation he felt around the boy. Something...

The hallway door opened and closed, and Susan and Ethan returned. Ethan passed the kitchen table and went to Luke. Held out his hands, palms up. "Play?"

Luke smiled and slid down onto the floor, probably happy to have the distraction from his girlfriend getting all googly-eyed over Jacob Morgan, and also, maybe, in an attempt to show Susan that he was perfectly comfortable playing with kids, in an effort to hopefully impress her. Score some points.

"Only a few minutes, Ethan. It's already past your bedtime."

Ethan pretended not to hear his uncle, and Jacob rolled his eyes at Susan, who laughed.

"So, Lance, how long you staying? Good while?"

Again with the questions. Why couldn't Jacob Morgan pull out his phone and stare at Facebook or play Candy Crush like every other well-behaved adult in the country?

"As long as work takes," Lance said. Then, to flip the cards, "And what do you do for a living? More than chop wood, I take it."

Jacob Morgan laughed and pointed at Lance. "Good one. Yeah, a little more than that. I still own the hardware store, but I hired a manager to run the place. I share the profit with him. Not a bad gig for either of us, really. I do some farming, some handiwork 'round town for folks, some of the businesses. This and that."

Susan said, "What he's not telling you is his parents left him, like, a bazillion dollars."

Lance suspected Susan meant the words as a joke, but it was instantly obvious it made Jacob uncomfortable. The man nodded, forced a smile. "My parents invested well in some land about a decade before they died," he said. "It's certainly helped." Then he looked to Ethan. "Especially since this little guy came along.

"And on that note, Ethan, it's time to go."

Ethan didn't protest. He simply played one more quick round of hot hands with Luke and then stood up from the floor. "Okay," he said.

And then Lance sucked in a sharp, quick breath, clenching his teeth and almost doubling over, as if he'd just experienced a pregnancy contraction. It wasn't so much painful as overwhelming. The room seemed to wobble in and out of focus, the hairs on his arms and neck feeling as though they were standing straight up, like he was part of a load of laundry, fresh out of the dryer.

It was the sensation he'd picked up from Ethan, only intensified ten times over. Maybe a hundred.

And then his vision cleared and the room came back into focus and he saw that all the other adults in the room were standing around like nothing at all had happened. They weren't even looking at him, wondering what'd gone wrong, why he'd gasped.

And then he saw that all their eyes were locked on to something, all staring in the same direction.

Lance turned his head to follow their gazes.

Ethan stood directly in front of the basement door, staring at the chipped wood, his hand slowly reaching up toward the knob.

Jacob spoke up. "Ethan, no. That's just a basement, and it's locked."

Another blast of electricity made the room wobble in Lance's vision, but it was weaker this time. Not enough to bother him. Again, the others didn't seem to notice.

Ethan reached for the knob again, and Jacob was across the room, swooping the boy up into his arms. "Ethan, I said no!"

Ethan instantly burst into a fit of tears and childish screams. "But she's down there! She's down there!"

Jacob offered a barrage of rushed apologies and thanks for the pizza and was at the front door in a flash, Luke and Lance and Susan all trailing. Jacob gave a final goodnight and wave and then was gone, switching on the lantern he'd left on the porch, disappearing down the steps and around the side of the house. Ethan's cries echoed in the night air. "She's down there! She's down there!"

The three of them stood in silence at the front door.

*Oh my God*, Lance thought. *He's like me.*

LANCE FLOATED DOWN THE HALLWAY, LIGHT AS AIR. SOUND was muffled, distorted, as if he were underwater. The walls of the farmhouse closed around him, a vignette in his peripheral vision. He was moving, but his body was on autopilot. He wasn't even sure he was breathing, but he must be, because as he reached the kitchen, he had enough air in his lungs to whisper the words, "He's like me," delivered in a voice of such astonishment, such absolute shock, that both Susan and Luke looked up from where they'd been cleaning up the kitchen table and said together, "What?"

Lance heard them, faintly, soft voices lingering far off in the distance as his head reeled and his mind scrambled and some part of his entire life uprooted and shifted itself with enough force to make his stomach queasy.

There was confusion at first, followed by a fundamental understanding that brought into focus a feeling of happiness and relief strong enough to force an unexpected laugh from Lance's lips.

*I am not alone.*

Even though the boy Ethan was only six years old, he was

living proof, the first solid piece of evidence Lance had ever encountered that there were others like him. Others who shared his gifts.

There were the Reverend and the Surfer, sure, but they were something different. Lance did not understand the full breadth of their powers and abilities, but he was certain that in this unspoken war, they were on the opposing side.

But the boy ... innocent.

Like Lance had been when he'd been young and his mother and he had struggled to keep up and comprehend Lance's abilities.

Lance had so many questions, was dying to know if Ethan was just like him—the conversations with the dead, the telepathic tendencies, the instant downloads with just a touch of flesh on flesh. Could he control any of it? Could he do more?

*He's six years old, Lance.* He had to slow himself down. Ethan was a child. Lance tried to remember being that young, what it'd been like to have the realization that he wasn't like everybody else. Could see and hear things the rest of the world could not.

It had been confusing.

Terrifying.

If it hadn't been for his mother, her patience and grace and absolute love for her only son—her protection...

And Lance was swarmed with another thought that made his heart quicken and his breathing intensify with excitement. A thought ripe with possibility.

He replayed the moment of Ethan's outburst in his head. The way the boy had gone toward the door and reached for the handle. The way Jacob Morgan had at first tried to calmly dissuade his nephew, then rushed to his side to pull him away, as if sensing the tantrum was on its way. Which made a certain level of sense, as parents often knew their children's habits and tendencies better than any other—and Lance doubted Jacob Morgan and Ethan's situation would be any different, given it seemed Jacob had been the boy's guardian for nearly his entire young life.

But what struck Lance as odd was the fact that, despite the suddenness with which Ethan's tantrum had erupted, the words he'd screamed had been clear as day.

("She's down there! She's down there!")

Lance, for one, was in on the game. He'd already experienced some sort of supernatural message he was still presuming to have come from Mary Benchley, so he hadn't question Ethan's words.

But neither had Jacob Morgan.

Whether the man was taking his nephew's claims at face value or, more likely, simply playing along in an effort to placate the screaming child, the natural response from most people would have been, *Who's down there?* Or maybe, *There's nobody down there*, in that soothing parental voice one uses to set a child's mind at ease.

Jacob Morgan had gone with neither. Had said nothing.

Lance considered this for a long time, standing idly in the kitchen while Susan and Luke continued to stare at him.

*Maybe he knows*, Lance thought. *Maybe he knows Ethan is special. That's why he was in such a hurry to get out of here. He recognized the boy slipping into one of his ... episodes.*

If that was the case, Lance *needed* to talk to the man. His head was spinning, full of questions.

Lance's vision cleared and he saw Luke and Susan standing behind the table, waiting.

"Tell me everything you know about that guy," Lance said, looking at Susan.

"Well," she said, pulling out a chair to sit. "For starters, he's on the list you gave me."

She held up the yellow sheet of legal paper and Lance eyed it. He had forgotten all about it.

And that's when something else struck him, another shift in the landscape. He'd been trying so hard to figure out why he'd been brought to Ripton's Grove, ultimately accepting it was because of the potentially unsolved mystery behind the Benchley family murder.

But now he wondered if it had been about the boy from the very beginning.

## [ 24 ]

LANCE STOOD AND WATCHED AS LUKE AND SUSAN CLIMBED into the Jeep, gave a final wave, and then started to back down the driveway, the sounds of tires on gravel growing fainter before quieting altogether.

He shut the front door and locked it. Double-checked the windows and the back door. All secure. Though at this point, he wasn't sure the doors being locked mattered much. Somebody had access to this house. Somebody that wasn't supposed to. But Lance didn't allow himself to be concerned with thoughts of intruders right then. He found the odds of somebody entering the house for a third time in twenty-four hours slim, if not completely nonexistent. Especially when on their last visit, they'd assaulted a woman and sent her to the hospital. They had to at least think the police might have taken a bit more of an interest in the place now. Have a deputy swing by a few times during the night to make sure everything was calm and orderly. Lance knew no such thing would happen. This place was a black spot on the town's map, and it seemed that Sheriff Kruger was keen on keeping it that way.

But there was more keeping Lance from worrying about

possible nighttime assailants. He was too distracted. His mind was still coming down off the high of discovering, after all these years, that there were others like him. At least one, anyway. But if there was one ... it only fueled the theory that there would be more. Out there somewhere. All probably wondering the same things as Lance. Wondering if they were alone and questioning everything they were and desperately seeking any sort of answer, explanation, and, most importantly, camaraderie.

Lance sighed and sat down at the table, pulling his last bottle of water from his backpack and cracking the top. He took a small sip, then a full gulp, and then another. It was tepid, but it also seemed to help cool his thoughts, allow his body and mind to slow down, his heart rate to steady and his breathing to normalize. He took another swallow and then refastened the cap and said, "Okay." He stared down at the wooden table, refocusing his mind. "What do I do now?"

The list that had magically ended up in his bag from the sheriff's office was on the table, refolded and looking innocuous. After Jacob and Ethan had left, and Lance had regained enough control of himself to have a conversation with human beings again, he'd told Susan that he had reasons to believe that anyone on that list might have some sort of insight into what happened the night the Benchley family was killed.

Susan's eyes had scanned the list, not even flinching when she saw her own name, and then nodded. "Makes sense," she'd said. "Where'd you get this?"

Lance shook his head. "Nope. Remember, you'll just have to trust me."

Susan didn't take offense. "Well, I suppose you're curious as to why I'm on here. But I'll tell you right now I'm not surprised."

Lance waited. Said nothing.

"Sheriff asked me to come in to answer some questions a couple days after it all happened. I was happy to help, of course.

Or at least try to. And, well, I mean, I wasn't worried or anything. I knew I didn't have anything to do with…" She looked around the room, as if suddenly remembering where she was. "I knew I had nothing to do with what happened here."

Luke was leaning against the kitchen counter again, but now he stood straighter, curiosity burning in his eyes. "So why'd they want to talk to you, Suze? You've never told me this."

Susan shrugged. "I haven't really told anybody. My parents, of course, but that's it. It was a long time ago." She paused, took a deep breath and said, "Apparently, I'm the last person in town to talk to Mary Benchley before she went away. Like, literally. The last words she spoke to anyone before she was gone — anyone that's come forward, that is—were to me." Susan must have seen the surprise in both Lance's and her boyfriend's eyes, because she quickly laughed and held up her hands. "Calm down now, boys. Do you want to know what she said? She said, 'Thank you.'"

Lance and Luke looked at each other, clearly disappointed in the revelation. Lance repeated, "Thank you?"

Susan nodded. "Yep. I'd just started working at Mama's, and Mary had come in to pick up a pie to go that her mother had called in an order for. I'm the one who gave it to her. She came in the restaurant, we chatted for just a minute or two—just general chitchat—and then she thanked me and she was gone. Sometimes I replay it in my head, that scene. I try to glorify it and convince myself that maybe she had a different look in her eyes, that her voice carried more meaning than just thanking me for handing her a pie. Like maybe she was thanking me for being her friend, not being part of the immature cesspool of rumors and rude remarks that is high school. But honestly, the more I replay that moment—and trust me, I've done it a lot over the years—I'm not sure she even really saw me that night. Truth is, she looked distracted. Vacant. Like she had a lot on her mind.

I gave her the pie and she left. That's exactly what I told the sheriff."

Lance nodded, filing away the bit about Mary looking distracted. He supposed that the knowledge that she was about to be shipped off to a boarding school might weigh heavily on a teenage girl's mind. But maybe it was something else altogether.

"And what about Jacob Morgan? Why's his name on there?"

Luke's eyes grew a little harder. "Yeah, I'm wondering the same thing."

Lance suppressed a chuckle. Luke was jealous.

Susan didn't seem to notice. "Oh, I thought you knew," she said to Luke. She turned to Lance. "Jacob's the one who called it in. He's the one who found them the next morning."

Lance put the rest of the pieces together before Susan had finished explaining. Statistically, it all made sense. Jacob Morgan was the closest neighbor the Benchleys had had, as far as Lance knew. Either something sent up his hackles, and he sensed something was wrong enough for him to make the short hike to check on the family, or maybe he was supposed to be there for some other reason. Had had his morning plans quickly and grotesquely derailed.

"He'd been headed out of town for a week or so to help a friend do some renovations on a new house," Susan said. "He was stopping by before he left to ask Mark Benchley to keep an eye on his place while he was gone. Apparently they did these favors for each other. Joan tells me that Mark and Jacob were fairly good friends, despite the age difference. Used to have lunch together a lot in town. Anyway, he got here and ... well. You can imagine."

Lance could.

"The police took him right in. I remember that morning, because things felt electric. Like you could feel the current of gossip pulsing around town. By lunchtime, everybody was convinced Jacob was the killer, not knowing it was actually him who'd found him and called it in. But by later in the day, after the police had done their thing and examined the crime scene and whatever else they do, they had let Jacob go and the finger was pointed squarely at Mark Benchley. Which of course, given his reputation, didn't surprise too many people. Not as much as it should have, anyway."

Lance soaked in all this information. Processed it and tried to categorize it into mental filing cabinets for further review. There were more questions he wanted to ask, but he was tired ... and his mind kept drifting back to Ethan.

Susan and Luke had left then, leaving Lance with the house and his thoughts. They'd told him to call them if he needed something, or wanted to hang out again, and Lance could sense the excitement in them, see the flash in their eyes. They believed he was going to figure this out, like they were playing a game of Clue and all Lance had to do was keep eliminating things until nothing was left but the truth. And they were enjoying playing the game.

He'd seen the same thing in Leah's eyes back in Westhaven. She'd had a personal stake in the game, sure, but the excitement and enthusiasm were all the same. Maybe it was something about small towns, the lack of other things to do, that made people so willing to jump into a murder investigation. For them, it was an episode, an excursion away from a mundane reality. For Lance, it was a way of life. They didn't understand that. Couldn't understand that.

Leah had started to.

And then he'd left her.

Lance downed the rest of the water and tossed the bottle at the sink. It missed, the bottle striking the counter and then bouncing on the floor with sharp crackles as plastic met wood. He sighed, stood. Retrieved the bottle and set it on the counter.

He rested his hands on the edge of the counter and stretched his back, arching it until it cracked and loosened. He stared into the window above the sink, at the reflection of—

The door to the basement was open.

Lance spun around and looked.

The door was closed. The bolt still locked.

He looked back to the window and saw it was still closed there as well.

He sighed. "Okay, I get it," he said, as if capitulating to the house.

He dug in his backpack until he found the small flashlight he carried. A tiny thing powered by one AAA battery, but powerful all the same.

Then, exhausted and wanting nothing more than to sleep, he opened the basement door, clicked on his flashlight and started down the steps.

## [ 25 ]

THE STEPS WERE OLD, AND THEY CREAKED AND SQUEALED with every slow step Lance took, but they were built solid all the same. Plenty of support beams and a smattering of nails that almost made the wood look speckled in the bright cone of light thrown from Lance's flashlight. There was no railing to grab hold of for balance, just the walls on either side for the first few steps down and then you were on your own. Just you and the boards and a fight with gravity you hoped to win.

Lance checked again for a light switch on his way down. Found nothing. Let his flashlight swish and swoosh in wide arcs, sweeping across ceiling and walls and steps, illuminating clouds of dust and a latticework of cobwebs.

The boards whined and dust puffed from his shoes as he stepped, leaving behind a ghost trail of prints.

The air was thick with earth and soil and stone. Cool, but somewhat unpleasant.

It smelled like a tomb.

*If this were a horror film, right about now would be when the door slammed shut behind me and my flashlight went out*, Lance thought.

Not that he honestly expected those things to happen. While Lance did find the spirit world to conform almost comically to many of the tropes displayed in Hollywood, it almost never did so on cue. Sometimes, he wished it would. Everybody loves the familiar.

No, the door did not slam shut. And, no, Lance's flashlight did not suddenly need a change of bulb or battery. In fact, when Lance reached the bottom step and then stepped softly down onto the hard-packed dirt floor, something brushed across his ear and, after a mini-heart-attack that he was glad nobody was around to see, he shined his flashlight to his right and found a pull cord attached to a hanging overhead light. He reached up and tugged it, expecting nothing but thrilled to see a single uncovered bulb spark to life. It was dull and had the same yellowed tint as the lights in the aboveground portions of the house, but in the basement, it might as well have been the sun, forcing the bad things to retreat back into the shadows.

Lance lowered his flashlight, leaving the beam on and burning bright in case the old bulb hanging from the ceiling decided it had had enough and winked out. He stood in place and did a slow circle, examining the room.

The basement was empty except for a well-worn wooden workbench against the wall to Lance's left, long devoid of any tools but scuffed and scarred and full of cuts and nicks and evidence of heavy usage from a time before. In the back corner of the room, behind the stairs and nestled in the shadows where the light didn't quite fully reach, were mounted rows of what looked like metal shelving spanning from waist height to nearly above Lance's head. The shelves were bare, except for a single gallon paint can sitting on one of the midlevel shelves, its outside dotted and splashed with dried remnants of a dull white color Lance suspected was the original color of the farmhouse's exterior.

But there was nothing else. No spirits standing and waiting patiently for him, ready to spill their secrets and help him make everything right in the world. No monsters lurking in the dark ready to drag him down into the depths of places unknown. Just a dirt floor, a lonely workbench, and a single can of old paint on shelves that had likely not held anything important since the Benchley family had been killed and their belongings purged from the house. And probably never would again.

Lance called out, "Hello?" He waited, then tried, "I ... I think you know I'm here to help. Can you speak to me?"

There was nothing but the muffled creaks of the house upstairs as a gust of wind blew across the top of the hill outside.

Lance looked around the room, turning slowly and trying, for some reason, to appear unaggressive. Friendly. He received no answer. No words, no messages, no prickle of electricity like he'd experienced earlier when...

He tried again. "The boy," he said. "Ethan. He could hear you? Sense you?" Then Lance took a gamble, hoping he was right about his earlier assumption about whom he might actually be attempting to contact. "Mary, how did he know? Is he like me? And why could he hear you, but I couldn't this time?"

A flutter, small and tickling in Lance's stomach. A slight buzz in his ear, like a gnat had just flown in one side and out the other. Followed by a pang of absolute sadness, no more than half a second at most, but deep and strong enough that Lance felt at once completely consumed by the grief, his eyes suddenly full of tears and his heart pleading for relief.

And then it was all washed away in the blink of an eye, and Lance stood in the basement in the dull yellow light with the flashlight at his side and a desire to see his mother's face again trumpeting in his mind like a full-blown marching band.

He coughed and took a deep breath and shook his head, forcing himself to process what had just happened.

He'd managed to get through. Something he'd said. Was it calling Mary by her name? Was it the mention of Ethan?

"Mary," he tried again. "What happened here?"

The basement was silent, and Lance's frustration bloomed.

"Then why am I down here if you don't want to help me?"

He thought of the reflection from the kitchen window, the open basement door. It was an invitation. It had to have been. Whether sent by a friendly spirit or an evil one, there was no other explanation. *Something* had wanted Lance to descend the steps and see what was down here.

He walked the perimeter of the room, sweeping his flashlight beam across the floor and ceiling and corners. He stopped at the workbench and ran his hand over the surface, feeling the smooth wood and the pockmarks from tools. He searched for a drawer or a compartment. Found none. Looked for scribbled or carved messages. A clue. Any clue. Anything at all.

But the basement was empty.

Lance tugged on the pull cord too hard as he made to leave and head back up the steps, and it snapped at the chain. He let the cord fall to the floor at his feet and walked back up to the kitchen, closing the door behind him.

He headed to bed. The house seemed to be finished speaking to him for the time being. Lance figured it would know how to wake him if it changed its mind.

In the morning, he'd walk down to see Jacob Morgan. Talk to the man and see if he knew what his nephew really was. But more importantly, Lance hoped to chat with Ethan alone.

Lance carried to bed with him a glint of hope, an excitement that, if not for his mental exhaustion and many miles walked and an entire hillside climbed, would have likely made it difficult to sleep. He wished the sun was up and the day started so he could spend more time with Ethan immediately.

But along with the hope, being dragged behind it like a ball and chain, was the nagging, unmistakable sense that he was missing something.

Lance kicked off his shoes and fell onto the bed of a dead girl. Sleep grabbed hold within minutes.

[ 26 ]

THERE WERE NO DREAMS THIS TIME. NO RIDING ON EMPTY buses. No men with their faces blown off. The sleep was deep, and it was purely black. A long blink of the eyes, only to have them open to the faint early-morning light highlighting the window around the blinds in Mary Benchley's old bedroom.

Lance rubbed sleep from his eyes and yawned, sitting up on the bed and taking stock of himself. He was still in one piece, with no visible injuries he could see or feel, so he was happy to know his idea that the home invader would not strike again so quickly was accurate. It had been a calculated gamble.

He stood and stretched and padded over to the window in his socks, peeking out the blinds. Mary's windows overlooked the driveway and front yard, and while there was a hint of sunlight still hidden behind the crest of the trees in the distance, the sky was mostly overcast. Lance could feel the chill from the window. Breathed out onto the glass and drew a smiley face in the condensation with his finger. "Good morning," he said to the face. "Sleep well?"

The face did not answer.

Lance looked down to the driveway again and noticed that Victoria Bellows's Mercedes was gone.

"Well, you know what they say," Lance said to his finger-drawn friend, who was beginning to fade away. "The early bird gets the luxury SUV."

He turned and grabbed his toiletry kit from his backpack and went to the bathroom.

The upstairs bathroom had a shine to it that it hadn't the day before. The sink and tub were a brighter color, and the faucets and fixtures had a new life to them. The ring around the toilet bowl was mostly gone. There was the artificial smell of pine in the air. Victoria Bellows had done a good job. Lance hated that she'd been attacked. He felt he owed her more than a bouquet of flowers.

He brushed his teeth and flossed, then looked into the mirror in order to assess whether he needed to shave or not. He could usually pull off a few days' stubble without feeling gross or thinking he looked like a fool. He ran a hand over his cheeks, feeling the roughness that had grown, examined the five-o'clock shadow look he had going. He chose not to shave.

He splashed some warm water on his face, still clean and refreshing in smell and taste, and then dried off with his t-shirt. And when his eyes met his reflection in the mirror, he was hit again with that strange prickling at the base of his skull, a repeat of yesterday morning's episode, when he'd foolishly tried to reach his hand through the mirror's glass because he felt it had been calling out to him, urging him to take action.

And here the feeling was again. He couldn't deny it was real, present and suggesting. The tingle at his neck grew, and his stomach fluttered with an anxiousness that was clearly fabricated. Something was tugging at his gut; something was drawing him closer to the mirror again. Lance stood and stared. Turned his head from side to side, raised himself up and down on his

194

toes. He followed his face in the mirror, then focused his eyes on the background as he moved, looking for some anomaly between the mirror's reflection and the reality of the bathroom.

He saw nothing different.

Yet the feeling persisted.

Lance reached out and rapped his knuckles on the glass, causing a metallic rattling as it vibrated in its frame. He waited. Nothing knocked back from the other side. Lance gripped the mirror on either side and gave it a slight jerk up and down, left and right. It did not move. It was mounted solidly on the wall. He swung the medicine cabinet door open again, took in the fly graveyard once more and found nothing else of interest, and swung the door closed again.

He sighed and stepped back. Stared at the mirror for another full minute. Looked at it for what it was, instead of what it might be. *There's something off about it*, he thought. Then he remembered that yesterday, he'd thought the same thing, realizing that the mirror was mounted much higher up than most mirrors he came across in life.

Then another thought collided into this one. Joan's mention of Mark Benchley being a man of above-average height.

Lance added these things up. The mirror was high. Mark Benchley was tall.

The feeling pulling at his stomach started to grow.

*People put things in high places that they don't want others to reach*, Lance thought. *Or things they don't want them to find.*

Lance stepped back up to the vanity, stretched his arm up to reach the top of the mirror and let his hand search blindly across the top of its dusty surface.

His fingers brushed against something. It was small, and cold and solid. He wrapped his hand around it and—

*A basement. No windows and a hard-packed dirt floor. Wooden steps leading up to a closed door. A wooden work table along one wall with neatly organized boxes and jars of nails and nuts and bolts and other things that only had any use for a man who knew how to use them. A pegboard was above the table, tools precisely hanging in their spots. They showed signs of use, but also of care. Well-sharpened blades and deeply oiled leather. Glinting steel and shining metal. There was a sprinkling of sawdust on the floor near the work table.*

*A lone lightbulb hanging from the ceiling. The light it cast was dim, but another light was flickering in the corner. A kerosene lantern sat idly on the floor, casting shadows along the wall under and around the rows of metal shelving. The shelves held toolboxes and industrial-type storage containers. There were a handful of paint cans. There were extension cords coiled tightly and stacks of newspapers piled high but well aligned and balanced, their edges crisp and flush with the wall.*

*The wall was not flush with the adjacent wall. Where the wall with the shelving should have met its neighbor, forming a back corner of the basement, there was a five-foot gap. There was some sort of track system inlaid in the ground and in the ceiling. The entire wall had shifted over, sliding neatly behind the stairs, just far enough so that the edges of the shelves did not collide with the edges of the steps.*

*It was a door.*

*Light spilled from the opened mouth of the wall.*

*"So you see, Ray, when the Japs or the Chinks or whatever group gets pissed off enough and comes and starts bombing us, I can come down here and lock myself in and be nice and safe until it's all over."*

And then the basement shifted forward and the opened-mouth doorway in the wall came rushing forward in a blur and Lance was standing in the opening and—

*The room beyond the wall was long and narrow. The size of a bedroom that had been squished at its sides. There was a long*

196

*encasement of fluorescent lighting on the ceiling at the center of the room. A pull cord dropping down a foot or so. The light was powerful, enough to illuminate the entire room. Along one entire wall were floor-to-ceiling shelves full of canned food and gallons and gallons of water. There were gas cans along the floor, and a stockpile of lanterns lining the wall beside them. Piles of batteries and both CB and AM/FM radios. Stacks of paperback books and a couple old board games. At the far side of the room were a sink and a toilet. A shower curtain and rod were hung from the ceiling in front of the toilet, serving as a bathroom door. In the center of the room was a futon. It was in the folded-down position.*

*A boy and a man lay atop it, looking up at the ceiling.*

*"And of course you and your mom and the rest of yous can come, too. It might be a little tight, but we'll make it work."*

*The man was tall and wore faded overalls with a short-sleeved white t-shirt underneath. Boots on his feet. The outfit of a country man who worked with his hands and worked the land. Built things and grew things and enjoyed the fruits of his labor. He was in his forties, maybe, but looked older. Heavy creases on his brow and cheeks, skin like leather.*

*He poked the boy playfully in the ribs, turning and saying, "It'll be fun, won't it, Ray? Like a big sleepover. Like the kind you probably have with your friends, right? You can stay up as late as you'd like—because if it comes to that, what's the point of a bedtime, am I right?—and we can read each other stories and play board games and it'll be a grand ol' time!"*

*The man laughed and poked the boy again, and the boy grinned and squirmed away and the man laughed some more and said, "Hey, I got an idea. Why don't we play a game now? What do ya say, Ray, my boy?"*

*The boy, who looked not much older than he'd been when he'd pulled the garden hose in his backyard and tripped the little* girl because he was angry that she'd splashed him, grinned and nodded his head. "Okay," he said.

"Good! I could use a little fun," the man said. "I've been working too much. Too much, I tell ya!" The man crinkled his brow and tapped his temple, making a show of pretending to think. Then his eyes lit up big, and he smiled and said, "I know! Why don't we play our secret game?"

They boy's face fell. His eyes dropped to the futon's mattress and he said nothing.

The man, seeing the boy's apprehension, did not respond with sympathy. Instead, his eyes grew hard, narrowing to slits. His voice came out hushed but hot.

"Ray. Come on, now. Be a good boy. What's the matter, too good to play a game with an old slog like me? Do you think when your mama comes and picks you up, she's gonna want to hear her boy didn't behave? Do you want me to tell her that, huh? She'll be real mad, I bet. Disappointed in you, too." The man shook his head. "I wouldn't want that, Ray. I'd hate to see your mama upset, wouldn't you?"

The boy said nothing. He kept staring at the mattress.

"Ray?" The man's voice was even quieter now, but scarier all the same. "I'm starting to get mad."

The boy looked up and met the man's eyes. "Okay," was all he said.

The man's face lit up again, an instant transformation back into the happy, playful person he'd been moments earlier. He hooted a laugh. "Hooray! Ray's going to play!"

The boy didn't so much as blink. He just sat stone-faced and waited.

"And remember," the man said, "it's our secret game. That's what makes it so fun, right? I'd be really mad, Ray, if you ever told somebody. I want this to be our thing, okay. Something special for just you and me, okay?"

*The boy said nothing. Waited.*

*The man, apparently satisfied, said eagerly, "Okay, let's get ready."*

*He unfastened the buckles of his overalls and flung the straps over his shoulders, then worked to shimmy them down around his ankles. Then he pulled down the threadbare boxer shorts he'd been wearing underneath, fully exposing himself. He was already growing hard.*

*Quietly and with the poise of someone much older than his true age, the boy reached down and began to—*

Lance gasped and felt himself flung back into the bathroom. The world coming back into focus with a speed that was almost blinding. He closed his eyes and counted to ten, getting his breath under control and letting his heart slow. Then he slowly opened his eyes.

He saw his reflection in the mirror. His eyes darted up to the top of the mirror, then back down to his hand. His right hand was closed in a fist. Something was inside, digging into the soft flesh of his palm. Lance raised his hand and opened it, examining what he'd found—what had held within it a terrible memory that no person should ever have to see.

It was a key.

[ 27 ]

LANCE STARED AT THE SILVER KEY IN HIS HAND. IT WAS small, but heavy. Thick and durable, not flimsy and easily bent like most cheapos you had made in hardware stores or at the checkout counter at the Walmart Tire Center. He tossed it gently in the air, feeling its heft.

Then he considered what he'd seen. His eyes went unfocused again as his mind drifted back to the flash of memory the key had jolted him with. Most of Lance's instant downloads came from a human touch, and although he knew he could never quite seem to make sense of from who he received them, or why, there was still something incredibly unsettling about receiving one of these flashes from an inanimate object. It was even more unexpected than the ones he received from other people, because at least with human contact, Lance could have a sense of expectancy, even if the odds were slim. With inanimate objects ... well, he wasn't going to go around all day expecting to have an item's history presented to him every time he went shopping or opened a door or picked up a fork in a restaurant. The Universe had at least spared him that consideration.

It had only happened twice before.

Both items had presented him with horrible scenes that he knew he'd never forget.

Today's was no different, but it was also relevant.

Lance remembered Victoria Bellows's words, how she'd told him that after the Benchley family murder, the sheriff had gone around telling people that he should have known better. That too much evil had already happened in the house and it made sense that more would follow.

Now Lance understood. Ray Kruger had been molested in the farmhouse. How many times?

(*"Why don't we play our secret game?"*)

How much had that little boy who would grow up to be the town's protector suffered at the hands of a twisted older man?

And who else knew about it?

Every time Lance had tried to dig for more details about why Ray Kruger was so protective of—and repulsed by—the farmhouse, he'd received coy answers, changes of subject, and hushed whispers. But never any valuable information.

Did the whole town know and simply wish to protect their sheriff's privacy? Was the abuse of a small boy a secret that an entire town was trying to keep buried? Lance could understand that. It was a terrible thing. Not something you'd want tossed around in casual conversation.

But Lance felt there was more.

As usual, there was always more.

Lance looked at the key again, thought about the wall that had slid open in the basement.

He didn't want to go down there again. Not now. He wanted to put his shoes on and jog the short way down the hill and find Jacob Morgan and try and talk to Ethan. As much as Lance was invested in trying to figure out what had happened to the Benchley family—especially after hearing the echo of some of the events that'd taken place the night they had been killed (*Who was the fourth person?*)—he could not dampen his excitement and elation at finding another person who shared his abilities. He had so much to ask, and so much to teach the young boy, if possible. Help him come to terms with who he was and what life would be like for him.

Lance again remembered the feeling he'd gotten when he'd stepped off the bus in Ripton's Grove the evening before last. He'd been hit with such a compelling drive to stay here. He'd felt that pull of being needed, more than he'd felt in a long time.

Ethan had to be the reason for that. The Universe was finally giving him something in return. A small gesture to say *You are not alone.*

Lance finished up in the bathroom and returned to the bedroom to pull on his shoes, and then he was moving down the stairs, his backpack snug on his shoulders and the key he'd found—that terrible key—tucked safely into the pocket of his cargo shorts.

And instead of walking out the front door, he found himself turning and heading down the hall to the kitchen. Opening the basement door. Heading down the stairs. Despite the sun having risen, the basement was still nearly pitch black, the light coming down the stairs from the kitchen doing little to fight back the dark down below. Lance could just make out the pull cord he'd ripped down lying coiled on the ground, and he stepped over it and used his height and long arms to reach up and fumble in the dark until he found what was left of the bit of chain hanging from the fixture and pinched it between his fingers and tugged. The bulb snapped to life.

Lance turned around and looked at the wall behind the stairs, the metal shelves, the paint can, and was amazed at how different it all felt now that he knew what was behind the wall.

And what had taken place back there. A secret place. A secret game. A disgusting crime.

Lance walked closer to the wall, his steps feeling heavy, his stomach grumbling. He needed to eat. He needed coffee. He needed answers.

He hoped he'd get all these things soon. But for now, the wall had his attention. He stood three feet away, then two. Then he reached out, slowly, and rested his palm on one of the empty shelves. Braced himself for another memory, another flash of the past.

He got nothing but a bit of dust on his palm.

He grabbed the edge of one of the shelves in both hands and pulled, gently at first and then with more effort, finally leaning in, throwing all his weight into it and feeling the cords in his neck stand out as he strained.

The wall did not so much as flex. It had no give whatsoever. Lance wasn't too surprised by this, but he had to try. He walked back and forth along the length of the wall, pulling his flashlight from his backpack and scanning the surface, looking for a handle or a lever or some sort of trigger that would open the wall.

Then the key in his pocket suddenly seemed to weigh a hundred pounds, weighing down his thoughts.

*Of course,* Lance thought. *Lance, you idiot. Sometimes you're such a dumbass.*

Now he was looking for a keyhole.

He spent ten minutes shining his flashlight over the entire surface of the wall, floor to ceiling, side to side. Again, his efforts were in vain. Lance remembered Joan telling him that ol' Uncle Joe had been an engineer for the Army and could build anything. If he'd built a way to open the wall, he'd sure hidden it well.

The air in the basement was cool, but Lance felt the dotting of perspiration on his forehead and temples. A dampness was at his lower back, causing his t-shirt to stick. He was about to pull off his hoodie, but his stomach gave another grumble, and Lance knew that the longer he stayed in the basement, the longer it would be before he could have his conversation with Jacob Morgan an Ethan. Which, unless Jacob offered Lance some coffee and a stack of pancakes, meant the breakfast Lance planned on devouring at Mama's would be pushed even further away.

Sometimes hunger was a real pain.

He took one last glance at the wall and couldn't shake the feeling that something important waited for him on the other side.

While inside the farmhouse had been chilly, as the cold fall morning air had seeped through the old house's walls, when Lance stepped out the front door and onto the porch, he breathed in deeply and saw the white cloud of his breath as he exhaled. Each passing day seemed to be getting colder and colder, taking longer for the sun to warm things up. Lance loved fall, loved the chilled mornings and the crisp evenings. He stood for another minute on the porch, breathing in the clean mountain air, and then pulled the hood of his sweatshirt over his head and started down the steps. Rounded the corner of the farmhouse and found the trail. Followed it down the way he'd walked up yesterday afternoon.

There was a stillness to everything. An overshadowing calmness that seemed to have fallen among the trees and the rocks and the creatures. Lance's footsteps seemed very loud. The only noise aside from the occasional breeze stirring up leaves and rustling branches that had started to go bare.

He was at Jacob Morgan's house within a few minutes, standing on the path and peering through the trees at the small home. Just like yesterday, Lance thought the place looked more like a small hunting cabin than home, but he didn't pass judgment. The scattered pieces of split wood were gone from the yard, all neatly stacked and ready in a heaping pile. The chopping block remained, but the axe was gone as well. Stored away, taken care of. Lance watched the house for a full minute, watching for any signs of life. A shadow in a window, a reflection of light, the sounds of muffled voices carried to him on the breeze like a telegram.

There was nothing, except a small tendril of smoke snaking from a crude chimney at the side of house's roof.

Lance adjusted the straps of his backpack and stepped into the woods. Dead leaves and fallen twigs and branches crunched and snapped underfoot. Now he did hear the scurrying of small animals, suddenly alarmed at an intruder in their midst. Lance felt oddly like he was trespassing, creeping through the woods and into somebody's yard, but with no driveway or entrance from the path that he could see, he didn't dwell too much on it.

He emerged from the tree line and stepped into the grass. Finding his strides growing longer and quick, he stopped just short of the cabin. A single step led up to a modest covered porch. Two rocking chairs sat at opposite sides of the front door, one large, one small. Two-thirds of the Three Bears. The building was old, there was no mistaking it, but Jacob Morgan had obviously used his handyman skills to keep the place up. It was small, but it didn't appear shabby or forgotten. It had been cared for. Lance admired Jacob Morgan's work, his commitment to keep his home modest, yet presentable. A combination of rustic and quaint.

Lance stepped up the porch step and knocked on the door. Two quick *thwops*. He took a step back, waited. Heard nothing from the other side of the door. He tried again, another two knocks, only this time more forceful. The window next to the door rattled as he did so.

Still nothing. Lance counted to thirty in his head before he slowly reached out and grabbed the handle, knowing what he was doing was wrong yet unable to stop himself. Thankfully, the door was locked. Lance wasn't sure he would have been able to keep himself from trespassing any further. His curiosity about the boy was too high. The potential too great.

Lance sighed and turned and walked down the steps, heading around the side of the cabin to the rear. Here, he found the driveway. A crude gravel trail that led down a small decline and then connected with what looked like a dirt road. Lance followed the dirt road with his eyes, tried to imagine where it led. Most likely it fed into the main road that wound up the side of the hill from town.

There was no vehicle in the driveway. *They're not home*, Lance thought. He quickly tried to think about where they might be. Where he could find them.

Then he remembered what day it was.

Sunday.

Sunday morning.

("*She watches him in Kids' Group at church on Sundays.*")

The snippet of last night's conversation doused Lance's fire of excitement.

Jacob Morgan and Ethan were either at church or headed there. Susan too, likely.

Lance contemplated his options. He could wait. Take a seat in one of the rocking chairs and wait for the sound of tires on gravel. Or he could go to the church, hang out in the parking lot and wait for the doors to open and the stream of people to trickle out.

Either option carried with it a whiff of stalker. Despite

Lance's urgency, he didn't want to appear aggressive, or too eager. And he certainly didn't want Jacob Morgan to feel he was being accosted.

The third option seemed best. Breakfast at Mama's.

Lance needed coffee. Boy, did he need coffee.

And since he had more questions, he might as well talk to the town's best source of information.

[ 28 ]

Halfway down the mountain, Lance started to feel light-headed, his arms and legs taking on a bit of a floating feeling. He closed his eyes and took three deep breaths, counting to ten each time. With the final exhale, he opened his eyes and shook his head to clear it. He felt better, but he scolded himself for waiting so long to eat. He was running on empty. With his size and metabolism, last night's pizza was ancient history in terms of fuel. But this was nothing Mama's pancakes wouldn't solve.

He slowed his pace and tried to put his mind to work, keep himself occupied with thoughts other than his empty stomach and low blood sugar. He made a mental list of things that he knew, or at least had been told, about the night of the Benchley family murder. Then he made a list of all the things he didn't know. Questions he had. Item number one on this second list was obviously *Who had killed the Benchleys?* But there were two other items that Lance felt more pressed to answer first, thinking that perhaps the answers to one or both of these might have some bearing on the answer to the question of the Benchley family killer.

What was Sheriff Ray Kruger's real involvement?

The vision Lance had seen of the sheriff's abused childhood certainly played a role in the man's preoccupation with the farmhouse. On some disturbed level it seemed to Lance that the sheriff was both simultaneously repulsed by the home and somehow concerned about its well-being. There was a deeper connection here that Lance was missing.

Why had Mary Benchley's body been burned?

Lance hadn't given much thought to this part of the story until last night, when he'd relayed to Susan and Luke that the cleaning company didn't come to the farmhouse because they believed that Mary Benchley had been a witch. It was then that he'd remembered the fact that her body, or at least what very little was left of it, had been found burning on a brush pile in the backyard. Assuming that Mark Benchley had not killed his family and himself, why had the killer left Mark and Natalie Benchley's bodies where they'd fallen after the shotgun blast had done its work, yet he or she had gone through the trouble of disposing of Mary's body in an entirely different manner.

*Some sort of sacrifice?* Lance thought. *A ritual?*

Thoughts of what he'd encountered in Westhaven trickled in, forcing Lance to acknowledge that something as sick as human sacrifice could certainly not be ruled out as an option. Maybe there were witches in Ripton's Grove, but Mary Benchley wasn't one of them. Had she been their victim?

Why?

Lance stepped out of the woods and into the park. Out from under the cover of the trees, the temperature picked up a few degrees. Lance lowered his hood and headed toward the parking lot, back the same way he'd come after the Bellowses had dropped him off yesterday afternoon. There were a few morning joggers in the park, winding around the path. Those who were not quite God-fearing enough to put Him before their cardiovascular system. An elderly man sat alone on a bench near the baseball fields, staring across the empty playing area with something like nostalgia on his face. A folded newspaper sat beside him, weighted down by an iPhone. Lance considered his flip phone, how the older gentleman on the bench had infinitely more access to information and services and the rest of the world in the palm of his hand than Lance could ever have. He really should try and upgrade. But the phone had been a gift from his mother, all those years ago. It was the last thing he had from her. And he couldn't quite bring himself to give it up quite yet. It would feel too much like chipping away at her memory. He remembered the look of excitement on her face the day she'd given it to him. She'd put it inside a thousand-piece jigsaw puzzle box and then wrapped it in newspaper. Lance had torn away the paper to find a picture of what looked like a hundred kittens surrounded by balls of yarn and wicker baskets. He hated cats, and his mother was well aware of this. She'd found her joke hilarious. Lance had been too happy with the surprise inside the box to even give her a hard time about it.

And then Pamela Brody had shown Lance that she'd purchased a matching phone for herself, and they'd spent the rest of the afternoon sending silly text messages to each other and calling each other from different rooms of the house.

Lance found himself standing in front of Mama's, smiling like a fool. He had no idea how he'd gotten here but was thankful he'd somehow managed to cross two streets without getting plowed over by a truck. Or a police cruiser.

He pocketed the cell phone memory and made his way past the handful of cars in the parking lot, then pushed open the door.

The dining room was mostly empty. The booth right by the door was taken, as were two of the tables along the rear wall near the kitchen. The smell of bacon and coffee hit Lance like a wave, and his stomach grumbled in excitement. He stood by the hostess stand and waited, scanning the room again and looking for Joan.

A woman pushed through the kitchen door, carrying two plates of food to one of the tables along the wall. She spotted Lance and said, "Sit anywhere you'd like, sir. I'll be with you in a flash." She was tall and lean, with red hair and a heavy dose of freckles. Maybe midthirties. She was all smiles and graceful movements. She'd called him *sir*.

She was not Joan.

Lance smiled and nodded and made his way to back corner booth. Where he'd sat yesterday. Where Sheriff Ray Kruger had sat and read his Kindle the night before that, staring into that black-and-white screen and trying to suppress who knew how many awful memories.

Lance slid his backpack into the seat next to him, and when he looked up, the red-haired woman was at the table, smiling with big bright teeth that almost looked too large for her mouth. She smelled like strawberries and sugar, and her hair looked like something from a shampoo commercial.

She was not Joan.

"Good morning!" she started. "I'm Jen, and I'll be taking care of you this morning. Can I get you something to drink? Water, juice, coffee?"

"Coffee, please," Lance said. "Black." Then he proceeded to order the same breakfast he had the day before. Jen stared at him while he spoke, smiling and nodding and never letting her eyes leave his. It was almost unsettling. When he finished his order she said, "Got it. Anything else?"

"Actually, yes," Lance said. "Is Joan working this morning?"

Jen was all too happy to answer. "She should be here in..." She checked her wristwatch, a small silver thing that sparkled in the light when she brought it up to her face. "Maybe another hour. She and I alternate the Sunday morning shifts. That way we can let the other one get to church."

Disappointed, Lance thanked the woman, and she went back to the kitchen to give his order to the cook.

The thought of Joan in church was comical. Surprising, actually. She didn't seem the type. But then Lance figured it was possible she went every other week purely because she didn't want to miss out on any good gossip. With towns as small as this, drama would be everywhere, church not excluded.

Lance's coffee and food came, and once he assured Jen that he didn't need anything else, she left him alone to devour his food at a rate that made him appear as if he were in some sort of contest against unseen competitors. Jen came by and refilled his coffee and took away his empty plates, and with his stomach full and his body beginning to feel normal again, Lance sipped on his fresh cup and decided that he didn't want to just sit in the booth and wait for Joan to show up. Plus, if she was coming in after church, a lunch rush would likely soon follow. She'd be too busy earning tips and listening for juicy details to stop and have another heart-to-heart with the town's newest reporter.

Lance paid the check and left Jen a nice tip. As he handed over the cash, Jen leaned in closer and whispered, "You're him, aren't you? The fella writing the book about what happened up at that farmhouse?"

Lance said nothing.

Jen leaned closer and her voice grew even quieter, her eyes darting around to see if anybody was listening in. "Between you and me," she said, "I always knew Mark Benchley was trouble. He just had this look about him, you know? Something about his eyes, the way he looked at people." She shrugged. "It was creepy."

Lance was quiet for a second, then asked, "Can you tell me where the library is?"

Jen smiled with those big white teeth and told him it was two blocks behind the courthouse. Lance didn't have to ask for directions. He just had to head toward the bell tower.

Lance thanked her and left, calling over his shoulder as he opened the door, "Tell Joan that Lance says hi."

A new idea had struck, and since he figured he had to wait till church let out before he could talk to Jacob Morgan and Ethan, he had the time to kill to check something out.

Pun intended.

## [ 29 ]

THE STREETS OF RIPTON'S GROVE WERE ESSENTIALLY empty, only two or three cars driving lazily through downtown as Lance used the courthouse's bell tower as his North Star and walked the sidewalk. The cloud cover was still gray and rolled across the sky like a protective film, giving the whole town a very noir appearance. Lance, feeling very much like an private investigator, didn't miss the irony. *If I had one of those smart-phones, I could put my headphones on and listen to some jazz and really set the scene.*

He made a left turn and walked by the courthouse, looking up at the bell tower. The architecture was impressive—almost gothic in appearance—and Lance wondered what year it'd been built. How long had Ripton's Grove been Ripton's Grove? How many generations had walked these streets and opened businesses in these buildings? How many sheriffs had there been before Ray Kruger ... before Bill Willard?

How many murders?

Lance walked another block and found the library, a one-story concrete building with a green roof and a small glass atrium at the entrance that looked up to the clouded sky. There were large flowerbeds around the building with dark mulch and bushes that looked freshly trimmed. No flowers now, though. Gone until the spring, when they'd yawn and stretch their limbs and pop open with color.

The place looked very inviting, just as a library should. Lance stood on the sidewalk and allowed himself a brief image of his mother, wandering amid the stacks of the Hillston Public Library, her fingers tracing the spines of books and her head cocked at such an angle, with the tiniest hint of a grin on her face, that she appeared completely at ease. Blissful. Home.

How many hours had they spent together in that library? How many hundreds of books had they read? Since Pamela Brody had worked there part-time, Lance and she had spent many evenings there after the last guests had left and the front doors had been locked, just lounging silently on the couches and chairs scattered about, silently reading whichever new adventure they'd started. There was something magical about being alone in a library. Just you, surrounded by endless books, letting your imagination take you away.

The front doors of the Ripton's Grove Library opened with an electronic purr, and a woman and small girl exited. The woman, with a stack of books tucked under her arm, was holding the little girl's hand and practically having to tug her along the walkway because the girl was trying to hold open her own book and look at the pictures with one hand. Lance smiled at them as they passed. The woman smiled back.

He walked up the walkway and entered the library, looking up through the high glass ceiling of the atrium as he made his way in, knowing how much his mother would have loved to sit right in that very spot, book in her lap, reading under the stars late into the evening.

Being just the single story, the library's floor plan was simple and meant to utilize the space. A large open area in the front held two banks of computer stations for patrons to use, as well as a handful of large tables. To Lance's right were the restrooms and water fountain, to his left the front desk. Two women with gray hair stood behind the desk, each using a handheld electronic scanner to zap the barcodes in the backs of a large stack of books on the counter between them.

Lance walked over, hearing the faint *beep-boop* from the women's scanners with each new book they zapped. When he reached the counter, both women looked up slowly like some sort of two-headed guard dog. Their expressions were stoic, if not unpleasant.

"Can we help you?" the one on the left said, peering over the top of her glasses, which were pushed down on her nose.

Lance smiled. "Yes, ma'am, I hope so." He cleared his throat. "Does your library keep an archive of the town's local newspaper?"

This time, the woman on the right answered. She set her scanner down and straightened her posture. A small gold cross swung from her necklace. Her glasses were atop her head, and she pulled them down and settled them in place. *Better to scrutinize you with, my dear*, Lance thought.

"Of course we do," the woman said.

"Great," Lance said. "I was hoping you could help me find a particular issue, or at least point me in the right direction to get started in the appropriate timeframe. Are they digital archives, or physical?"

The woman on the left scoffed. "*Digital*, he asks." She shot the woman on the right a look that made it apparent she was questioning Lance's intelligence, perhaps ready to point him in the direction of the children's section and ask him if he preferred Sesame Street or the Muppets. "You see these here guns?" She held up one of the electronic scanners for Lance to see. "We just got these in the last two years, and they don't work right half the time. I don't know why folks can't just read a gosh dern paper with their hands any more. Why's everything have to be on a daggone television screen?"

"Yes, ma'am. I don't know, ma'am," Lance replied, unsure what to say or how this conversation had gotten out of hand so quickly. Or, honestly, whether the woman had actually answered his question. But he wasn't deterred. "So, may I have access to the archives, please?"

The woman on the right sighed. "Do you have a library card?"

Lance figured she already knew the answer to this question. "No, ma'am. Do I need one if I'm not taking anything out of the building?"

The women looked at each other, their eyes searching for a reason to protest. Finally, the woman on the right sighed again and said, "Follow me." She turned and walked out from behind the counter and rounded the corner out of sight.

Lance thanked the remaining woman, who nodded and gave a soft grunt, and then hurried around the corner to follow the woman with the gold cross necklace.

She was standing at a closed door near the rear corner of the building, the rows and rows of bookshelves casting shadows on the wall and forming more of an alcove than a walkway. The woman was searching through a small keyring when Lance approached, sliding them along the ring excruciatingly slowly in search of the correct key. Lance felt he could have picked the lock quicker, and he didn't even know how to pick locks.

Without a word, the woman suddenly shoved a key into the lock on the door handle and turned. There was an audible click, and then she pushed down and swung the door open wide, standing aside for Lance to enter. The door had a frosted glass pane with black stenciled letters that read: ARCHIVES – SEE FRONT DESK.

Lance stepped inside the room, which was cooler than the rest of the library had been. There were no windows, and when the woman reached inside the door and flipped the light switch on the wall, the overhead lighting was dim and mostly unhelpful.

"Apparently it's easier to read the screen this way," she said, not hiding the disapproval in her voice. She nodded to the back wall, where a large microfiche reader sat on a wide table. The entire rest of the room was lined with storage cabinets, no doubt containing decades worth of Ripton's Grove's history.

"Have a seat," she said.

Lance sat. Obedient. He wanted to stay in the woman's good graces.

Without question or instruction, the woman with the cross around her neck walked to one of the cabinets, leaning in close to read the labels on the drawers. She moved to the next one over, tapped one of the drawers with her finger and then yanked it open. She riffled through what looked like folders from where Lance was sitting, her fingers flicking through sheet after sheet, and then she paused, her thumb and index finger pinching one of the sheets and raising it out just slightly. She peered down at it, her eyes squinting behind her glasses. Then she pulled the sheet completely free and shut the drawer.

The sheet was roughly six inches long and reminded Lance of a smaller version of the old transparency sheets his teachers used to use with the classroom projectors when he was in elementary school. He could just make out the small squares of images on the sheet—the shrunken-down pages from past newspapers.

The woman stood at his side and worked the microfiche reader with hands that'd performed this task a hundred times before. Maybe a thousand. She showed Lance how to turn on the screen and then moved toward the door.

"When you're finished, come back to the front desk and I'll come clean up."

Confused, Lance said, "Excuse me, ma'am?"

She'd been halfway out the door but stopped and came back in. "Yes?"

Lance nodded toward the microfiche reader. "I didn't tell you what date I was looking for."

The removed her glasses and placed them back atop her head. She rubbed her eyes with her hands. "A group of us women play gin once a week. Last night was at Joan's house."

*Oh. I see.*

"I know who you are," the woman said. "And I guess I know why you're here. If that's not what you're after"—she pointed to the blank screen behind Lance—"just set it aside and look in the drawers for anything else you need. *Don't* refile the sheets. I'll take care of that."

Lance said nothing. Nodded.

The woman turned to leave, stopped, then turned back to face Lance. Even in the dim light, he could see her eyes were glistening. Pooling with tears.

"Listen," she said, her voice stern and lecturing, "Natalie Benchley was a saint. You hear me? A *saint*. And Mary was never anything but polite and sweet and pretty as a peach." The woman stopped, wiped at her eyes. "Whatever it is you're writing, you better do right by them, you hear? You better respect them."

Before Lance could answer, the woman turned and left, closing the door softly behind her.

*Boy*, Lance thought, *there's a lot of pressure when writing an imaginary book.*

But, despite his joke, he felt he understood where the woman was coming from. In fact, he thought he was starting to understand why the whole town seemed to be so concerned and so secretive about the entire incident involving the Benchley family's deaths. In towns this small, underneath the drama and gossip and surface-level lies, there was still an undeniable sense of family.

Lance was not part of the family. But he was digging around in the closets, all the same.

He sat and waited for a full minute, staring at the closed door and seeing the faint outline of the stenciled words on the outside of the frosted glass, waiting to see if the woman would return, offer another warning. Satisfied that she was likely back at the front desk, speaking of him in deplorable adjectives to her cohort, Lance spun around in the chair and flipped the switch to turn on the microfiche screen.

The screen lit up bright, enough to force Lance to sit back and squint his eyes until they adjusted. Then he leaned closer again and saw the big bold letters of the headline that dominated the entire top of the front page of the newspaper issue the woman had loaded for him. She was right; she had known exactly what he wanted. The headline read:

### Family Dead After Apparent Murder-Suicide

Lance studied the word *apparent* for a few seconds, wondering at what point it had no longer fit. How long had the Ripton's Grove Sheriff's Department really investigated what had happened there? If Mark Benchley had been innocent, how much of a chance had he really been given in the eyes of the public and law enforcement?

The image below the headline was a picture of the farmhouse, police cruisers parked in front and along the side. Lance skimmed the article, picking out key words and phrases and learning nothing he hadn't already been told by people in town.

He wasn't here for words.

When he was leaving Mama's, Jen had given her opinion on Mark Benchley, citing that he had a certain look about him.

221

Hearing this, Lance thought it might be time to try and track down a picture of Mark Benchley, and maybe the rest of the family as well. Put faces to the names, and also to the voices he kept hearing at the farmhouse. He couldn't really imagine it would help much, but again ... he had the time to kill.

The article about the murders continued on another page, and Lance fumbled with the knobs below the screen until he had the correct page in focus.

His jaw dropped. His heart leapt into his throat.

He leaned in closer.

The picture that accompanied the rest of the article about the Benchley family murder was a shot of the family all together at what looked like some sort of neighborhood picnic. There was a long table set up behind them covered with food, with lots of people milling about. Trees and playground equipment dotted the background, and Lance recognized the area as the park at the base of the mountain.

Mark Benchley was an average-looking man, but above-average height, towering over his wife and daughter by a good foot, at least. His hair was thinning and his belly was soft, but all in all, he appeared normal. He wore blue jeans and loafers and a button-up shirt.

Mary Benchley looked to be maybe twelve or thirteen in the picture, a small spotting of acne on her forehead, her body looking as though it were still trying to figure itself out. But her face was pretty and her smile was a knockout, and Lance figured that she would likely have grown up to be a very attractive young lady.

But it wasn't Mark Benchley or his daughter, Mary, that had nearly caused Lance to fall out of his chair.

Natalie Benchley stood beside her husband, looking proud and happy. She had a plate of food in one hand, and the other arm wrapped around her daughter's shoulder. She wore a tank top and shorts and flip-flops. She looked comfortable in every sense of the word.

But there was one imperfection.

A scar on her chin. Just to the left of center.

Lance had seen the scar and then stared into the picture of the woman's face, had seen the image reverse itself in age, growing younger and younger until the face was of a little girl of maybe six or seven. Her mother scooping her up in her arms while the blood flowed from the fresh gash from where she'd fallen and struck the patio.

A little boy, maybe a year or two older, standing by with tears in his eyes, guilt weighing heavy on his heart and mind.

A little boy who would suffer unspeakable abuse and then grow up to be sheriff.

Lance sat back and looked at the image for a very long time. Another piece of the puzzle falling into place.

Natalie Benchley had been Sheriff Ray Kruger's younger sister.

[ 30 ]

WHEN LANCE APPROACHED THE TWO-HEADED GUARD DOG at the library's front desk, both women eyed him with looks that said *What could he possibly want now?*

"I'm all finished," Lance said, adjusting the straps of his backpack. He looked at the woman on the right, the one with the gold cross. "Thank you for your help." Then he smiled at the woman on the left, not wanting her to feel left out. "I hope you both have a great day."

He didn't look back as he walked through the atrium, sneaking another peek up at the cloud-covered sky through the glass ceiling and then stepped out the front door.

He stood on the sidewalk and took a deep breath, filling his lungs. The traffic was picking up on the main streets. He could hear the rumble of engines and the squeals of brakes that needed work coming from beyond the courthouse. He pulled his cell phone from his pocket and checked the time. It was just past noon.

Church would likely be out now.

He walked up the side street for two blocks until he was back in front of the courthouse, then he made a right turn, away from the direction of Mama's—he was much more eager to speak with Jacob Morgan than Joan right now—and figured he could cut down another street and circle back toward the direction of the park. Then he'd hike back up the hill and hopefully catch Jacob and Ethan at home. If they weren't there, maybe having stopped for lunch, Lance told himself he would wait. His belly was full and he'd had his coffee and he was pumped fresh with adrenaline after his discovery about Natalie Benchley's familial ties to Sheriff Ray Kruger. There was a Dean Koontz paperback somewhere in his backpack that he'd started twice without finishing. He could fish it out and give it another go while he waited.

Lance rounded a corner and saw he was correct about the traffic uptick. There were five cars stopped at the stoplight, and as Lance walked by and glanced inside the windows, he saw most of the drivers were dressed in their Sunday best. Shirts and ties and jackets and conservative dresses. No evangelical shorts and a t-shirt around these parts. The songs played and sung during worship services in Ripton's Grove would be the standby classics like "Amazing Grace" or "How Great Thou Art" instead of anything more contemporary that one might be able to threaten to dance to.

A few of the drivers looked at Lance before quickly darting their eyes back to the road, the cars in front of them, the stoplight. The light turned green and the cars moved slowly on. Back to homes where families would sit down to share a meal, off to Mama's or other restaurants where they'd maybe join friends and enjoy a few laughs.

A routine.

Normalcy.

Things Lance wondered if he'd ever taste again in any sense of the word. Right now his only routine was to have no routine.

He looked down at his sneakers on the sidewalk, tilting his

head down and letting the steady breeze ruffle his hair. It was getting too long. He'd need to get a trim soon. Haircuts were the type of trivial thing that Lance often found slipping through the cracks of his life now.

"Lance! Hey, Lance!"

Lance stopped and looked up. Searched for the source of the voice. He looked across the street and saw he'd ended up directly across from R.G. Homes. Rich Bellows, wearing black dress slacks and a white dress shirt, the tie loosened around his neck and hanging askew, was standing half out the door, waving frantically to get Lance's attention. Lance allowed a pickup truck to pass by and then crossed the street.

"Hi," Lance said.

Rich Bellows nodded a greeting and then pushed the door open completely, suggesting Lance should come inside.

Lance looked over his shoulder, back across the street, and then left and right. He found the courthouse's bell tower and then looked down at the buildings beneath, mentally tracing his steps from there to here.

This hadn't been the direction he'd meant to come. He'd started out on the right path, but somewhere along the way, he'd lost his focus, had let his mind wander, and his feet had brought him right here to Rich Bellows's doorstep.

Why?

Lance entered the office.

Then Rich Bellows closed the door, turned the deadbolt, and shut the blinds.

*Well ... this may not have been my best move.*

Lance didn't move. Rich Bellows didn't make him feel any more comfortable when he said, "Lance, I think you need to get out of town. Today. As soon as you can."

Lance thought about this, then chose his words very carefully. "But, we have a lease agreement."

Rich Bellows stared at Lance, his face showing first misunderstanding, then confusion. Finally he allowed himself a grin. Lance grinned back, and Rich let out a short burst of laughter, followed by a long, sad sigh.

"What's going on, Mr. Bellows?" Lance asked. "What's *really* going on? Why do you think I need to leave?"

Rich rubbed at the side of his face, trying to decide what to say. "I don't want you to get hurt."

"The way you say that," Lance said, "it doesn't sound like it's you who'd be doing the hurting. Am I right?"

Rich took a step forward, and Lance stepped back quickly, his hands coming up defensively.

Rich stopped and shook his head. "Relax, okay? You're right. I'm not who you need to worry about." He motioned behind Lance. "I was just going to go back to my office."

Lance lowered his hands but kept his body alert. "If not you, who should I worry about?"

Rich nodded toward the door behind Lance again. "My office."

Lance stepped aside. "After you, sir."

Rich did not seem to notice or care that Lance was allowing him to go first as a defensive tactic—to avoid possibly getting attacked from behind by some coward. He walked past Lance and stepped into his office, sidestepping around the desk and collapsing into his chair like a man who was exhausted from a hard day's labor.

Lance entered the office and stood just inside the doorway, leaning against the wall. He crossed his arms, decided it looked too aggressive, and then uncrossed them, burying his hands in the pockets of his cargo shorts.

He said nothing. Waited while Rich Bellows stared down at his desk, eyes lost. Finally, he looked up at Lance and said, "It was the flowers."

"Sir?"

"You seemed like a really nice guy the night you came in here looking for a place to rent. I even went home and told Victoria all about you. So, I guess"—he sighed and leaned back in the chair, running his hands through his hair—"I guess I was never quite convinced it'd been you who attacked her in the farmhouse yesterday morning, but I was so *blasted* angry, Lance. I felt so violated, to think somebody had come after her and hurt her. I ... I wasn't thinking straight, and I was looking for somebody to blame—other than myself—and you were the first person I could think of. I used you as a scapegoat. That's why I was so adamant with the sheriff that they should bring you in. I mean, they probably would have anyway, since you were the one staying at the house, but ... I could have done more to vouch for you."

Rich paused and looked to Lance, searching to see if he was following him. Lance nodded once.

"But then you showed up at Central Medical yesterday with those blasted flowers, and I thought to myself, *Rich, what an—pardon my language—asshole you are, to accuse this nice young man of such an awful crime.* You didn't even know my wife until yesterday morning, and you were thoughtful enough to check in on her and bring her a gift. She loved them, by the way. Put them in water as soon as we got home, and I had to stare at them on the counter this morning all through our breakfast. All the while thinking how it was all my fault, yet you were the one who got pulled into the sheriff's office and treated like a criminal."

Lance, ignoring what he figured was Rich Bellows eventually coming around to an apology of sorts, asked, "Sir, that's twice now you've alluded to what happened yesterday as being your fault. Why is that?"

Rich looked down at his desk again, and his face grew pale,

like he was getting sick. He took a deep breath and swallowed once, twice, then looked at Lance and said, "I may have been an accomplice. Indirectly, mind you, but that's not ever going to help me sleep at night."

Lance gave the man a minute before saying, "I'm going to need more, sir. It's hard for me to put any stock in your request that I leave town based on your vagueness. You understand, right?"

Rich seemed to consider this for a long time before saying, "Why are you here, Lance?"

Lance couldn't help it. He barked a laugh. Rich looked at him, confused. "Sorry," Lance said. "I'm just beginning to think that's what the epitaph will be on my gravestone. 'Here lies Lancelot Brody. Why was he here?'"

Rich didn't so much as smile. "You told me you were a consultant. But everyone in town seems to think you're writing some sort of article or true crime book about the Benchley murders."

Lance said nothing.

Rich sighed again and stood up, pushing the desk chair to the side and leaning over to rest his palms flat on the desk. "Lance, I truly don't believe you're a bad person. I don't know why you're here, and you don't seem keen on telling me, so all I'm going to do now is ask that whatever I tell you never leaves this room. Remember, I'm trying to *help* you here. Okay? I'm looking out for your best interest." Then he added, "And what I'm about to tell you, while I don't know that it's technically a crime, I just... if Victoria found out. I don't know the repercussions, Lance, and—well, if it comes to a head, then it does, and I'll take the responsibility like a man. But I don't want my life ruined, Lance. Not so much for my sake, but for my family's."

Lance looked Rich in the eyes and said, "Sir, you have my

word. This is just between you and me. I'm not here to ruin any lives or add any fuel to the gossip train."

Rich searched Lance's face for a long time, contemplated his honestly. And whether it was that he did bring himself to fully trust this stranger before him, or whether his apparent guilt would no longer allow him to remain silent, Rich said, "After the murders, and about a week after R.G Homes purchased the property, I got an email from an anonymous sender. A random address with letters and numbers, no name. It was a simple offer —a *partnership* is how they put it. They'd give me five hundred dollars a month, every month, on a date of my choosing, and all I had to do was email them back at that address anytime anything was done involving the Benchleys' farmhouse. Maintenance work, cleaning crews, landscaping, and"—he gave Lance another guilty look—"new tenants. Anything. The email told me to go check the mailbox out front to see how serious they were, and sure enough, there was an envelope right along with the other junk I get, with five one-hundred-dollar bills inside."

"So you went along with it?" Lance asked.

Rich looked at him, and Lance saw some of the guilt melt away and be replaced by defensiveness. "I've got a wife and two kids who I want to give the world to, Lance. There's nothing on this earth that makes me happier than to see them happy. I don't know if you've noticed, but Ripton's Grove isn't exactly a booming real estate metropolis. Five hundred a month ... well, let's just say it was a nice cushion. It took some of the pressure off me and kept Victoria in that Mercedes she loves so much and helps keep our mortgage paid. Do you understand?" He ran his hands through his hair again. "I mean, I didn't see how it would possibly hurt anybody. Why would it?"

"You didn't think it was strange?"

"Of course I thought it was strange," Rich said. "But..."

"But five hundred dollars," Lance finished for him.

Rich's mouth closed with an audible pop. He nodded and his face turned red. "Do you have a family, Lance?"

Lance felt the twinge of pain, a stab like a dagger in his heart. It was a low blow, and he suspected Rich knew it. But he remained calm. "No, sir. I have nobody."

Maybe it was the way that Lance had phrased his answer that kept Rich Bellows from pressing on, or maybe he'd realized he'd gotten too personal when, as he'd said at the start, he was only trying to help.

Lance digested Rich's story. Thought about potential implications. Said, "So you think that whoever attacked Victoria yesterday is the same person who's been sending you the five hundred every month."

Rich nodded. "Or ... if it wasn't specifically them, they had a hand in it. Hired somebody, maybe. But there's more to it than that. I started thinking about what I told you the other night when you showed up, how everybody who rented the old farmhouse left, saying it was haunted. Well, we both know that's silly, right? Places aren't haunted."

Lance said nothing.

"So," Rich continued, "I started thinking that maybe whoever is sending me the cash is making the place *seem* haunted. I don't know, going over there and rattling chains or slamming doors, or ... *whatever*, just to scare whoever is renting the place into leaving." He paused and took a breath. "Lance, I think there's somebody out there that is trying hard —really hard—to make sure nobody stays in or around that house very long. And now, after yesterday, they're getting more direct about it, and I don't know how far they're willing to go. It's not a secret the whole town is talking about you, and whatever it is you're out to accomplish here—*up there*, I should say. And I think you've got whoever attacked Victoria worried. I think they're scared you're going to do exactly what they've been trying to keep everyone else from doing all these years."

Lance felt a prickle of realization at the base of his skull. Rich Bellows was definitely onto something. "What is it they're afraid of?" Lance asked.

Rich shook his head. "No idea. But I think it's for you to decide if whatever it is you're after is worth getting hurt over, or worse." There was the faintest shimmer of tears in Rich's eyes by now. "I've already got my own wife's blood on my hands, Lance. I don't want yours, too. Leave. Today."

Lance stayed where he was, leaning against the wall with his hands shoved into his pockets. He watched Rich Bellows recompose himself and then sit back in his chair. Rich pulled the tie completely loose from his neck and tossed it onto his desk.

Lance asked, "Do you have any idea who it might be, the person who's sending you the cash?"

Rich shook his head, then changed to a sort of seesaw back-and-forth motion. "Well," he started, "There's only one person in town I know who would potentially care about that property enough to do something as extreme as this. But..." He shrugged.

"But what?"

"He wouldn't have to pay me to get the information. He could just walk right in the office, or call me on the phone, or hell, stop by the house for dinner and ask me to do him a favor. And I'd do it for him, no problem. Why not?"

Lance understood. "You're talking about Sheriff Kruger."

Rich nodded. "I am."

"What happened that night hit him pretty hard, huh?" Lance asked, seeing how much Rich would delve into unprovoked. "The fact that it was never really solved?"

Rich gave another shrug. "I don't know about the whole *unsolved* part. I think the odds that Mark Benchley had a breakdown and killed them all are still fairly high. But, yes, it hit Ray hard. He's never been the same."

"And nobody likes to talk about that much around here, do they?"

Rich's eyes narrowed and his brow creased. "You've noticed?"

Lance laughed. "Hard not to, sir. Every time somebody mentions the sheriff's name and the farmhouse or the murders in the same conversation, it's like they're scared to get slapped on the wrist."

Rich nodded but offered nothing more.

Lance said, "I know Natalie Benchley was Kruger's sister, sir."

Rich's eyes widened, and then his face fell into a disbelieving grin. "You've done some research."

"Sure."

Rich sighed and leaned back in his chair further, putting his feet up on the desk. The heels of his dress shoes were worn and the laces tattered. The five hundred a month certainly wasn't going to his personal wardrobe.

"Look, nobody's real sure what the relationship between Ray and his sister was. Rumor is he would never step foot inside the farmhouse. Hardly ever visited," Rich said. "But he *loved* Mary. I swear, when you saw the two of them in town together, if you didn't know any better you'd be convinced Ray was her father. You'd see 'em at the park shootin' hoops, or in Mama's—always in the back booth, mind you—eating and talking like they'd never run out of topics. He went to all her school events. I think it half broke his heart when he found out she was going off to that boarding school. Worst part is, I don't think he even knew it was happening until after the fact. I don't think *anybody* did."

Rich paused for a moment, as if trying to find his place.

234

"You see ... well ... Ray never had any children of his own. Never been married, or even had a girlfriend that any of us folks who've lived here our whole lives has seen. He's a great guy— smart, polite, a sly and dry sense of humor, and a heck of an honorable profession. But it's like ... it's like he's closed that part of his life—the part that might involve a woman, *intimacy* I guess you'd say—off from everything else." Rich shrugged. "Some folks think he's gay and is happier in the closet than out. But I don't see it that way."

It was then that Lance realized he might be the only person in Ripton's Grove who had some insight into the true reason Sheriff Ray Kruger was the man he'd become.

"So people don't mention the sheriff's connection to Natalie and Mary Benchley because they're trying to spare his feelings? Protect his privacy? Is that it?" It seemed extreme to Lance, but he supposed he'd heard of crazier things. Had *seen* crazier things.

Rich Bellows looked at his watch. "I've got to get going. Victoria'll have lunch ready any minute now. And the kids are sure to be grumpy and tired." He picked up his tie off the desk and draped it over his shoulder. He looked at Lance. "Two weeks after the night the Benchley family was killed, a reporter from some paper up north came into town, digging for a scoop, a scandal—hell, I don't know how you guys operate. But he basically stalked the sheriff one day and cornered him in the parking lot of Mama's and started asking questions about whether or not there was anything Ray felt he could have done differently to prevent what had happened. If he'd see any signs beforehand, or if Natalie had mentioned anything to him that might have been a call for help."

*Oh, boy.*

"Ray didn't like that," Rich said. "The reporter spent three days in Central Medical, and the Ripton's Grove sheriff's office caught a break and settled out of court. But it was still a lot of money, Lance. *A lot.* Anywhere else, Ray would have lost his job, for sure. But around here—well, you know. Small towns. We know who Ray really is."

*Not entirely*, Lance thought. He put a few more of the pieces together in his head and asked, "So the sheriff inherited the farmhouse after his sister and family were killed?"

Rich nodded. "He actually inherited it when his uncle Joe died, but he told Natalie she could have it. They were having a tough time, apparently, and Ray helped her out. Personally, I think that's one of the reasons the whole thing shook Ray so hard—you know, aside from the fact that his sister and niece were killed. I think he feels responsible. I think he blames himself because if he'd kept the house, and Natalie and her family hadn't moved in, maybe they'd all still be alive."

Rich headed through the office door and Lance followed. The sky had grown darker, and outside the windows looked gray and bored. "So Ray got the house back after the murders and contacted me almost immediately to see if we wanted to buy it. He said he didn't want any part of the place. Can't say I can blame him, right?" Rich tugged on a sport coat that'd been draped over the phantom receptionist's chair. "Honestly, I didn't want the place, but Ray was willing to take next to nothing for it, just to be done with the whole thing, and I figured the land alone was worth the investment. So I took him up on the offer."

Lance had learned so much from Rich Bellows, he felt he should take the man over to Mama's and buy him a whole meatloaf. But then he remembered that Rich had likely been the cause of Lance being potentially attacked and figured he'd call them all square.

Rich looked at Lance as he took his key ring out of his coat pocket. "It's not Ray, is it? The one sending me the money?"

Lance shook his head. "No, sir. I don't think so."

Rich nodded, as if this was the answer he'd been expecting. "Any idea who it is, then?"

Lance nodded, letting a cold truth sink in. One that he had probably been suspecting this entire time but had only now managed to fully convince himself of. "It's whoever really committed those murders. I think they're worried somebody is going to find them out."

Rich grimaced, as if Lance's words had caused him physical pain, then he shivered. "So you're saying there's a murderer walking around Ripton's Grove?"

Lance nodded again. "Can't say for sure they're still here, but I'm thinking it's likely."

"And I've been on his payroll all these years." Rich shook his head, and his breath caught in his chest. "God ... what have I done?"

Lance said nothing. Slipped out the door and stood on the sidewalk, listening to Rich Bellows step out and lock the deadbolt. Rich's Explorer was parked on the street. As he walked toward it, his face carrying a fresh expression of sorrow, he called to Lance. "Want a lift to the bus station? I'll buy you a ticket anywhere you want to go."

Lance shook his head. "No, sir." He thought about Ethan. "I'm not finished here."

Rich looked at Lance with questioning eyes, but he got no response. "You won't tell anyone about the cash, right, Lance? You gave me your word, right?"

Lance shook his head. "I won't, sir. But I think *you* should. I think it's what Sheriff Kruger would want, don't you?"

Rich Bellows didn't say anything. He climbed into the driver's seat, cranked the engine, and then drove away, leaving Lance standing alone on the sidewalk.

## [ 31 ]

Lance stood on the sidewalk for a long time. He watched Rich Bellows drive away, back to his home, back to his wife and children and his life that he knew would be waiting for him. Lance wondered if the man would call Sheriff Kruger and tell him about the emails, the money. Lance doubted it. He didn't think Rich Bellows was a bad person at all, but Rich was too afraid to lose everything to admit he might have done something wrong at such a potentially large level. Aiding a criminal— a *murderer*—would weigh heavily on his mind for a long time, Lance was sure of that. Maybe one day Rich would fess up, but it wasn't Lance's place to do it for him.

Because what good would it do, really? If Lance marched straight to the sheriff's office right now and told Ray Kruger everything he'd just learned from Rich, what would happen? First, they'd have to believe Lance was telling the truth, which from recent experiences seemed like a fifty-fifty gamble. Second, if they did decide that Lance wasn't blowing smoke up their tails, then what? They call Rich Bellows and ask him to verify? Make him give up access to his email? Would they have to obtain a warrant for that information? The Benchley family murders had been six years ago—what would the process be for anything pertaining to such an old case? And say they did get access to Rich's email, then they'd have to get computer gurus to analyze it and probably work with other outside resources to try and get some sort of trace on the email's origin. Lance was no computer expert—flip phone, remember?—but he'd seen enough TV and films and read enough spy novels to know that there were enough ways to disguise email and web traffic that the whole thing could end up being a wild goose chase.

And it would take time.

Time Lance didn't have.

What was he supposed to do? Spend his days eating meat-loaf at Mama's and sleeping in the bed of a dead girl day after day, night after night, just on standby until the answers came in —*if* they came in? Or waiting for another sound bite from the mystery dinner theater performance that had been slowly revealing itself to him in the farmhouse?

He didn't have the answers, and as far as he could tell, there was absolutely no way he was ever going to get them. This problem was too big. It had too many moving pieces, too many unknowns. It had all happened too long ago.

And what good was the information he'd gotten about Sheriff Kruger's past, the abuse he'd suffered? The sheriff was a grown man—a troubled man, sure, and rightfully so, but he was grown. He could take care of himself. Ray Kruger's uncle was dead. His sister and family were dead. Lance couldn't do anything to fix any of that.

Whoever thought that Lance was a threat to fingering them as the Benchley family's killer, the joke was on them. Lance was no closer to adding any closure to that horrible night than he'd been the moment he'd stepped off the bus two days ago.

"The boy is all that matters now," Lance said to himself and the quiet city street. "He's the one I need to worry about."

Now, more than ever, Lance was convinced that Ethan was the real reason he'd been meant to stop in Ripton's Grove. Everything else had just led to their meeting.

He walked three blocks back toward Mama's and made a right, stopping at a small convenience store he'd passed on his way to Central Medical the day before. He stocked up on bottles of water, protein bars, nuts, and a few packets of instant coffee. He tossed them all into his backpack, ignoring the curious looks given to him by the woman behind the checkout counter, and then pushed out the door and headed back toward the park. Back toward the trail that would lead up the mountain.

It was time to talk to Jacob Morgan. If he and Ethan weren't home yet, Lance would wait as long as it took. Because honestly, he had absolutely nothing else to do in this town anymore.

---

The clouds continued to thicken, darkening the sky. Beneath the cover of the trees, the world seemed even darker. The wind was picking up, rattling branches and making the leaves sound like the crashing waves of the ocean as they bristled and swayed and collided with each other above. Lance walked with his head down, his hood up, staring at the trail and watching each step he took, one foot in front of the other. His backpack was weighed down with his fresh supplies, and already the satisfying feeling of his Mama's breakfast in his stomach was beginning to fade. He did not reach for a snack, however. Did not even feel the weight on his back. All his mind was focused on was Ethan.

Over and over again, Lance replayed the scene from last night. The way the boy had been entranced by the basement door—or more specifically what

(*who*)

was behind it. "*She's down there! She's down there!*" the boy

241

had cried. If Lance hadn't already heard the young girl crying to be let out himself, he wouldn't have understood—not fully, anyway. But he *had* heard. And Ethan—small, innocent, special Ethan—had heard her too. Mary Benchley had called out to both of them.

Something else still sat at the forefront of Lance's thoughts about that night. The way Jacob Morgan had reacted so quickly, almost from the moment Ethan had begun to walk toward the door. It was as though he'd sensed the boy was slipping into his *other place*, the place where he could hear the dead and see things that nobody—especially a young boy—should see. *He knows,* Lance told himself again as he reached the place where he'd turn and walk through the woods to Jacob Morgan's house. *He knows what his nephew can do.*

"I can help them," Lance said aloud as he crunched through a fresh crop of fallen leaves, the latest victims of the strong winds. "And they can help me."

The first thing Lance noticed was that the plume of smoke wafting from the chimney was thicker, denser. *They're home,* he thought. *Fresh logs on the fire, and they're home.* His steps picked up their pace, but he kept himself from running full-on in case Jacob Morgan was watching out the window. Lance didn't want to appear to be a threat ... or a crazy person. Depending on how his intended conversation went, that last part might be unavoidable as it was.

Lance walked up the porch step and approached the front door. The rocking chair to his right, the baby bear chair, was rocking gently in the wind. Lance pulled down his hood, attempting to look less like a burglar, raised his hand, and knocked three times.

He waited. Heard muffled voices from behind the door. The shuffling of feet.

Jacob Morgan opened the door slowly. The first thing Lance saw was the knife in his hand.

The second thing Lance noticed was that there was a smear of what looked like peanut butter on the blade. His heart quickly recovered from the spike in pulse it'd achieved at the sight of a potential weapon in Jacob Morgan's hands, and Lance offered his best smile.

"Lance, hi," Jacob said, opening the door wide, lowering the peanut-butter-smeared table knife. "What's up? Get bored up on the hill all by yourself? Thought you'd come down for what barely passes as civilized company?" Jacob chuckled at his own joke and motioned for Lance to step inside. Lance looked into the cabin, saw Ethan sitting on an old couch with a picture book in his lap. He had a finger on one of the pages, moving it slowly left to right, his lips moving as he sounded out words. He looked up, as if sensing Lance staring, and their eyes met briefly before Ethan returned his gaze to the book.

Lance stepped inside and Jacob closed the door behind him.

"Ethan, can you say hi to Mr. Lance?"

Ethan looked up from his book again, and obediently said, "Hi, Mr. Lance. How are you?"

Lance looked at this small boy on the couch, book in his lap, impeccable manners, and knowledge behind his youthful eyes. In that moment, Lance saw himself. Many years ago as a child, sitting in his home reading a book his mother had brought him from the library while she was busy in the kitchen, humming a tune while baking them a pie they'd share later while she asked him about what he'd read.

Lance smiled at the boy. "I'm doing very well, Ethan. Thank you for asking. How are you?"

"Good," the boy said, then quickly diverted his eyes back to his book.

"Good, what?" Jacob said. His voice stern.

Ethan looked up from his page again. "Good, thank you." Then he looked to his uncle. Jacob nodded once, and the boy was back to his book again.

"Can I offer you a sandwich, Lance? PB and J is sort of our post-church ritual. We'd be happy to have you join us."

Lance thought about the protein bars in his backpack. "If you're sure it's no trouble, that would be great. Thank you."

"No trouble at all. White or wheat?"

"Wheat, please."

"Good man," Jacob said. "Been trying, and failing, to get little man over there to switch to wheat instead of this processed white garbage. No luck so far." He shrugged his shoulders. "Kids, right?"

Lance nodded, because it seemed the only right thing to do. "Kids," he said.

"Just a second. One world-class PB and J on wheat coming right up. Make yourself at home."

Jacob turned and walked to the kitchen area, which took up the entire left side of the cabin's open space. Fridge, oven, sink, and a large woodstove in the front corner with a small pile of chopped wood beside it. A square table with four chairs separated the kitchen from the rest of the open space, which served as the living room. There was the couch, on which Ethan was absorbed in his book, two end tables, a coffee table, bookshelf, and small TV stand with a modern-looking television that looked incredibly out of place among the otherwise rustic décor. A wired antenna was mounted on the wall above the TV, its black cable snaking down the wall and out of sight. The rear of the room had three doors, which Lance assumed led to bedrooms and a bath.

Lance breathed in deeply. The whole place smelled of wood and spices and ... peanut butter. He turned and found Jacob

Morgan behind him, holding a small plate with Lance's sandwich.

Lance took the plate and said, "Thanks."

"You're welcome. Milk?"

"That'd be great," Lance said and walked toward the table.

A few moments later, Jacob Morgan was at the table as well, his own sandwich and glass of milk half-eaten and half-drunk. Lance chewed his sandwich and took a sip of his milk. Wiped his mouth with the back of his hand, and then wiped the back of his hand on his shorts. Both men seemed intent on eating and nothing more. But once the sandwiches were finished, Jacob Morgan looked at Lance with eyes that said, *Go ahead, get on with it.*

Lance took a deep breath, realizing he had no real idea where to start. Settled on, "I've got some questions, and they might seem strange."

As if he'd been expecting nothing less, Jacob Morgan gave off a small sigh and looked over to Ethan, who was still sitting quietly on the couch, finger still moving across the pages.

"Let's step out onto the porch. Get some air. That okay?" Jacob asked.

Lance stood and nodded. "Okay."

[ 32 ]

The sky was still darkened, the breeze still steady, but the air was not uncomfortably cool. In fact, it was Lance's preferred temperature. A perfect fall afternoon, if not for the blanket of dark clouds. Jacob Morgan wore faded blue jeans and a plain gray sweatshirt, his post-church attire. His feet were bare and he kicked a few stray leaves off the porch and into the yard, where the breeze snatched them up and they went scurrying down the hill and disappeared over the bank, back toward town.

Lance had a brief moment where he wondered if he should follow. Catch a ride on the wind and hightail it out of here before he did something stupid, said the wrong thing to the wrong person. Like mentioning to the nearly complete stranger on the porch with him that he could talk to and see the lingering spirits of the dead ... and more.

But he could not leave. Not now. Not while, after his entire life of wondering, he was so close to finding somebody else that shared his gifts.

Jacob Morgan turned and stuffed his hands into the front pouch of his sweatshirt. He leaned against the porch railing and said, "You can have a seat if you'd like." He nodded toward the papa bear rocking chair. "My ass is still numb from church, so I'm going to stand, if you don't mind."

Lance didn't mind. He mimicked Jacob Morgan's posture and stuffed his own hands into the pouch of his hoodie. He leaned against the wall of the house, facing the man. Leaned his head back and felt the rough wood scratch at his scalp. The two men stared at each other, and just as Lance was about to open his mouth to begin, Jacob Morgan cut him off, saying, "I suppose you're here to ask me about the morning I found the Benchleys. Is that right?"

Lance closed his mouth. Had to regroup. He'd become so focused on the mission to get answers about Ethan that once he'd actually arrived at the house, the entire Benchley family story had evaporated from his mind. He found that right then and there, he couldn't have cared less about what had actually happened that night in the farmhouse. Felt a twinge of guilt and shame in his gut as he realized he didn't care if their killer was still walking free along the streets of Ripton's Grove.

Lance heard his mother's voice in his head. *You're being selfish, Lance.* Could hear the tone of disappointment. He swallowed hard and his mind raced as he tried to figure out whether to allow Jacob Morgan to start off down this road of conversation.

And then Lance remembered that he was never in control. If this was the way things were supposed to begin, Lance would let them. He'd get his opportunity to ask about Ethan soon enough.

"Why do you think that's what I want to know about?" Lance asked.

Jacob laughed. "Come on, man, you don't have to be all mysterious with me. You were being coy last night at the farmhouse, and I didn't press that matter, but everybody knows you're here to write a book." He made air quotes with his fingers and said, "*Discover the truth.*" Then he laughed again. "Is that about right?"

So far, the ruse of being a true crime writer had worked well for Lance—so much, in fact, that if he had a computer, he might be compelled to actually *write* a damned book about this mess. It would certainly give him something to do on buses other than sleep and read. He figured continuing the charade would only help him at this point.

"Something like that," he said. "But you should know, I'm not a detective."

Jacob Morgan looked confused. "Meaning?"

"Meaning I'm not out to solve a case," Lance said. "My publisher"—*Your* publisher? *Boy, laying it on thick now, aren't we, Lance?*—"was intrigued by the nature of the crime, and I'm only here to present the facts as given by those who know them." Lance grinned, sheepishly but purely for show, and said, "Now, I won't deny I'm also supposed to make it a compelling read. You know, add suspense and mystery and make it as dramatic as possible. But I'm only gathering information. If the police say Mark Benchley killed his family, that's what the book will say."

Jacob Morgan was quiet for a moment, then said, "People really buy that shit?"

Lance nodded. "True crime was the third-best-selling genre in the United States last year." This was a one hundred percent made-up statement as far as Lance knew. But it sounded like a good answer that an actual true crime writer might have ready.

"What was first?" Jacob Morgan asked.

"Romance," Lance said instantly. "Chicks dig their love stories."

Jacob Morgan barked another laugh. "True enough, my friend. True enough."

A hard breeze blew across the hilltop, and the porch rattled and squeaked. Jacob Morgan looked at the support beam to his left and then knocked on it with his knuckles, as if reassuring himself it was secured and in place. "So you want to hear my side of the story, is that it? You found out it was me who found them and you want to know how it was?"

Lance nodded, eager to move on to the subject of Ethan but also very curious to hear what Jacob Morgan had to say. "That would be great."

Jacob nodded, looked to where Lance had his hands stuffed in his hoodie. "You gonna write any of this down or ... record it?"

Lance blushed and thought quickly. He pulled his flip phone from his pocket and snapped it open. Pretended to hit a few buttons on the keypad and then set it in the rocking chair next to him. "Okay," he said. "All set."

Jacob eyed the phone suspiciously.

Lance said, "Uh, you wouldn't believe the microphone on that thing. You know what they say—they don't make 'em like they used to."

Jacob nodded as if this made perfect sense, and then Lance watched as the man's face changed and his eyes narrowed and his thoughts slipped away from the porch and landed back on that awful morning.

---

Lance listened intently, his eyes never leaving Jacob Morgan's face as the man told his story. The details weren't much different than what Lance had already been given by Susan, but the perspective—the emotion—that was now presented differed greatly. Where Susan had recited the grisly details of where the bodies had been found with a sense that she'd been excitedly presenting a book report, Jacob Morgan's voice had wavered and cracked at parts, causing him to pause and look away, often out over the railing of the porch, staring blankly into the trees, or off toward the horizon where the hill sloped away and fell to Ripton's Grove. He would wipe a loose tear or two away from high up on his cheeks, and then he'd turn back to Lance—man-to-man once again—and continue.

Jacob Morgan had been headed out of town to help his friend Jack do some work on a new house he and his young wife had just purchased. "It was a total wreck of a place," Jacob said. "He sent me pictures. It was going to take a hell of a lot longer than a week, but that was a good enough chunk of time to start. Jack's terrible at that sort of stuff, and a contractor would have taken one look at the house and another look at Jack and ripped the poor bastard off." Jacob shrugged. "I was looking forward to getting away for a bit anyway. Not exactly a vacation, but it was good enough for me."

Jacob had driven up to the Benchleys' place to ask Mark to stop by the house a few times during the week, just to check on things. "It was just something we did for each other," Jacob said. "Help out here and there when we could. Share stuff from our gardens, help out with any handiwork now and again. You know," Jacob said with another shrug, "neighborly stuff."

Jacob had seen Natalie Benchley's body as soon as he'd pulled his pickup truck into the driveway. "At first I thought some laundry had blown off the line," Jacob said. "Looked just like some fabric sprawled out, half on the porch steps, half in the driveway. But as I got closer"—here was a time he'd had to look away, a time when his voice wavered— "I saw ... I saw it was Natalie. I didn't have any delusions about it." He shook his head. "She was dead. There wasn't no question about it. She was facedown in the yard, one arm outstretched as if she'd been reaching for something to hold on to, and on her back from the neck down was nothing but gore." He shook his head over and over as he spoke. "Just holes and blood and torn flesh and..." He

251

cleared his throat. "Like I said, there was no question she was dead."

Jacob had walked up the front porch steps and pulled the pocket knife he always carried from his jeans. "It was all I had on me at the time," he said. "I don't travel with my guns." He had entered the house and called out to see if anybody was there. "I knew they wouldn't be," Jacob said. "I knew whoever'd killed Natalie wouldn't be sticking around. But all the same, I kept my eyes peeled, ready to jam my blade into the unlucky bastard's neck if he gave me the chance." And he'd found Mark Benchley in the living room, sitting in his chair with the shotgun at his feet and most of the man's face gone. "I looked at the wall behind him for a long time before I ever even lowered my eyes to Mark," Jacob said. "It was like ... it was just covered in..." He trailed off. Another clearing of the throat. "It does weird things to you when you see stuff that's supposed to be *inside* somebody on the outside. Especially when it's splattered on the wall like some sort of goddamn art project." He shot Lance a look and frowned. "Sorry for my language."

Jacob had then gone upstairs. "I stood in the living room a long time, Lance. A long time. By this point, I figured if anybody'd still been in the house, they would have either come at me already or run away. This is going to sound funny, but you gotta remember, these people were my friends, and, well ... I guess I was in a bit of shock. That's what the doctors or the shrinks will tell you, anyway. But, even though I saw the shotgun lying at Mark's feet, and the way the gore was spread on the wall behind him, my brain never perceived it as a suicide. Not then, anyway. I went upstairs, just for my own sanity— wanting to say I'd checked the whole house before I called the cops. It was empty, of course. Then I went down to the kitchen."

Jacob had seen the smoldering remains of the brush pile fire through the kitchen window as he'd run the cold water tap to get a handful to splash his face. "Something about the smoke called to me," he said and then quickly shot Lance a look that asked, *Do you think I'm crazy?* He forced a weak laugh. "I know that doesn't make any sense, but I swear, it's like I couldn't take my eyes off that pile of brush and the slowly dying smoke puffing from its center. It's like it was pulling me in, Lance. Does that make any sense at all? It's like something was yelling at me, trying to get my attention and get my ass out there."

Lance felt his blood run cold. He did understand (*The mirror*), and he wondered if there were more people on this hilltop with hidden gifts than just he and Ethan.

Lance, the good journalist, said nothing. Only nodded for Jacob to continue.

Jacob had then found Mary Benchley. "I walked out the backdoor and I saw her. I mean ... I didn't know it was her. How could I? All that was left at that point..." This time he heaved and tried to hold back a great sob that spun him around, and he wiped his eyes and stared out to the trees for a long time, taking deep breaths. He turned around once he'd composed himself. "It was just bones, man. Just bones and not much else." He shook his head and his eyes still glistened. "Something told me it was her, man. Just like I'd felt pulled toward that fire, something just told me it was her. I mean, I hadn't seen her since ... well, since she'd gone off to school, but I just knew." He looked at Lance, and his eyes were those of a man who was begging to be understood. "I never told the police that part. I never told them about those feelings I'd gotten. I never told them I thought that pile of bones in the fire was Mary."

"Was the basement door open or closed when you were in the kitchen? Do you remember?"

Jacob Morgan looked confused. "I have no idea, man. Why does that matter?"

Lance shrugged. "Details are always important. Even if we don't know why."

Jacob Morgan didn't seem to know what to say to this.

"So I pulled out my cell and called 911 and then, well... you know the rest, I'm sure."

Lance nodded. "For the most part. How hard did they work to prove you were the one who'd killed them? I mean, that was the initial thought, right? According to everything I've seen and heard."

Jacob Morgan sighed and nodded. Laughed. "Yeah, that was a fun day or two. Nothing like being the town monster to really show you folks' true colors. I've never seen so many people turn their back so quickly." He shrugged, like a man who'd chosen to live in the future and forget the past. "But it got sorted out in the end."

"Did it?" Lance asked, and immediately wished he'd found a more tactful way to continue.

Jacob's eyes narrowed. "What do you mean?"

"Did the police get it right?"

There was a flash of something then, something across Jacob Morgan's face that said he was no longer simply rehashing information but was now engaged in something he wasn't sure he wanted to continue. His voice was suddenly accusatory.

"Are you suggesting that you believe I *did* murder the Benchleys?"

Lance pulled his hands free from his hoodie's pocket and held them up, shook his head. "No, of course not. But I am asking if you think Mark Benchley did. Other sources I've spoken with have said he was quite the family man. Loved his wife, adored his daughter. Why would he kill them?"

"Did your sources also tell you that Mark Benchley was a few bricks shy of a full load?"

Lance said nothing.

"They tell you he was a religious fanatic who would cast judgment so fast, if you blinked, you'd miss it?"

Lance nodded in agreement but added, "They also told me the two of you were friends."

*What are you doing, Lance? You're here to talk about Ethan. Why are you provoking this man? How is that possibly going to help you?*

Jacob Morgan leaned back against the railing, and his aggressiveness drained away. He looked down at his feet, cast his eyes across the wooden boards of the porch floor before he looked up and grinned. "Yeah, Mark and I were friendly. Truth be told, we probably wouldn't have been if they hadn't moved into the farmhouse, but after I went to introduce myself and then helped him out with a few little fix-me-ups, it just sort of happened. Mark wasn't a bad guy on the surface, honestly. Pretty normal, in fact, if you could ignore his Bible-thumping fear-of-God trances he'd slip into now and again. But seriously, he was a nice guy, and I can honestly say I enjoyed his company. He had a very unique worldview. It was ... I guess I'd have to say it was refreshing."

"But he killed his wife, and burned his daughter, and then shot himself," Lance said, unable to stop himself for some deep down reason he couldn't control.

Jacob Morgan didn't protest. He nodded his head. "He had demons, Lance. Just like all of us. His just got the best of him, I guess." He hawked some phlegm from his throat and spat it out over the railing. "Here's something else I never told the police, Lance, and you can decide whether you want to stick it in your book or not." He shrugged again. "I don't guess it matters at all now. But if I'd have known Mark was going to snap like that, do the things he did ... I'd have killed him myself before he had the chance to hurt those girls. Natalie was the sweetest woman. Funny, charming, hell of a cook. And Mary..." The tears were so sudden and so strong, Jacob Morgan was sobbing into his hands before Lance had even realized what was happening. Deep cries of anguish that were choked off by a man ashamed to have lost control in front of another man—a stranger, digging into a painful past. Jacob looked up from his hands, wiping his eyes. "Sorry," he said, forcing an awkward-sounding laugh. "She just had so much to live for, you know? She was so young, and just getting started. And that bastard *killed* her. His own goddamn daughter. *He* killed her!"

Jacob Morgan eyes were full of fire, his face electric with anger, but then he looked down at the rocking chair and saw Lance's flip phone sitting open, and his features softened again. He worked to regain control of himself. Finally, he said, "Sorry. I guess I always think I've moved on from it, but I'm always wrong. It still stings, even after all these years."

Lance nodded. "I can't pretend to imagine what it must have been like."

Lance had seen a lot of things in his life, and he could certainly imagine much worse than finding a few dead bodies, but it seemed like the right thing to say.

"I left," Jacob said. "After it all. I left. Went to help my friend with his house, and then just bounced around for a while. I kept thinking I'd be ready to come back, but every time I got ready to start the drive, I found myself heading in a different direction. And then my sister and her husband were killed in that car accident, and I found myself suddenly with a newborn child under my wing. And the only place to try and start a home with him was ... well, home. You know? So I came back, and here I am talking to a guy I hardly know about my deepest and darkest emotions."

Lance picked up the flip phone, pressed a few random keys, and then snapped it shut. "I'm sorry if that was painful for you, but I do appreciate you talking with me."

256

Jacob Morgan waved him off. "Glad to do it," he said. "I'd rather you hear the truth than tell the world a bunch of gossip bullshit. Even though I'm sure that would sell more books, right?"

"Can I ask you something about Ethan?"

Jacob Morgan's mouth snapped closed, and his eyes hardened and his arms crossed.

*Lance Brody, ladies and gentlemen. Master of segues, and the art of subtle conversation.*

Jacob Morgan's words were slow and direct, as if he were suddenly thrown into a chess match he neither had expected or fully understood. "Ethan has nothing to do with what happened to the Benchleys."

Lance shook his head. "No, of course not. I wanted to ask you something about what happened at the farmhouse last night."

"No."

"But—"

"*No.* Listen to me, I understand you have a job to do, and I understand I was a part of something that is never going to go away, and there will always be people like you showing up over the years to ask questions or ask what it was like. I've accepted that. But you have access to me only, *not* to my nephew. *Not* to a six-year-old boy."

Lance tried to gain some footing. "I understand, sir. But if you could just let me explain, I think—"

"We're finished here," Jacob Morgan said, moving toward the door. "Good luck with your book, but I'd like you to leave."

Lance, desperate and overwhelmingly surprised at how quickly this conversation—his one chance—had resulted in him getting completely shut down, went against everything his mind knew was right, against everything that had worked so hard to keep his secrets safe for years, and said, "I think he can see the dead."

Jacob Morgan stopped at the door, turned and stared at Lance. His face was working something out, his mind dissecting and examining Lance's words.

*He knows!* Lance's mind screamed. *He knows!*

Somewhere overhead, a crow cawed twice, and then all was still and quiet.

Jacob Morgan took a step toward Lance, and his voice was hushed. "Get off my property," he said, "or I'm calling the police." Then, slyly, "I'm sure Sheriff Kruger would love another reason to drag you into the station, don't you?"

Then he turned and went inside.

Lance heard the door's deadbolt slide into place.

[ 33 ]

By the time Lance had made the walk through the trees and up the remainder of the path to the farmhouse, the clouds had blackened like a smoker's lungs, and the wind had notched up enough to stir the fallen leaves in the yard into mini-cyclones and dancing waves of burnt oranges and browns. Lance walked through the yard with feet that felt heavy and a spirit that had worn down to just a thin strand, ready to snap.

He walked up the porch steps, his brain conjuring up the image of Natalie Benchley sprawled half on the steps and half in the dirt, her hand outstretched, reaching for ... for what? For him? Reaching for help?

Lance mumbled under his breath, the words carried off with a strong gust of wind that whipped at his hoodie and whistled through the porch. "Better reach for somebody else."

He pushed through the front door just as a far-off crack of thunder officially announced the impending storm. Lance didn't even so much as glance over his shoulder to the horizon. He slammed the door with a crack to rival the thunder. The windows rattled, the ceiling creaked. Lance made his way to the kitchen, thinking that the old farmhouse could go ahead and fall down, collapse on itself with him in it for all he cared. One more casualty, another notch on the house's belt. He could see the headline now, another back issue of the newspaper to add to the library's archive: **STRANGER THAN FICTION? TRUE CRIME WRITER DIES IN HOUSE COLLAPSE**.

And nobody would care. A few people might actually be relieved. Sheriff Kruger, for example. And the Benchleys' killer, happy the house had taken care of their dirty laundry for them. With Lance gone, things could go back to normal. People could let the house slide back into the background of the town's memories, back onto the high shelf in the garage, where they put things that no longer served much of a purpose but they weren't willing to toss away.

Nobody would care.

This thought wormed its way from the back of Lance's mind, dug itself out from a grave where it'd been sealed away and asked to keep quiet because while it might be true, Lance was allowing himself to believe he was to serve a larger purpose in life. His life was about more than just his personal well-being and happiness. His life wasn't about *him* at all, but about what he would do. The things his gifts would allow him to be for others.

*My sweet boy. Oh, what great things you'll do.*

His mother's words had pushed him, her memory a driving force. And while he knew he was special—that was the only word that seemed to fit, although Lance would argue that *unique* was his personal preference, because it carried with it a much less positive connotation—and his mother had, in her last moments on this earth, been gifted messages and maybe even visions of Lance's future by the spirits of the Great Hillston Cemetery, a future that was apparently worth her sacrificing herself for, he was now overwhelmed with a great sense of fail-ure, and along with it ... a desire to give up.

Despite his gifts and his knowledge and the overwhelming sense of duty he'd carried with him since the time he'd been old enough to even begin to understand his abilities, today, right now inside the farmhouse while a storm as dark as his current mood climbed up the doorstep, Lance was giving up. Not giving up on life, or a continuation of his apparent predetermined destiny—if you believed in such a curious word—but in Ripton's Grove, he was finished.

He could not go on.

He couldn't help the long-dead Benchley family—and did they actually need help in the first place? He'd not seen any of their spirits, no traces of ghostly bodies anywhere in the farmhouse during his entire stay. All he'd been given were some phantom words—a sort of prerecorded retelling of that terrible night they'd all died—and those didn't tell the whole story.

There'd been the incident with Ethan

(*She's down there!*)

that had started him on a dangerously desperate path of hope that the boy was like him and would...

Would what?

Come away with Lance? Leave his uncle and let Lance be his new guardian as they roamed the country together, Lance helping the boy to hone his skills and understand what he was and what he could become like some sort of supernatural-solving Batman and Robin?

How ridiculous that thought had been. How blindly ignorant.

Lance had gotten so emotionally invested in the idea of not being alone, he'd risked everything. He'd mentioned to Jacob Morgan that he thought Ethan could see the dead.

What would Jacob do with that information? What would he think about Lance, and who Lance really was?

It was still a stretch ... because honestly, who really believed in such things—seeing ghosts and talking to the dead? But still, it'd been a slip. And Lance could not afford many of those.

The Reverend and the Surfer had found him once, and Lance knew they would find him again. He didn't need to help the matter along by fanning the gossip fires about a young man who claimed to have supernatural abilities.

He found he'd ended up at the kitchen table, sitting at one of the wooden chairs, a half-empty bottle of water in one hand, its twisted-off plastic top in the other. He had no memory of sitting or digging the bottle from his backpack. Outside the kitchen window, rain lashed against the glass, the sky dark, both from the rain and from the sun that had settled down for the evening.

*What time is it?*

Lance pulled his phone from his pocket and gawked at the tiny display. Hours had passed since he'd started up the hillside from Jacob Morgan's house. Lance shook his head and rubbed at his eyes and checked the time again. Same result.

He'd been checked out. His mind had almost literally blocked out the rest of the world—time and space and any sense of being—and Lance had vanished into what he could only describe as a fugue state, sitting alone in an old house, contemplating all the moves he'd made, and also the ones he hadn't.

Alone.

He was all alone.

He looked down at the phone in his hand, watched as his thumb pressed the buttons to bring up the contact list, and then begin to scroll. The list was small, and it took only a few presses of the button to the get to the M section.

*Mom*

Lance's thumb hovered, wanting so badly to press SEND and listen to the call go to voicemail. Needed to hear her voice.

But did he really? Did he need to hear her and be taken

back to that night, back to the life before the one he lived now? Tossed headfirst back into the sinking feeling of tragedy and loss and broken heartedness that he'd been slowly and steadily climbing out of since the night she'd died?

*The number might not even work anymore*, he thought, and he was unsure which would be worse for his psyche: hearing his mother's voice again, or discovering that he'd *never* be able to hear it again.

Thunder boomed so loud Lance jumped from the chair. It had sounded like cannon fire, a war reenactment taking place in the backyard. The entire house had shaken, the kitchen table vibrating enough that it had scooted to the left a quarter of an inch.

Alone.

God, he felt so alone.

He used his thumb to scroll up in his contact list. Stopped at the L section. Stared at her name.

*No.* He stopped himself. *You know you can't.*

He scrolled down the S section instead. Needed somebody, anybody.

The rain caught the wind and slammed into the house. More wind gusted and circled and attacked. The noise was terrible, but the house held firm.

Lightning snapped and lit up the backyard in a freeze frame that was blinding.

More thunder rolled.

Lance navigated to Susan's name and wondered what he'd say if she picked up. They barely knew each other. Same with Luke. What could he tell them? How could he explain?

But the urge was strong. So strong he felt at once he couldn't put the phone away even if he'd wanted to. He just needed a voice, he reasoned with himself. *I just need a friendly voice.*

His thumb pressed the SEND button, and Lance put the phone to his ear.

It rang. Once, twice. Three times. After the fourth ring, Susan's voice picked up, cheerful and full of life. It was a recording, apologizing for missing the call but asking Lance to leave a voicemail and she'd return his call as soon as she could. It was polite and professional, and Lance was furious. Finally, his emotions took over, his rage surfaced like water breaking through a dam, and he tossed the opened phone onto the table, grabbed his half-empty bottle of water and hurled it across the kitchen, where it struck the wall with a dull thud and fell to the floor, its opened mouth pouring the remaining water across the wooden floor in a slow and steady trickle.

Another explosion of thunder.

Another white-hot flash of lightning.

Lance grabbed one of the kitchen chairs in both hands and lifted it above his head, smashed it to the floor, where the back snapped off the seat with a satisfying crack. Lance tossed the chair aside and grabbed his backpack, yelling to the house as he made his way back down the hall toward the front door, "I can't help you!"

He had to leave. Would walk in the downpour to the bus station and get out of town. He didn't care if it would take hours. He couldn't sit in the house anymore. He couldn't be alone with his thoughts anymore.

He needed out. He needed

(*my mom*)

help.

When he was two steps away from the door, somebody knocked.

Three almost inaudible taps that were drowned out by the noise from the storm.

Lance ripped the door open, anger burning deep in his eyes.

And then his eyes lowered, taking in his visitor.

Standing on the porch, soaking wet in his blue jeans and sneakers and buttoned-up flannel shirt, was Ethan. There was a flashlight in his hand that looked big enough for him to carry with two hands, its bright light shining down to the rough wooden boards beneath his feet.

"She said you could help me," the boy said, water dripping off his forehead and into his eyes. Lance thought there were tears mixed in with the rainwater. "The girl in the basement said you could help me."

[ 34 ]

AND THE REST OF HIS THOUGHTS VANISHED—THE ANGER and resentment and sadness disappearing as quickly as the flashes of lightning lit up the night sky.

"Help you how?" Lance asked, but he knew the answer didn't matter.

*This is why I'm here,* he thought. *I'll do anything he needs.*

He ushered the boy inside and closed the door, the bright cone of light from the boy's flashlight becoming a spotlight in the dark house.

Lance hadn't even realized he'd left the lights off. He'd been sitting alone all this time in a house as dark as his thoughts. He found the switch on the wall and flipped it, bathing the foyer in that awful yellow tint.

Ethan didn't answer the question. Instead, he stood just inside the door, shivering in his wet clothes. Lance moved swiftly, stripping off his hoodie and telling the boy to take his shirt off. The boy did, obedient, and Lance held the oversized sweatshirt out to the boy, who raised his arms and allowed Lance to slide it over his head. It fell to the boy's shins, the sleeves comically long, but the boy didn't seem to care. He wrapped his arms around himself and within a minute the shivering subsided. Lance picked up the wet shirt from the floor and hung it over the banister by the stairs.

"Better?" Lance asked.

Ethan nodded. "Yes." Then, "I mean, yes, sir."

The protectiveness Lance suddenly felt for this child was all at once overwhelming, as if he were being introduced to his own son for the first time. It was a feeling so foreign, and so unexpected, it nearly made his head swim and his heart flutter with elation.

But at the same time, something wasn't right. Something wasn't ... *him*.

Along with the joyousness, there was a faint buzz of something beneath the surface. Something familiar. Something electric that was almost unpleasant but...

He knew then what it was, the realization presenting itself with stark clarity. It was a slightly more subdued version of the feelings he'd experienced last night when Jacob and Ethan had visited, the feeling that had intensified with an almost crippling effect when Ethan had begun walking toward the closed basement door.

*He's like me*, Lance thought again. And he wondered if the boy was feeling the same things that Lance was. Was this some sort of cosmic connection between the two of them, two bare wires that spark when they touch?

Lance studied the boy's face. Ethan had used the sleeves of Lance's hoodie to wipe the water from his eyes, and it appeared that the tears had stopped as well. He looked stoic, almost dutiful. Like he was simply doing what was asked of him. He showed no outward indication that he was experiencing any of what Lance was.

*I'm stronger*, Lance thought. *I'm more sensitive to it.*

He had no idea what he was talking about. And why would he, really? This was an entirely new experience.

"Help you how?" Lance asked again, now that Ethan seemed more settled and at ease.

The boy looked at Lance sheepishly, shrugged. "I don't know."

Lance was not surprised. He'd done nothing in life if not gotten used to things being difficult to explain. "When did she tell you this? When did the girl in the basement tell you that I could help you?"

The boy knew the answer to this question and spat out, "Last night. Last night when I ate the pizza and played the game with the boy, she started talking to me."

Lance's heart sped up. It was the first solid, tangible evidence that he was right about Ethan sharing his gifts. "She talked to you?" he asked. "You could hear her voice?"

Ethan made a face that said he wasn't sure. He shook his head, then stopped, changed his mind and nodded. "I heard her up here." He tapped his head with his tiny index finger. "She was far away, but I heard her up here." Another tap.

"And she said I could help you? Is that all the girl said?"

Ethan nodded. "Yes, that's all."

Lance's excitement had grown so great, he didn't immediately allow himself to be deflated by the extreme lack of detail in Mary Benchley's instructions to Ethan. Instead, he pressed on. "Ethan, you said you could hear the girl in the basement, right?"

Ethan nodded.

"Could you see her?"

Ethan looked at Lance like he'd grown a horn from his forehead. Shook his head. "No, she was in the basement."

*Of course. Try again, Lance.*

"Ethan." Lance got down onto one knee and looked the boy in the eyes. "Have you ever heard other people talking in your head? Or"—this one was tricky—"ever seen people that nobody else could see? People that ... aren't really here, maybe."

"No."

No hesitation. No contemplation. A simple answer.

*He's either telling the truth, or he's a fantastic liar for a six-year-old.*

Lance sat down on the floor and considered this. Unless Jacob Morgan had filled Ethan's head with some sort of knowledge of what had happened in the farmhouse, it seemed too coincidental of a thing to make up on the spot. Plus, there'd been the buzz ... that electric tingling at the base of Lance's skull and the nauseous feeling in his gut. Something had certainly happened last night in the kitchen.

*Could it possibly have been his first time? Was last night the first time his abilities had ever been exercised?*

Lance remembered his own childhood and envied Ethan if that was the case.

Another question popped into Lance's thoughts, and he changed topics, his own head going too fast to keep up with. "Ethan, why did you come here? Why now?"

The boy shifted from side to side and hugged himself again and then started to speak in a rapid burst of words that caused his eyes to tear up again and his voice to waver. "Uncle Jacob is mad and he was scaring me, and I started crying, and then I 'membered the girl said you could help me, so I went out my window and ran up here and the storm was loud and scary and I thought it was gonna kill me dead."

*Jacob's mad*, Lance thought as Ethan used his hoodie again to wipe his nose. *Which part of our conversation set him off? Was it the part about Ethan ... or was it the Benchleys?*

And then Lance thought, with more fear than he'd been expecting, that maybe it had been *both*.

"Ethan, buddy, do you know why your uncle Jacob was

mad?"

Ethan answered as he tried to hold back his tears. "I don't know. He was yelling and scaring me and told me to go to my room, so I did, and then he yelled some more and I heard something break and that scared me more, so I went out the window because you can help me."

Lance nodded his head. "That's right, Ethan. That's right. I can help. I'll help you, I promise. Everything will be fine."

Lance said the words and placed a hand on Ethan's small, bony shoulder. He looked the boy in the eye and repeated, "Everything will be fine." But he knew that he should not be making such a promise. He couldn't take the boy anywhere except back to Jacob Morgan without it possibly being misconstrued as kidnapping, especially after Lance had been to the house and had his conversation with Jacob, where he'd asked what would certainly be labeled as *strange* questions about Ethan.

Could he call the sheriff?

And say what? *Hi, Sheriff, I've got Jacob Morgan's nephew here—you know, little Ethan—and he's really scared and doesn't want to go home.* There was a hint of domestic abuse in that phrase, which might get the sheriff's hackles up, but—

Lance saw movement from the corner of his eye. Ethan had started down the hall while Lance had been absorbed in thought. "Ethan?" Lance called after him.

Ethan walked slowly but with a steady purpose to his gait. He turned his head and spoke with the same matter-of-factness as a man who was giving the time. "She's still down there," he said. "And she wants us to come see."

*Us.*

"Us?" Lance asked, shoving up to his feet and hurrying after the boy. "She said she wants *us* to come see?"

Ethan didn't answer, but Lance saw his shadow on the wall

nod a single time.

In the kitchen, Lance flipped on the light switch and watched as Ethan stopped for a moment to investigate the broken chair on the floor, giving Lance a sidelong glance, and then the boy turned to the basement door.

A loud buzz exploded in Lance's head, causing him to cry out and grab his head with his hands. His vision blurred and he tasted bile in the back of his mouth.

Then it passed, and when he could see clearly again, Ethan had opened the door and was halfway down the steps, the beam of his too-big flashlight shining into what looked like the mouth of a cave.

Lance followed, the cool, damp air of the basement biting at his skin and causing goose pimples to ripple along his forearms. And then he stood on the last step, Ethan standing on the hard-packed dirt floor a step in front of him. Ethan swung the flashlight beam to his right and started to walk in that direction.

"Ethan?" Lance said, stepping down to the floor and reaching up for the little bit of pull chain that was left on the light fixture above his head. He fumbled for it in the near-darkness, found it, pulled. Watched as the basement lit up in a dim glow, and he found Ethan standing in front of the row of metal shelves mounted on the wall behind the stairs.

"Ethan?" Lance tried again.

The boy stood motionless, staring straight ahead at the wall, his flashlight hanging loosely at his side, ready to fall from his hand and rattle onto the floor.

*God, it's like that last scene from* The Blair Witch Project.

Lance had thought it a joke, but as soon as he'd finished thinking it, he found himself quickly looking over his shoulder, eyes peering into the rest of the dimly lit basement.

He saw nothing.

When he turned back around, he nearly screamed in

surprise to find Ethan turned to face him, staring directly at him. "She's back there," Ethan said.

Lance's gaze looked past Ethan and settled on the wall behind him. He knew there was a room back there. He'd seen it in that awful memory that had been stored away in the key he'd found atop the bathroom mirror. But there were two things that bothered him about this. The first was that he didn't know how to open the wall, and the second was the fact that Mary Benchley's body had been found burned on the brush pile in the backyard. Not the basement, and certainly not behind a secret door that apparently nobody knew about or knew how to access.

"We need to unlock the door," Ethan said, pointing to the wall.

*But he knows*, Lance thought. *This must be real, because he knows about the door.*

Lance walked closer and stood beside Ethan, gently taking the boy's flashlight from him and shining it across the wall, the shelves. He'd been over every inch of this wall earlier that day and had found nothing.

"I don't know how," Lance said, feeling his face burn with disappointment at letting the child down.

And then another zap of electricity started at the base of Lance's skull and climbed up into his head, and his ears buzzed and his eyes squeezed shut and he thought he was going to throw up and—

And it stopped as suddenly as it had come. Lance gasped in relief, sucking in large gulps of air, turning to look to Ethan to ask the boy if he was feeling any of this.

But Ethan wasn't looking at Lance. He was looking at one of the shelves, his arm and hand outstretched, pointing. Lance followed to where the boy was pointing, and when he saw what he ended up on, he sighed and mumbled a bad word under his breath.

"I'm an idiot."

The paint can, with its dribbles of dried paint splattered on its exterior, was exactly where it'd been when Lance had first discovered it last night, and when he'd examined the wall earlier that morning. And now, Lance wondered exactly how long the can had been sitting in that spot on the shelf.

*Forever* was the answer he arrived at. How inconspicuous, a paint can on a basement shelf. How completely forgettable, dismissible. And Lance had done just that. Completely dismissed the can as nothing but part of the scenery.

He took Ethan's flashlight and walked to the wall, watching the light reflect off the can's spots of bare aluminum. Lance reached up and tried to gently push the can to the side along the shelf.

It wouldn't budge.

He tried again, pushing harder, putting more weight behind it.

Nothing.

He set the flashlight on the shelf next to the can, the light bouncing off the wall and giving Lance just enough to see by, and he grabbed the can with both hands and tried to push and pull it left, right, forward, back. It didn't so much as wiggle.

Lance grabbed the flashlight again and bent down and shined it under the shelf, peering under and looking for what was holding the can in place. The metal shelf was maybe two inches thick, but there were no signs of screws or bolts or anything else keeping the paint can stationary.

Lance turned and looked at Ethan, raising his eyebrows. *Well, kid, you seem to be the one running the show. Any ideas?*

Ethan stared back. Said nothing.

Lance sighed and studied the can again. Stepped back and looked at the shelf, the whole picture.

*The shelf,* he thought. *The can has to be attached to the shelf somehow, and there's nothing underneath, and nothing behind it, so...*

An idea.

He stepped back to the shelf and reached up and used both hands to press down on the top of the paint can.

And the can sank into the shelf. Not much, maybe only half an inch, but enough. When the can had been depressed into the shelf, Lance heard the shifting of metal on metal, the clinking of some sort of interior mechanism hidden away inside the body of the shelf itself. He released the can and it popped back into place quickly ... and the shelf loosened the tiniest bit, sliding over to the left a quarter of an inch, if that.

Lance placed his palm against the right edge of the shelf and pushed. Watched as the shelf slid left six inches on tracks inlaid in the basement's wall, and then came to a stop.

Lance grabbed the flashlight and shined it on the newly revealed spot on the wall.

Found a small keyhole. A dull silver mouth for which Lance knew he had the key tucked away in his pocket. He quickly pulled the key from his pants and stuck it in the lock. Then, after looking back to Ethan, who was still standing and watching attentively without a word, Lance turned the key. He heard an entire chorus of clinking and clanking and hinges in need of oil softly screeching inside the wall.

When the noises had finished, Lance stood and waited for something more to happen.

Nothing did.

Lance pulled the key from the lock and pocketed it.

He walked down the wall to the corner where it met the intersecting wall. He shrugged, placed two hands on the closest metal shelf, and pushed.

The entire basement wall began to slide open, and Lance had a startling idea that he was opening a tomb.

[ 35 ]

THERE WAS NO CORPSE IN THE ROOM—A ROOM THAT HAD been presumably sealed and undisturbed for the better part of six years—but there was blood.

Just like the key had slid into the lock in the wall and opened the room with a satisfying clicking of tumblers and gears, a key also slid into place in Lance's mind. The secrets he'd been trying to unearth, the questions he'd given up trying to answer—they were here, waiting for him. He knew this instantly as he took his first breath of the stale air and was able to see the dark stain on the concrete floor revealed in the flashlight's sweeping beam. When he took a step closer, the flashlight reflected off something else, a metallic glint winking back at Lance as he approached. When Lance saw what it was, he stopped and turned to look over his shoulder. Found Ethan standing in the opened mouth of the wall, peering in with nervous fascination. "Stay right there for a bit, okay, Ethan? Nobody's been here for a long time, and I want to make sure it's safe, okay?"

Ethan wrapped himself up again in the long sleeves of Lance's hoodie and nodded, but his eyes were pleading to see more. Lance turned and stepped closer, finding that metallic glint again and moving toward it, a sick feeling growing stronger in his gut with each step he took.

He reached the grotesquely large black stain on the floor, which was directly in front of the futon, and for an instant it reminded him of spilled coffee, brewed strong and just the way he liked it. He would have liked some coffee right then, for he had a strong certainty things were going to start moving very fast, and he'd have to stay ahead of it if he wanted to accomplish what he'd been brought here for.

He reached for the pull cord attached to the bank of overhead fluorescents and gripped the chain, pulling gently. Above, a noisy flickering of lights sputtered briefly like the engine of a long-idle car choking itself awake and then came on. Lance looked up and saw only one row of the lights were working, but it was enough. He switched off the flashlight and set it on the ground, careful to avoid the stain that he knew wasn't coffee.

The metallic reflection was coming from a rolling IV stand positioned next to the futon. Two clear plastic bags hung like a cowboy's saddlebag from the hooks on either side. They each looked half-empty. Beside the IV stand was a rolling cart, a metal tray atop it full of a handful of medical and surgical tools. Lance recognized most by sight but could not name them. The whole scene looked eerily like something you'd see on one of those tours of an abandoned mental hospital where the guide would tell you chilling tales of patient abuse and archaic medical procedures that once had been thought groundbreaking but were later proven to be nothing but torture. Lance walked around the black stain and the front of the futon—the futon he tried not to think about with little Ray Kruger lying atop it, his pants and underwear pushed down around his tiny ankles—and nearly tripped on a pile of towels scattered along the side of the futon. Towels that had once been white but were now tie-dyed a dark crimson. Lance jumped away from the towels as he might if he'd accidentally stepped on a rattlesnake. He looked down at them for a long time, his mind trying to add the IV stand and the bloody towels and the black stain together in some sick calculation that would show him an answer.

"What's there?" Ethan's voice, nervous and curious.

Lance looked up and saw the boy staring at him. Contemplated telling him the truth or trying to keep him calm.

*What would my mother do?*

The truth. She'd always told him the truth.

Lance chose a compromised answer. "Ethan, listen to me, okay? I think somebody got hurt down here. Pretty bad, too. So I really need you to stay right there unless I tell you different, understand?"

Ethen did not protest. Did not inquire further. Just nodded his head and kept his arms wrapped around himself, his eyes wide as he watched Lance's every move.

Lance stepped carefully around the towels and stood next to the IV stand, grabbed each of the plastic bags and read their labels in the half-lit room. One appeared to just be saline. The other was something called oxytocin. Lance, having misplaced his nursing degree, found this information less than helpful. But regardless of his understanding, one thing was clear: somebody had been down here and had needed medical attention. But who, and for how long?

Lance stepped back, allowed himself to fully take in the room. When he'd opened the door initially, he'd been overwhelmed with the memory of what he'd seen when he'd found the key atop the mirror, and those images played through his head and drew his eyes directly toward the futon in the center of the room. Now, with the lights above and his attention refocused on the grand picture, Lance saw additional details.

Things that at once painted a new picture. One that chilled his blood.

A pink-and-blue bedspread atop the futon, now a tangled and twisted mess, pushed far down toward the foot of the bed and spotted with blood; a small nightstand placed next to the futon on the opposite side from the IV stand, atop it a hairbrush, thin wisps of hair tangled in the bristles, bottles of vitamins, a small stuffed pig, pink and plush, and a copy of one of the *Twilight* novels, a bookmark sticking out from somewhere near the end.

Lance turned around and looked toward where the toilet and sink were. The shower rod was still there, only the curtain was much different than the one he'd seen in his vision from Ray Kruger's childhood. The curtain here was a pink-and-blue print matching the bedspread on the futon.

There was a scented candle on the counter by the sink, burned most of the way to the bottom.

Lance took another long look around the room.

*Somebody lived down here*, he thought. *Somebody was trying to make this a bedroom.*

He looked back to the *Twilight* novel on the nightstand. To the hairbrush with the strands of hair stuck in it. Recalled the black-and-white image of the Benchley family from the newspaper archives at the library. The hair in the brush was light in color. He looked at the book again, considered the subject matter.

Mary Benchley's hair had been much lighter than her mother's.

Lance remembered the voice he'd heard calling out from behind the locked basement door. A young girl pleading to be let out.

"She was kept down here," Lance said. He looked back to

the IV stand, wishing he had a smartphone to Google what oxytocin was used for. "Why?" he asked the room.

His vision went black and his head buzzed and his stomach churned, and he fell forward onto the futon, his sneakers slipping on the mess of stained blankets on the floor. He managed to choke out a muffled gasp, felt his lungs constrict as he sucked in a deep breath of air as his vision cleared as quick as it had darkened and his stomach settled.

Lance pushed himself off the futon and stood, blinking to clear his eyes, which had started to water. When he could see clearly again, he saw that Ethan had stepped inside the room, crossing the floor halfway to the futon.

He was pointing again.

Lance stepped back around the futon and followed the boy's outstretched hand, and his gaze landed on a stack of paperback books piled behind the nightstand.

"She wants you to read it," Ethan said.

Lance, despite his love of literature, was in no mood to curl up with a good book. But he remembered the last time Ethan had pointed at something—the paint can—and did not argue.

The nightstand cast a long and dark shadow along the floor, bathing the stack of books in black. Lance retrieved the flashlight and switched it on, then kneeled down in front of the stack and examined the titles, hoping one of them would be called *What Really Happened*, or maybe *Read Me First*.

No such luck. The titles were all old Westerns and a couple early Stephen King novels. Their spines were all deeply creased and worn, cracked with heavy usage, and Lance imagined they'd come from a dime store or library sale many years ago. None of the books looked like they'd be any help.

Lance was about to ask Ethan if he could maybe coax a few more details from his silent partner, but when the beam of his flashlight did another pass over the stack of paperbacks, something new caught his eye.

The fifth book down had a solid black spine that Lance had dismissed on his first scan of the titles, assuming it'd been part of another book. But as his flashlight had slid along the titles a second time, he'd more clearly seen the small slit of space between it and the book above and realized it was a book of its own. There was no printed title or author on the spine. Lance carefully lifted the four books atop it, one by one, and set them to the side. He shined the flashlight beam onto the front cover of the black book, and a gold-embossed word jumped out to him.

*Journal.*

Ethan's words—*She wants you to read it*—gained greater clarity.

Lance reached out and grabbed the journal. The leather was soft and—

He sucked in a sudden rush of air. His eyes widened and the hair along his arms and back of his neck stood on end. A second later, he expelled his breath in a great *whoosh* and fell back onto his butt, dropping the flashlight onto the floor next to him.

Like the key he'd found atop the bathroom mirror, the journal had electrified his mind with information. He hadn't had to read the pages—had known he likely didn't have the time. The pages had given themselves to Lance, and what he'd learned was both relieving (because the pieces had finally fallen into place), and devastatingly heartbreaking.

Lance looked at Ethan and felt great sadness for the boy.

Ethan was not Jacob Morgan's nephew.

Lance pushed himself from the floor, his mind spinning to decide what he should do next, when there was a thunderous noise from upstairs as the front door crashed open.

*"Ethan!"* Jacob Morgan's voice was full of rage.

Ethan's eyes shot open wide, and he ran to Lance's side. Lance bent down and wrapped one of his arms around the boy, enveloping him. His eyes scanned the wall where it opened back into the regular basement. Found what he was looking for; a small lever that presumably opened the door from the inside. Ethan would be able to get out on his own if things went poorly for Lance.

Lance used one hand to tuck the journal into the rear waistband of his shorts, covering it with his t-shirt, and used the other to lift Ethan's face to meet his own. Footsteps were pounding on the floorboards above—Jacob Morgan moving swiftly and angrily down the hallway toward the kitchen.

"Ethan, listen, I want you to stay here. Stay quiet, and don't come out unless I tell you, okay? There's a lever on the door you can pull to get out if you really think you need to, but I want you to wait, okay? I want you to wait for me. Your uncle's very mad, and I want to try and help him, okay? Do you understand?"

Ethan's eyes were full of fear and worry. They glistened with tears, but to the boy's credit, none fell down his cheek. He nodded.

Lance, only because it simply felt right, kissed the boy atop his head and then stood, making his way quickly across the floor and out into the basement. He gripped one of the metal shelves and pulled, slamming the hidden door closed.

"*Ethan!*"

Lance stood still by the bare workbench in the corner and watched with a certain level of dread as Jacob Morgan called out again and stomped down the stairs, his boots coming into view first, followed by his legs, and then his upper body.

Jacob Morgan reached the last stair and then stepped down onto the hard-packed dirt, eyes burning and locking onto Lance.

He was carrying a hunting rifle.

*I've really got the worst luck in basements*, Lance thought.

[ 36 ]

Jacob Morgan was dripping wet, water falling from the brim of the ball cap he wore and splashing into the dirt at his feet. He'd tossed a jacket on over his shirt, but it was unzipped, and the fabric of the shirt beneath clung to him, accenting a muscled physique.

He gripped the hunting rifle with hands so tight the knuckles were white.

He spoke through gritted teeth, hissing the words at Lance. "Where is he?"

Lance cleared his throat. "Who?"

Jacob's hands twisted the rifle from across his body, inching its aim closer to Lance's direction. A subtle threat. "Ethan. Where is Ethan?"

Lance's heart hammered in his chest. He took slow, deliberate breaths, trying to calm it, keep his poise. His knack for casual conversation had saved him on more than one occasion. "Why would he be here? There's no more pizza."

"His shirt is on the banister upstairs. There's nowhere else close he could have gone to, and I'm going to take out your kneecap with a bullet if you don't tell me where he is in three seconds or less."

"Who?"

Jacob shook his head and raised the rifle, taking aim at Lance's legs. "Stop playing dumb. It's not going to work. *Where. Is. Ethan?* Three ... two..."

Lance swallowed and said, "You mean your son? You want to know where your son is?"

Lance saw the jolt of shock ripple through Jacob Morgan's body. It wasn't much, but perceivable all the same. The man's eyes narrowed further, met Lance's. "You don't know what you're talking about. Ethan's my nephew."

"Stop playing dumb," Lance said. "It's not going to work."

He reached slowly behind him, praying to any god that might exist and be tuned in to the correct frequency that Jacob Morgan wouldn't view the motion as a threat and shoot him through the heart before Lance had had a chance to make his big reveal. He reached beneath his shirt and pulled the leather journal free from the waistband of his shorts, then held it up in front of him.

"I know who he is," Lance said. "And I think you've been looking for this for a long time."

Jacob Morgan's eyes lit up like Christmas lights and his jaw dropped open at the sight of the journal, doing nothing but confirming to Lance that he'd been correct in the theory he'd managed to piece together since Mary Benchley's journal had shown itself to him.

"You knew she kept this, didn't you?" Lance asked. "You'd probably even seen it before. Maybe up in her room one day, after the two of you ... well, you know. Hey, what *is* Virginia's law on statutory rape, anyway?"

"*I never raped her!*"

Lance shrugged. "Court might have said differently. And

I'm positive Mark Benchley would have had a different opinion than you. Am I right? What was the age difference again? She was, what, fifteen or sixteen? You were somewhere in your twenties, deflowering Daddy's little angel?"

Lance was intentionally trying to rile Jacob Morgan up, trying to set him off his game. It was Lance's experience that while angry people tended to be more violent, they also tended to be less attentive to their surroundings and the entire situation at hand. Their anger threw up blinders.

But Lance was also aware that the only reason Jacob Morgan hadn't shot him dead yet was because Lance knew where Ethan was.

Lance took two slow steps closer to the man, keeping the journal in front of him at all times. It seemed to be Jacob Morgan's focal point.

Jacob shook his head again. "You don't know," he said. "I *loved* her. And she loved me."

Lance took another step, waved the journal out in front of him, back and forth like a matador distracting a bull.

"Maybe," he said. "But love can make people do stupid things, right? Is that why you killed them all? Because you loved her?"

Jacob Morgan kept shaking his head back and forth. "You don't know," he said again.

Lance stopped, now maybe six or seven feet from the man. He held the journal out and tapped it with a finger on his free hand. "I know everything," he said. "Let me tell you, and you can tell me where I've gotten it wrong. Maybe you can tell me the side of the story where you come out *not* looking like a murderer. If you can do that, maybe I'll tell you where your son is."

Jacob Morgan's eyes narrowed again, not liking being told

what to do. "Maybe I go ahead and shoot you now. How about that?"

Lance made a show of pretending to think about the offer. Shook his head. "I don't think so. Finding your son is more important to you than killing me."

"I could kill you after."

Lance nodded confidently, but inside he was very much aware that if he didn't get out of this basement, Jacob Morgan's threat would likely come true.

"You could," he said. "I guess we'll both just have to wait and see."

Jacob Morgan said nothing to this, so Lance took a deep breath and started to talk.

"It all makes a weird bit of sense, to be honest," Lance said. "Ever since I got to town, there's really only been two main names that have come up as suspects in the Benchley murders: Mark Benchley, and you. As it turns out, *both* of you killed them."

This drew a confused expression from Jacob Morgan.

"Oh, don't get me wrong, now. You're the one who pulled the trigger, but"—Lance held the journal up again—"it would appear that the accusations of Mark Benchley's fanatical religious beliefs were exactly spot-on."

Jacob Morgan didn't move, but Lance could see he was focused, listening to the story Lance was beginning to tell. After all these years, Lance imagined it was probably somewhat cathartic for the man to finally revisit that night with another human being, to have the truth laid bare.

"Mary told her mother that she was pregnant," Lance continued. "The two of you had kept your relationship a secret for a few months—you sneaking over when Mark and Natalie were in town, Mary stopping by your house on her way home from school or running errands. You both did a swell job of keeping things hidden. But then Mary got pregnant—what happened, anyway? Did the condom break, or did you just decide to risk it one time? I mean, with all due respect, you were already having sex with a minor, I would think the least you could do was use some protection. But you know what they say ... hindsight. Twenty-twenty." Lance shrugged. "Sorry, I digress.

"Mary got pregnant, and she got scared and she told her mom. The two of them kept it a secret from Mark for a while—and from you—but eventually Natalie decided that the right thing to do was to tell him the truth. She told Mary that Mark loved her more than anything and he might be upset at first, but they would get through it together as a family. Turns out, Natalie Benchley didn't know her husband as well as she thought she did."

Lance paused, gauged Jacob Morgan's reaction. The man stood, stone-faced and attentive.

*He's never heard any of this*, Lance thought. In his mind, he fast-forwarded through the rest of the journal's pages, the rest of the heartbreaking story, and realized he was right. From what he could tell, Jacob Morgan had only come into the story at the very end—the night he'd killed them.

"Something snapped in Mark Benchley when he found out Mary was pregnant," Lance said. "Mary wrote, and I'm quoting here, *Dad looks at me like I'm no longer his daughter, but a disgusting sinner damned to hell. But he doesn't realize it's he who's playing the role of the devil.* She was quite the writer," Lance said. "She painted a horrible picture, but she did it with striking detail."

Jacob Morgan shifted from one leg to another, the hunting rifle still gripped tight.

"That's when they pulled her out of school under the ruse of shipping her off to a boarding school. Mark was too humiliated to have his teenaged daughter start showing up to class with a baby bump and maternity pants. She was *unclean* in his eyes. She'd become the very type of person he'd preached was destroying the world that God had intended. And he was so self-ish, so ironically vain, he hid her under a rock. Or, in this case, under a house."

Jacob Morgan's mouth opened to speak, but he stopped himself. Coughed, cleared his throat, and tried again. "She was ... she was here the whole time? The entire pregnancy?"

Lance nodded and then pushed on. This next part was even more disturbing.

"With Natalie being a nurse, Mark figured she could give Mary all the medical attention she needed. And that might have worked—but then Natalie made a mistake."

Jacob Morgan waited, clearly hanging on Lance's every word.

"She convinced Mary that an abortion would be the best thing for everyone."

"Oh, God," Jacob said, almost without realizing it, it seemed. And Lance imagined what a terrible idea it must be to realize how close a living, breathing child you'd fallen completely in love with had come to not existing at all. To being murdered before they'd ever even been given a chance.

"Mark Benchley, ironically, didn't like this," Lance said. "Despite Natalie only trying to help ease the problem, Mark called her a would-be murderer, said she was just as unworthy of the Holy Kingdom as Mary. He said he could no longer trust her. And that's when he made her quit her job. He kept her home, only letting her go out to town if he accompanied her. With Ray Kruger as the sheriff, Mark knew he couldn't completely sequester Natalie to the basement like he had Mary, but—and again, I'm telling you exactly what Mary's got written here"—Lance held up the journal, reestablishing it in Jacob Morgan's view—"Natalie told Mary that Mark said he'd kill them both if they tried to run from him, or tried to get help to get away. And he told Natalie that if she tried to go behind his back, he'd sacrifice Mary. He said he was only doing what was right in God's eyes, and that if they disobeyed him, it was the same as disobeying the Lord and they would have to be punished."

*What a terrible position to be put in*, Lance thought. *Natalie's love for her daughter was what kept Mary alive, but it's also what killed them both.*

Lance paused, then added, "It's funny. I've always been told that God is all about forgiveness. Isn't that why they send a priest to visit death-row inmates before they're executed? To wipe the slate clean before they take their last ride?"

Jacob Morgan did not answer. He didn't appear to be focused on anything at all, his gaze staring straight through Lance, and probably down a deep dark hole that led back to that awful night.

"They managed to survive," Lance continued. "Mark kept his watchful eye on them, but the two of them survived together down here. He'd bring them meals, sometimes allowing Natalie to come up and cook—sometimes he'd get takeout. He escorted them upstairs to the shower and never let them close the door. Mary said he always looked like he'd been crying. His eyes always bloodshot and his nose red from wiping it. He asked Natalie what they needed—from a medical standpoint—and he'd drive two towns over to buy it all." Then, with a sinking feeling of sympathy for a dead girl he'd never met, Lance added, "He never let them go to a doctor."

Jacob Morgan's eyes glistened with tears, and he removed one hand from the rifle just long enough to quickly wipe at them. He sniffled loudly but still said nothing.

"She was nearly a month early," Lance said. "She started

having contractions, and Natalie told Mark it was going to happen at any moment. And it did."

Lance coughed, choking back emotions that began to surface as he recited from the journal pages that had uploaded themselves into his mind and saw the scenes playing out. A terrified young girl, trapped in a basement by her psychotic father, giving birth to a baby boy she'd never get to know.

"But they weren't prepared," Lance said. "Things didn't go well for Mary."

Lance remembered the large dark stain on the floor by the futon, the twisted and bloody towels.

"Obviously, the baby survived," Lance said. "But the last thing Mary wrote in her journal"—he could see the page in his mind, the handwriting faint and scrawling, palm-smears of blood in the margins and above and below the words—"was this." Lance opened the journal now, flipped to the back and found the page that perfectly matched the image he'd just conjured. Swallowed back threatening tears and read, *"Baby is beautiful. Baby is perfect. Mama says I'll be okay, but I know she's lying. I feel like I'm fading. Lots of blood. But I don't feel the pain."* Lance stopped here and looked up. "Then, a few inches down the page from this she added, *Jacob is here. How? He's yelling at Daddy. I'm going to show him his son. I love them both so much.*"

Lance closed the journal with a sound that seemed very loud in a basement that had fallen very silent. Above them, a clap of thunder went almost unnoticed. The rain continued to fall.

"You showed up and you killed them when you thought they wouldn't let you see your newborn son, is that it? Mark Benchley told you that you'd never see them, and you killed him? Natalie, too, when she tried to run?"

At these words, Jacob Morgan's eyes studied Lance's face. "How...?" he started. "How do you know he said that to me?"

Lance said nothing. Waited.

There were tears on Jacob's cheeks now, carving hot lines down his face.

"How did you know to come over that night?" Lance asked. "I've told you my part, now tell me yours."

Jacob Morgan closed his eyes, squeezing out tears. He wiped them away with the back of one hand and said, "I could never understand it. I never knew why she left. I know Mary was younger, and I know the age difference would have been a problem for a few years, but does that really matter? Can you look at me and tell me age matters with love?" He didn't wait for an answer. "Which is why I was so stunned when I came over here one Sunday evening to see if everything was okay, because Mary hadn't shown up at church, and that's when Mark told me she'd left for a boarding school.

"I begged him to tell me what the school was—you know, so I could send her letters, or care packages. But honestly I just wanted to know where I had to drive to go see her, to find out what happened between us. Because it had all been going so well, you know? And if she was going to break my heart, I wanted her to do it to my face. That might sound selfish, I know, but I wasn't going to let her just disappear and pretend that what we had together would fade away.

"But Mark would never tell me. Neither would Natalie. They said Mary had been having a tough time in school, with bullying or some bullshit, and they didn't want to risk the new school information getting out into the wrong hands. Man, I was so furious. But what could I do? I called every private school I could find in the state and got nowhere."

Jacob sighed, shrugged his shoulders. The hunting rifle rose and fell with the motion. Lance kept his eyes on it. "So I gave up," Jacob said. "I convinced myself that I was crazy to think somebody as young as Mary could have ever been serious about our relationship, and I tried to move on. And I did, Lance. I did move on. Or at least I thought I had. But then Natalie texted me that night, and everything changed." He looked at Lance like a man trying very hard to make a difficult to understand point. A look that was almost sympathetic, as if he knew the person on the receiving end of the forthcoming information would never truly grasp the meaning. "That night was the worst night of my life, Lance. But, it was also the greatest night. It was the night I found out I had a son, and for the first time I finally understood what love felt like."

There was a part of Lance that thought he understood what Jacob Morgan was saying. But the other part, the part that was still very much focused on the hunting rifle gripped in the man's hands, was not letting go of the other major event the night Ethan had been born.

"You killed them," Lance said. "Does that not bother you at all? Is that the sort of father you want to be for your son? You murdered his grandparents and burned his mother's body on brush pile like she was a discarded shrub. Do you actually want me to sympathize with that? Feel sorry for you? Whatever happened that night, at the end of the story, you still come out a murderer."

Jacob shook his head again and sighed, but when he spoke, Lance noticed that anger slipping its way back into the words. "You don't understand! When I got here, Mark was crazed. I'm serious, it was like he was possessed. He wanted me dead, I could see that the moment I walked through the door. And Natalie? She was terrified. More for her own daughter's life than anything else. She understood the severity of what had happened during the birth. That's why she texted me. She managed to get Mark's phone away from him long enough to send me a message. Do you have any idea what it's like to be sitting at home reading and suddenly get a text that says the son you didn't know you were having had just been born and that the mother's life was in danger and you need to come right away?" Jacob shook his head. "I tried messaging her back but got nothing. So I took off up the hill. Natalie was waiting for me at the door, frantic, terrified, begging me to help get Mary to the hospital. Mark was waiting too, and he had a shotgun."

This was the part of the story Lance had been waiting for. The bits of dialogue the house had played for him the past few days were of the moment in the story Jacob Morgan had arrived at just now. All he needed to hear was Jacob Morgan's confession, and then he'd try and see if he'd get killed trying to escape the basement and get to the sheriff.

"Mark wanted to kill me," Jacob said. "I think it's obvious he never knew I was the father until right before I'd arrived. Natalie and Mary must have managed to keep that much a secret from him, probably because they knew how he'd react. I don't know if they did it so much to protect me, or to protect Mark. Trying to keep him from committing murder." Jacob shrugged. "I guess it was both.

"Anyway, things got heated. Mark was threatening to shoot me and I was trying to stay calm, trying to diffuse things. Really all I wanted was to see Mary, and my baby boy. I could hear her pleading from the basement door, wanting somebody to let her out. And I could hear Ethan crying. I was trying to get to them, but Mark kept shoving that damn gun in my face. I was paralyzed, Lance. Didn't know what to do. I hadn't even laid eyes on him yet, but when I heard my son crying out, something inside me broke. I would have died to save him, but the only way to do that was to stay alive a bit longer. And that ... well, that's where I lost it."

Lance took a step closer, crossing his arms and trying to look nonthreatening. Added another half step. "How so?"

"I tried to get past Mark, and that's when he got physical. We pushed each other around a bit, and Mark reared back with the gun to swing it at me, and the butt of it sucker-punched Natalie in the gut. She cried out, and that's when she panicked. She jumped into the mix with us and kneed Mark in the balls. He dropped the gun and doubled over, and she pushed him over and got his keys from his pocket and sprinted down the hall toward the front door. She yelled back to us that she was going to get help, and I called out for her to wait, but I didn't move. I didn't try to stop her or go with her, and when I saw Mark Benchley push himself off the floor and pick up the shotgun, I froze. My whole world slowed down. Sound muffled. All I could seem to hear was my own breathing.

"And Mark shot her. I watched and did nothing while he ran toward the door and stood on the porch and fired the gun into his wife's back."

Lance couldn't believe what he was hearing.

"And that's when everything changed," Jacob said. "It was as if Mark fell out of whatever trance he'd been in. He dropped the gun and turned around and looked at me, and his face was pure terror. He said, 'What have I done?' and before I could answer, we heard two thuds from the basement stairs and then a baby started to cry at the top of its lungs. A heart-piercing wail. Mark and I looked at each other, and all the anger and the rage melted and we both sprinted toward the kitchen. I got there first, and I threw open the bolt and yanked open the door, and..."

Jacob stopped. Took a breath that wavered with tears. "They were at the bottom of the stairs, sprawled out on the basement floor. Mary must have ... she must have died right there on the stairs. She must not have been very high up—maybe she knew something was going to happen before it did, and she'd started to make her way down—but she didn't make it all the way. Those two thuds... I'll hear those two thuds in my head until the day I die.

"I ran down to her, but as soon as I got close, I knew I was too late. Her eyes were open—she had such beautiful eyes. Ethan was tangled in her arms, his head miraculously resting on her chest. He was crying at the top of his lungs, wrapped in some sort of baby blanket. I don't know how long I sat there, staring into Mary's eyes and listening to that little guy wailing, but finally I felt a hand on my shoulder and looked up to find Mark, standing there with tears and snot pouring down his face." Jacob shook his head again, as if trying to clear out the memories, or maybe finding himself disgusted all over again as they came to light. "He kept saying it over and over. 'What have I done? What have I done?'"

Jacob sighed again and looked Lance in the eyes. "I killed him, Lance. I killed Mark Benchley because of what he'd done. He killed his wife. He killed his daughter—the mother of my son—and he could have killed my son, too.

"He was gone, Lance. Mentally, it was like he'd checked out after he came down and saw Mary. But that didn't make me hesitate. I'd never felt anger like I felt that night, Lance. I've never felt that primal urge to end somebody's life like I did. I coaxed Mark upstairs and sat him in that chair and then went and got the shotgun." Jacob paused then, a small smirk coming across his face. "I think he knew. He knew what was going to happen, but he didn't care anymore. He didn't fight. Didn't say a word. I wrapped his hands around the barrel and shoved it under his chin and then I blew his fucking head off."

Both men were quiet then. Staring at each other, both unsure what was next.

Lance pieced the story together, thought about Ethan in the

hidden room to his left. Understood. "You burned Mary's body because you didn't want anybody to know she'd just had a baby. You'd just committed murder, nobody knew about Mary's pregnancy except you and three corpses, so you got rid of the evidence. Only you remembered Mary's journal later, and you were afraid she'd written that you were the father of her baby in there somewhere. Only you could never find it, could you? That's why you've been paying Rich Bellows to let you know when anybody gets near the house. Because you're afraid they'll find it before you do. You're paranoid they'll find the journal … or maybe anything else that could implicate you. So you've been lurking around, scaring people away—or, I don't know, threatening them. You were here my first night, too, weren't you? Checking out the new tenant?"

Jacob Morgan didn't deny anything. He nodded and said, "They would have taken him away from me. They would have taken my son away, and I would have never seen him again. But don't you get it? I was trying to protect *him*, too. I didn't want my son's life to be marred by the story of what happened the night he was born. That his grandpa was a lunatic who kept his mother a prisoner. That his grandma was murdered and his mother died after childbirth. That story would follow him around the rest of his life. He'd never escape it. He'd be looked at like a freak. It would have ruined him."

Lance shook his head. "You don't know that. People are a lot stronger than we think." Then he pushed the final few puzzle pieces into place in his mind. "So you hid Ethan away, made up the story of finding the bodies the next morning, and then skipped town with your son until you felt you would be able to come back and sell the story of him being your sister's kid. Did you even have a half-sister?"

Jacob shook his head. His voice came out raspy. "No. After what happened, I drove all night to a buddy of mine's house a few towns over—somebody I'd trust with my life—and gave him Ethan. Then I came back and dealt with the aftermath here. Afterwards, I left and took Ethan and spent a year and an insane amount of money getting things in order. Both medically —God, I had no fucking idea what to do with a newborn—and in terms of documentation. I made up the story of the half-sister so I could give Jacob my last name. People around town didn't ask a lot of questions. If it doesn't directly pertain to the people here, they don't much care about it. My made-up half-sister was an outsider. Unimportant. But people love Ethan." Jacob grinned. "They've loved him from day one."

The amount of lies and deceit and tragedy that Lance had seen and heard in the last few minutes was astounding, enough to make you question why human beings are even allowed to exist. We do terrible things.

With the awful truth finally exposed, Lance knew it was time to make his move. He took a small step closer and said, "Doesn't it upset you? Not being able to tell your son that you're his father? Doesn't it piss you off to see him grow up and learn new things and do new things and not be able to say to people that you're a proud father, instead of a proud half-uncle?"

Darkness fell over Jacob Morgan's face, his eyes hardening again and his posture straightening, stretching the man to his full height. An imposing, intimidating gesture. He raised the hunting rifle and aimed it squarely at Lance's chest. "Okay," he said, "I told my story. Tell me where my son is." He added, "After everything I've done to protect him, do you really think I'm going to hesitate in killing you? Especially now that you know the truth?"

Lance shrugged. "I'd hoped you would consider it."

This time, it was Jacob who stepped closer. There was now maybe three feet between the men. "Hope again," Jacob said. "Where is he?"

Lance held up his hands and nodded his head. "Okay, okay. He's in there." He pointed to his left and nodded his head toward the wall—the door to the hidden room—and when Jacob Morgan's eyes glanced that direction and his head turned slightly along with them, Lance ducked down and used his legs and speed to drive himself forward, pistoning up and under the barrel of the rifle and throwing all his weight into Jacob Morgan's torso.

There was a sound like thunder, only intensified by a million, as the rifle went off and then went clattering to the floor as Lance drove Jacob Morgan into the ground. The man cried out and cursed, and Lance got back to his feet and kicked him in the face, Jacob's head snapping hard with the blow.

Then Lance was moving. Bolting up the stairs two at a time without looking back, all the while trying hard to convince himself that Ethan would be safe behind the basement wall, and despite the fact that Jacob Morgan was a murderer, if he did manage to coax Ethan into opening the wall, Lance knew the man would protect the boy.

As Lance bounded into the kitchen, he heard Jacob Morgan call after him with some very unpleasant words, and then there came the sound of the man's boots on the stairs. Not moving as quickly as Lance, but moving all the same. Lance moved to slide around the kitchen table, toward the back door. Planned on running blindly down the trail and hoping he could make it into town.

Lance stopped. It wasn't long, maybe not even a unit of time measurable with any normal time-keeping device, but there was the tiniest moment of hesitation. Standing across the kitchen, directly in front of the back door, was the man from Lance's dream. The reflection man in the bus's window, the man he now knew to be Mark Benchley, with the blood-splattered white t-shirt and the missing face. He stood like a sentinel by the door,

300

one arm, speckled with blood, pointing the opposite direction, down the hall toward the front of the house.

Lance didn't stop to ask questions, and when he blinked, the man was gone.

The boots behind him were closer, and he turned and ran down the hall. The front door was open, and a strong gust of wind rocked it back against the house. Through the opened doorway there was a zap of lightning on the horizon and—

*Are those blue lights?*

Another noise like thunder erupted from inside the house, and a bit of the door frame exploded in a burst of splintered wood. Lance did not bother to look back. There was no point. Any moment of hesitation at this point would end with a bullet lodged somewhere in his body. He grunted and summoned all his strength and power he could from inside him and sprinted through the opened doorway and—

"Freeze!"

Lance heard the word shouted to him and was momentarily blinded by the flashing blue lights. But he didn't stop moving. He ran across the porch and leapt through the air off the top step. As he was airborne, a feeling of weightlessness overtaking him and causing time to take on a slowed-down, dreamlike state, he was able to take in the scene in front of him. Found the black Crown Vic he'd seen his first night in Ripton's Grove parked sideways in the drive, a blue flashing orb emitting the blinding light from atop the front dash. Headlights casting bright cones of white light. Sheriff Ray Kruger was standing in front of the car. Legs spread. Pistol in hand and aimed at Lance.

In the distance, at the end of the driveway, Lance saw a new set of headlights approaching, the faint silhouette of a Jeep Wrangler turning into the drive.

The rain made things fuzzy, blurring everything with a sheer veil.

Lance's eyes locked with the sheriff's, and the man shouted something.

Something Lance couldn't make out.

Then Sheriff Ray Kruger pulled the trigger. The gun fired.

The bullet found its target.

Lance landed hard on the ground, his legs crumpling beneath him. His body rolled once, twice, and then was still.

## 37

LANCE SAT IN THE PASSENGER'S SEAT OF LUKE'S JEEP. IT was seven o'clock in the morning, and Lance had been at the sheriff's office for what felt like days, giving statement after statement after statement. Finessing the truth to bend and mold around the lies he was forced to tell in order to protect himself, until the facts blurred together with his nontruths so convincingly that the deputies, and more importantly, Ray Kruger, had finally been convinced that Lance was innocent of any wrongdoing.

But Ray Kruger wasn't finished with questions.

Lance had landed on the wet grass and his sneakers had slipped out from under him and he'd gone down hard on his tailbone, clinking his teeth together and somehow managing to avoid severing his tongue. He'd rolled twice on the ground and then sat still, allowing himself a momentary rest before he'd spun around, twisting his body backward to crabwalk away from the house and toward Sheriff Kruger.

On the ground outside the farmhouse, half-sprawled on the porch steps, half-sprawled in the grass, Jacob Morgan was face-down and not moving. A perfect imitation of how the man had described finding Natalie Benchley. The hunting rifle was at his side, just out of reach of his splayed hand. Sheriff Ray Kruger moved in quickly, the pistol still locked in his hands and trained on Jacob Morgan's body. Then the cuffs were out and ready, but the sheriff leaned in closer, stared at Jacob's body for a moment before bending down further and placing his fingers to man's neck. Then Ray Kruger stood, pulled his cell phone from his pocket, and placed a call.

"Holy shit, is he dead? Dude, are you all right? What the hell happened here, man?"

The voice was muffled. Lance's ears had still been ringing from the cannon-like explosion of gun fire inside the house. He looked up and saw Luke standing at his side, Susan close behind.

"You wouldn't believe me if I told you," he'd said.

Luke's eyes were wide, and he looked over to where Sheriff Kruger was headed back in their direction. "Dude, you got some serious air coming off that porch. Took me back to when we played each other. I forgot how high you could jump."

And then Sheriff Kruger was there and telling Luke and Susan to get back in their car, and looking down at Lance like he was seeing him—*really* seeing him—for the first time.

And then everything had been a whirlwind.

Police cars and an ambulance and a firetruck had all flashed and screamed their way onto the hillside, heavy tires digging deep ruts into the wet and muddied yard.

Deputies and paramedics had scrambled here and there, barking orders to each other but also all looking to Kruger for direction.

Lance assured the young male paramedic who'd approached him that he was fine, and after a brief examination, the man had agreed.

Jacob Morgan had been loaded onto a stretcher and

wheeled away, his wrists cuffed to the side rail of the gurney. From the looks of it, he was conscious, but barely. A large bloody bandage had been haphazardly applied to the gunshot wound the sheriff had inflicted on the upper right side of his chest. An oxygen mask was over his face. They loaded him into the ambulance and it drove off, flashing lights like fireworks in the night sky.

And then Ray Kruger had walked up to Lance with a look on his face that said the man was expecting a terrible answer. "Where's the boy?" he asked. "My guy says he's not at Morgan's house."

Lance looked the sheriff in the eye, and instead of the tired, sad, haunted man he'd become, Lance saw the eyes of a young, innocent boy, playing with his uncle in the basement of the house directly in front of them. Suffering things he wouldn't come to fully understand until many years later.

Lance pulled the key from his pocket and handed it to Kruger. Told him what he'd find.

Ray Kruger looked down at the key in his hand for a long time, and Lance didn't want to know what the man's mind was conjuring. Then the sheriff nodded, turned and looked at the house, which had taken on a towering, menacing appearance in the stormy night, and walked up the porch steps and across the threshold, letting the house swallow him whole.

Later, in the same interview room Lance had been placed in when he'd been accused of assaulting Victoria Bellows, after the many rounds of questioning and statement taking and fact checking and rechecking, Lance had been left alone for maybe only ten minutes, but after the long night, that'd been enough time for his eyes to grow heavy and sleep to creep up his spine. He'd just about face-planted into the desk when the interview room door had creaked open and startled him awake. He found Ray Kruger standing in the doorway, two Styrofoam cups of coffee in his hands. He elbowed the door closed and sat down at the table, handing one of the cups to Lance.

"Thank you," Lance said. He sipped it. It was terrible, but also the best coffee he'd ever had.

The sheriff sipped his, too, eying Lance, but never saying a word.

Lance, never one to shy away from breaking the ice, said, "So, you have a great-nephew."

And just like that, everything in Sheriff Ray Kruger's face softened. His eyes lightened and his lips twitched up in what could only be described as the makings of a smile. "Yeah," he said, taking a long sip of coffee that Lance thought was only a ploy to hide the look of elation on the man's face. "I guess I do."

*Family is powerful*, Lance thought. *Family is what this man has always cared about the most.*

"Morgan confessed to everything," Kruger said. "I went and had a chat with him after they got him patched up. Showed him the journal. He cracked like a nut. I think this has been weighing on him a long time. He doesn't care what happens to him. All he keeps asking is what's going to happen to Ethan."

Lance thought about this. "What will happen to Ethan, sir?"

"That's for me to worry about," Kruger said.

Lance said nothing. Nodded once. But his mind had been shown flashes of future memories Ray Kruger would make with his new great-nephew. Adventures in the park, Little League games, school plays. A toy badge and a set of flimsy plastic handcuffs for Christmas because Ethan said he wanted to be sheriff when he grew up.

*Family.*

Family was a wonderful, strange, powerful thing.

Family, Lance had deduced during his long hours of giving statements and waiting in interview rooms, was why he'd mistakenly believed Ethan possessed abilities similar to his own. The boy hadn't lied to him when Lance had asked if Ethan had ever heard voices in his head before, or seen people who weren't really there. Hearing Mary Benchley in the farmhouse had been Ethan's first— and likely only—experience communicating with the dead.

Family.

Lance remembered his own connection with his mother. The direct line of thought and instinct and communication that had seemed to exist between them. A link. Unbreakable. Forged at Lance's birth. Mother and son.

The same link had existed between Ethan and Mary, although much weaker and diminished after Mary's death. Lance had reasoned all these years that for a spirit to present itself required some great energy, some great purpose. Mary Benchley's spirit might not have been completely trapped on this side of the veil, had found it impossible to present herself to Lance for whatever reason the governing rules of the Universe dictated, but she'd been able to use him. Those moments when the world had wobbled and his vision blurred and his head buzzed and his stomach rolled—that had been Mary, tapping into Lance's power and abilities, using him as a sort of signal booster to reach out and touch her son. Helping them both to discover the truth.

It had been a first for Lance, being used in that way. He wondered how many more firsts there would be. How much of his own ability he still didn't understand.

Then there was a long period of silence. Lance sat opposite the sheriff, and the two men sipped at their coffee and enjoyed the quietness, the calmness of the room. It had been a long, terrible night for both of them.

"My uncle molested me in that house when I was a child," Kruger said. And even though this was not new information to

Lance, he still nearly spat his coffee into his cup. "More than once. I've never told that to a soul."

Kruger's eyes stared deep into his coffee cup, getting lost in the blackness. He spoke slowly. "Tonight was the first time I've stepped foot in the place in almost thirty years."

Lance said nothing.

"I knew that room was down there," Kruger said. "I never knew how to open it, because Uncle Joe never let me come down until he had the door open, but I knew it was there. I keep thinking ... the only way that Natalie could have known was if Uncle Joe showed her, too. And if he showed her the room ... does that mean...?" Kruger trailed off, his eyes sinking deeper into the coffee. "I never imagined there'd be anything back there. Even after that night when they died ... I ... I fucking convinced myself there was no way anybody had gotten into that room. I *lied* to myself for years. A fucking *coward*. Too afraid to go in a house because of some bad things that happened to me a long time ago. I was the only person alive who had the information needed to find the last piece of evidence to help us figure out what really happened that night, and I sat on it for six years." He shook his head. "The worst part ... I'd still be sitting on it if you hadn't shown up."

Kruger looked up then, his eyes ripe with tears. "I'll never forgive myself for that, Lance. Never in my life will I forgive myself for being such a coward."

Lance said nothing.

Sheriff Kruger downed the rest of his coffee in two large gulps and threw the cup across the room. It floated in the air like a fallen leaf and landed softly on the ground, dribbling drops of spilled coffee.

"You're going to have to try, sir," Lance said. "For Ethan." Then: "For Natalie, and for Mary. For your family."

And then Kruger had cried. Choked back sobs and large

splashes of tears on the table. A man shedding his past, stripping away the remnants of a demon he'd been carrying for nearly his entire life. A man with a new future.

When he'd finished, Kruger wiped his eyes with his hands and looked at Lance, no hint of embarrassment on his face. He asked, "How did you do it? How did you figure this out?"

Lance thought about his answer for a long time before finally shrugging and saying, "Right place, right time. I guess we can thank the Universe."

Sheriff Kruger gave Lance a long look that told him he was well aware there was more to this story, but he was going to take Lance's answer at face value. The man nodded once, shook Lance's hand, and said, "Thank you."

And then Lance's cell phone and backpack were returned to him and he was allowed to leave.

---

After a quick stop at R.G. Homes, where Lance had very politely asked Rich Bellows for his deposit back, which he was given, and had not so subtly suggested that Rich tell Sheriff Kruger about the emails and money he'd been receiving from Jacob Morgan, Lance told Luke that he'd walk the rest of the way back to the bus station.

"Are you sure?" Susan asked, stepping out of the rear passenger side. She looked exhausted, and leaned against Luke along the side of the Jeep. "We don't mind, do we, Luke?"

Luke shook his head and kissed the top of Susan's head as she nestled it against his shoulder. "Don't mind at all," he said. "We can go get some breakfast first, if you want. I'm starved."

Lance looked at his two friends, envied the affection between them. Loved them for their kindness. People like Luke and Susan helped remind him of the good there was in the world.

"I appreciate it," Lance said. "But I think I'm ready to hit the road. I think I'm done here, you know?"

They both nodded. Susan's eyes were growing heavy.

Luke stuck out his fist. "If you're ever back this way, give me a shout. We'll get a pickup game together."

Lance bumped his fist against Luke's and nodded. "Sounds great. Thanks for chauffeuring me around town." Then he looked at Susan.

It had been her who'd saved his life.

While Lance had been giving one of his initial statements at the sheriff's office, he'd asked Ray Kruger how the man had known to be at the farmhouse. How had Lance been so lucky to jump off that front porch and find the sheriff waiting?

"Susan Marsh called the station saying she'd gotten a disturbing voicemail from you, said she heard a bunch of commotion, like things slamming and breaking. She sounded terrified and worried and said she was going to go up herself if nobody here would." The sheriff had shrugged then. "Any other day, I might have sent somebody else. But something about tonight..." He trailed off. "Anyway, you're lucky I didn't shoot *you* instead. I'd heard the gunshot but saw your hands were empty when you jumped off the porch like goddamn Evel Knievel."

Lance remembered his phone call to Susan. The way he'd felt so compelled to call and then so angry when she hadn't answered. He silently thanked the Universe. Didn't tell the sheriff how little luck had to do with it.

After thinking of a million things to say to Susan, Lance finally settled on, "Thank you. For everything. I'd probably be dead if it weren't for you."

Susan pushed herself off her boyfriend and sleepily gave

Lance a hug, slipping her hands beneath his backpack to give him a proper embrace.

Lance hugged her back.

And then they left, piling into Luke's Jeep and driving down the street. Probably to live the rest of their lives together.

Lance walked the opposite direction.

Bought a bus ticket. The first one out of town.

Waited half an hour to board and then climbed up the bus's stairs with a handful of other travelers, most of which were staring like zombies down at their smartphones.

He found a seat near the front and tossed his backpack into the seat next to him.

Leaned his head back and closed his eyes.

As the bus pulled away, Lance started to drift off to sleep, the image of Luke and Susan leaning against Luke's Jeep standing out in his mind like a sudden recollection of something he'd forgotten.

He let this image float in the forefront of his thoughts for a long time before he finally opened his eyes and lifted his head. Dug in his pocket for his phone and pulled it out.

Flipped it open.

Scrolled through his contacts until he got to the Ls.

## 38

It was nearly nine o'clock in the morning, and most of the weekday breakfast rush was over at Annabelle's Apron, Westhaven's upstanding citizens having hustled off to their nine-to-fives after scarfing down plates of eggs and gallons of coffee.

Leah, who'd only been working at the diner for about a week, was in the back corner booth, counting her tips with Samantha, the other waitress on duty this morning, and laughing about the plate of bacon Samantha had spilled in Hank Peterson's lap.

Samantha squealed as she told the story. "And you just know he wanted me to reach down there and pick it up. Probably be the most action he's gotten in twenty years!"

Leah laughed and folded her stack of money neatly, placing it back in her apron. "You mean other than Margie, right?"

This caused the girls to break into a hysterical fit of laughter that made Margie slide through the door from the kitchen and give them a stern look. This only made Leah and Samantha laugh harder, and after a small grin of her own and a shake of her head, Margie disappeared back into the kitchen.

Samantha slid from the booth and said, "Come on, we better get back to work before she has us waiting on Hank full-time."

Leah nodded and started to slide out of her side of the booth when her iPhone vibrated in her pocket.

She pulled it out and checked the screen. She had a new message.

Her heart jumped into her throat and her hands started to shake when she saw the name of the sender.

She failed to enter her passcode correctly twice before finally getting it right.

The message was short—three words, to be exact—but they brought to Leah's face a smile that was unrivaled.

"Hey," Samantha said, "what's got you so happy there?"

Leah looked up and found the other girl holding a half-full coffeepot, staring at her with curious eyes.

She looked down and read the message again.

And again and again and again.

*I miss you.*

## EPILOGUE

Two weeks later, Ripton's Grove's sheriff, Ray Kruger, sat at his desk, looking out over the sea of scattered paperwork and an ancient desktop computer that he hadn't used for anything other than solitaire in a decade. On the opposite side of the desk, sitting in a worn and sagging office chair that had been sat in by countless concerned and worried citizens over the years, was a tired-looking man of maybe fifty years old with a head full of shaggy gray hair. He was rail thin and wore a suit that might have fit him well a long time ago but now was many sizes too big.

Sheriff Ray Kruger held the newspaper clipping in his hand and looked down at the image—a tall, athletic boy, captured in the act of what appeared to be a high school basketball game.

"And you say this boy is your son?" Kruger asked, looking up from the picture and meeting the gray-haired man's eyes.

The man nodded and said in a weary voice, dripping with sadness, "I'm really worried about him, Sheriff. Haven't heard from him in months. Have you seen him? I heard he might have passed through here."

Ray Kruger looked down at the grainy newspaper print again. Looked into the boy's face for a long time.

Felt something tugging at his gut. Some might say it was a cop's intuition, if you believed in such a thing.

Sheriff Ray Kruger handed the clipping carefully back to the man in the chair across from him. "I'm sorry, sir. I can't say I recognize him at all."

And then the gray-haired man did something that Ray Kruger found very strange. He turned his head and looked into the corner of the room, his eyes narrowing as if focusing in on something that wasn't there. Then the man nodded and left without a thank-you or a handshake.

When the man was gone, Ray Kruger turned and looked into the corner behind him. Saw nothing except a dusty set of golf clubs and a faded KRUGER FOR SHERIFF campaign sign resting against the wall.

What Kruger couldn't see was the spirit of Sheriff Bill Willard, staring at the closed office door and thinking to himself, *The bastards are coming for you, Lance. I hope you're ready when they get there.*

## AUTHOR'S NOTE

Thanks so much for reading **DARK SON**. I hope you enjoyed it. If you *did* enjoy it and have a few minutes to spare, I would greatly appreciate it if you could leave a review on Amazon saying so. Reviews help authors more than you can imagine, and help readers like you find more great books to read. Win-win!

**DARK SON** is the 2nd full-length novel in my Lance Brody series, and is preceded by **DARK BEGINNINGS** (Prequel Novella) and **DARK GAME** (Book 1)

-Michael Robertson Jr

For all the latest info, including release dates, giveaways, and special events, you can visit the page below to sign up for the Michael Robertson, Jr. newsletter. (He promises to never spam you!)

http://mrobertsonjr.com/newsletter-sign-up

Follow On:

Facebook.com/mrobertsonjr

Twitter.com/mrobertsonjr

## More from Michael Robertson Jr

### LANCE BRODY SERIES

Dark Vacancy (Book 4)

Dark Shore (Book 3)

Dark Deception (Book 2.5 - Short Story)

Dark Son (Book 2)

Dark Game (Book 1)

Dark Beginnings ( Book 0 - Prequel Novella)

### OTHER NOVELS

Cedar Ridge

Transit

Rough Draft (A Kindle #1 Horror Bestseller!)

Regret*

### Collections

Tormented Thoughts: Tales of Horror

The Teachers' Lounge*

*Writing as Dan Dawkins

Manufactured by Amazon.ca
Bolton, ON

31901581R00187